Half-Shell Prophecies

A NOVEL OF THE MYTHOS

Ruthanne Reid

4th Floor Publication

PHOENIX, AZ

Ruthanne Reid/4th Floor Publication

www.ruthannereid.com

Book Layout ©2017 BookDesignTemplates.com

Ordering Information:

Quantity sales. Special discounts are available on quantity purchases by corporations, associations, and others. For details, contact the "Special Sales Department" at the address above.

Half-Shell Prophecies/ Ruthanne Reid. —1st ed.

ISBN 978-0-9852600-9-5 (ppbk)

ISBN 978-0-9852600-8-8 (ebook)

Contents

To the awesome community of The Write Practice:
You rock.

"Prediction is very difficult, especially about the future."

–NIELS BOHR

CHAPTER 1

Puppy-Dog Eyes

T HIS KIND OF PUB is always gloomy, you know? It's like the owners are inviting chicanery. Might as well hang a sign on the door that says *dark deeds welcomed here.*

Whatever. I won't be here long. Bran is easy to spot thanks to the light in his hands.

I have to admit it: he's striking. He leans over his rough wooden table with the perfect amount of poise and slumping, somehow combining strong shoulders and ill motive just enough that no one bothers him. Of course, they could also be leaving him alone because of the light leaking through his fingers.

Maybe I'd better start at the beginning? Yeah. A little less exciting, but it'll make a lot more sense.

My name is Katie Lin, and two months ago, I adopted a baby dragon.

Well. Technically, the dragon adopted me. Also technically, the dragon is now with my uncle, who's keeping it because also-also-technically, the baby is *really* the fulfillment of a prophecy about the "Starling Child" and might be able to lead the Red and Black dragon clans closer to peace.

It sounds grand, doesn't it? Epic adventure of a lifetime?

Maybe for someone who *didn't* grow up in a magical household. I stepped out of that life a long time ago, and I ran all the way to America to prove it.

My uncle knows where I am. The rest of my family doesn't, and I intend to keep it that way.

I had a sweet little setup in the woods of New Hampshire: a pretty little one-bedroom rental, a decent job translating and digitizing paperwork at a venerable old legal practice in Portsmouth, and no ties to anyone around me.

I mostly live without magic, too. It's nice. Nicer than you think.

Do you have any idea how unpredictable life gets when everyone has magic? The Ever-Dying—purebred, non-magical humans—read books and think magic would be so neat. Well, it's not neat. It's frogs in your underwear drawer because your brother is twelve. It's suitors who only want you for your ancestral uterus and assume waking you at midnight with a sky full of rainbows and singing trees is the way to prove they deserve to have it.

It's going to school with others of your kind and when they're told your last name is Lin, losing any chance of making friends because nobody wants to mess with *that* branch. And I do mean **Branch**.

See, my family is of the Kin. Kin—the only kind of "human" who can do magic—which simply means some non-human thing diddled our ancestors, giving us the gene. There are a lot of Kin out there, too, but only nine family names ended up symbolized by the infamous Branch of the Kin.

Look, see it there in the Wheel?

No? Look closer.

Behold the Branch of Kin—which is all symbol-y because we "branch" off from the magic-users, get it? My family, the Lins are the pointy leaf one right at the top.

Yeah, you bet your patootie it's condescending, but we didn't get a say. Yet another reason I wanted out.

Anyway. I nearly got my wish. Sure, a baby dragon showed up on my doorstep, but I delivered him to safety and got back home with only a mild crush on the Fey who helped me (a victory, I assure you— Fey are *really* pretty, and he was nicer than most).

Back to work. Back to ordinary dentists and taxes and nobody caring that my last name is Lin. Back to awesome neighbors who helped me shovel snow (or sent their kids to do it, which is the same thing), and awesome cider and beautiful trees and square American accents and nobody making live snakes spring out of their fingernails or walking around waving big iron wands like swords.

It all went south the day Bran the Crow King showed up at my door.

Picture this.

I was on my way to work. Real work, a real job—which required me to be there on time, which meant leaving ass-early in the morning due to icy roads and thirty-five miles per hour speed limits because New Hampshire.

Despite the cold weather, I was spiffed up in stockings and heels, a cute little trumpet skirt with matching jacket, and a pearl-button blouse (Old Employer Syndrome has its quirks), when I opened my front door to find it occupied.

The Crow King. Bran to his friends, of whom I was not one. The last time we met, he'd kidnapped my uncle and trapped him in a Roc's head *for no reason.*

He's Shadow's Breath—one of the People of the Darkness—and his real form is huge, red, and strangely cracked like old earth. He has big black horns and big blue eyes and a dark aura so strong it's a physical force. But of course, he wouldn't show up like *that.*

The form he took was drop-dead handsome in a Hollywood-pirate-rogue way. His rumpled black hair was just soft enough to emphasize his sparkling blue eyes and nut-cracking-sharp jawline. Last time I saw him, he'd worn a plain white tee and jeans. Today—on *my* porch, *uninvited*—he'd added a black buckle-and-button wool number that probably cost more than my car, manly boots a Japanese rocker would be proud to wear, and a smile.

"Kate!" he said.

I slammed the door.

Okay, I thought. I needed to get to work. Mr. Danner didn't care about inclement weather or traffic jams; he cared about results, and he wouldn't appreciate me hiding out in my house all day. I peeked through the peephole.

Yup, Bran was still there. "Kate!" he called again. "We need to talk!"

I didn't want to waste a sick day on him, dammit. "No, we don't! Go away!" Did I mention that last time, he also made noise about impregnating me because he'd always wanted some Lin in his bloodline? Told you being magical sucked.

He didn't go away.

I swear I considered climbing out the window, silk be damned. I considered calling the police—but if he stayed and they came, he'd hurt them, and if he left and they came, I'd look crazy. I would've considered other things, but that annoying banging sound was really getting in the way of my planning. Oh, wait. That sound was my head, knocking against the door in abject and complete frustration.

Bran was still there.

I decided to strong-arm it.

"Kate, we need to talk," he tried again as I physically shoved him out of my doorway (he let me, okay?) and locked up.

"No, we don't. Go away." Downside of ice in winter: you can't really *run* anywhere, especially in heels. I settled for a sort of slow, sliding march, trying to say with my every inch that this conversation was over.

"I need your help," he said, following.

"Nope." *Beep beep* went my key fob. Fifteen more feet.

"I really do, and you're the only one who can help me."

"Ask my uncle. Oh, wait, is he not your friend anymore after what you pulled?" I wobbled, turning *pulled* into a longer word than planned.

"Of course he is." Bran looked shocked. "Why wouldn't he be?"

Told you the whole Roc-head thing made no sense. "Leave me alone," I said. Bran was royalty. I should probably have said "please." I didn't. Oh, well.

The bastard got between me and my door handle at the last moment. "Please. Please." He got down on his knees in the snow. "Please."

He wasn't supposed to say "please."

Could I get in on the passenger's side and slide over the armrest? Well, I could, but not without giving the world a show. "Bran. Can I call you Bran? I don't owe you anything. You're terrifying to me. You kidnapped my uncle. Did I write you? Did I leave you my email address? No! Leave me alone!"

Damn. I was shouting. This little cul-de-sac only housed me and the Gigueres, and they were a vigilant little family. I looked over.

Nobody was opening blinds or doors yet. But they would if this kept up, and they'd ask if I were in trouble and needed help.

And this guy would hurt them. He wouldn't see anything *wrong* with it.

Beyond that bit of reasoning, I could never explain what I did next. "Get in the damn car. Passenger side. You're coming with me to Portsmouth."

The weird thing is he did what I said without arguing.

He said nothing as I navigated the roads, muttering at traffic lights that didn't go my way and hoping old Danner wasn't in the office yet.

My car was considerably heavier on the right-hand side with him sitting in it. This was not how I'd pictured my morning. "So aren't you, like... in line to be king of the Darkness, or something?" I said, which was inane and probably rude, but he's the one who barged into my life, *so*.

"Unfortunately, yes."

"Okay. That's not usually an 'unfortunately' kind of thing." It was hard not to look at him. I know the form he wore wasn't real, but damn, he'd done it right: the hint of stubble, the proportion of jawline to the length of throat he showed above his wool coat, the long-fingered hands that rested on his well-appointed lap—hands that managed to look dangerously powerful and dangerously beautiful at the same time.

All for me? He shouldn't have.

I braked to let a school bus pass (an empty one—told you this was early in the morning) and made a slow right turn onto Highway 101. Finally, plowed and salted roads! Praise bc!

He still looked out the window. All the authority I'd sensed when we met the first time was still there; this was not a man to cross, not a man whose ire you'd be smart to raise. This was a man who could command the shadows to do what he said.

But there was something else there—something pressing the authority down, something hiding the ego and pulling his attention far away from me: fear.

I swallowed. That wasn't good. If this guy was afraid, whatever was after him had to be awful.

Bran sighed deeply. "It's my grandfather."

Was I supposed to know what that meant? "Okay?"

"The Raven King."

I damn near drove us off the road.

One braking recovery later, we crept along at the speed limit while lunatics passed me on the left. I said nothing; my hands trembled like windshield wipers across dry glass. "That's... bad."

"Yes. Yes, it is. He's after me. I have nowhere else to go."

I laughed.

Of course I laughed! The Raven King? He's ancient! Crazy power-ful and crazy *crazy*! And what, now he was coming after the guy in my car? Welp, I was dead. He was dead. We were both dead.

It's long been my theory that if you can't laugh when death snarls in your face, you're just going to cry, and that's useless. Might as well laugh and have a good time on your way down.

Bran let me laugh. Weirdly enough, I think he understood why.

"Are you nuts?" I finally said. "What am I supposed to do, get blood on you?" I navigated onto Interstate 95—which, to my happiness, had been even more effectively plowed. I was making good time. For all the good it did me.

"No, you're not getting blood on me." He didn't even smirk or turn it into a weird flirt; the guy must have been genuinely terrified. "You're going to help me find Notte and fight my grandfather back."

Have you ever had a weird day so weird that you suddenly became certain you were dreaming and decided to treat it as such until it proved itself real? Me neither, but this one came close. "Bran. Honey. I can't help you."

"Yes, you can."

"No." Turn signal, go *around* the slow granny. "No, I can't." Wind-shield wipers on to shove the random flurries out of my vision. "I'm not even in practice. I can't do anything fancier than spells to make tea and remove really bad stains."

"I knew you'd say that."

"I don't think you knew I'd say *that*."

"No, I knew you'd say that, so I brought proof." He reached into his coat pocket and pulled out half a clamshell.

"Um," I said, like one does.

"The answer is the lost Lin," said the half-a-shell in a high, tinny voice, vibrating slightly in his hand. "Find her, and she can take you to one of his children. From there, your path will be easy enough."

It took me a moment to speak after that.

"What. The hell. Is that?" I said, taking my exit.

"I'll tell you when you agree to help me," he said with a smirk.

Great. Now a clamshell was ruining my life.

Portsmouth, already. It's such a pretty New England town, even prettier than Cabot Cove in *Murder She Wrote*. The speed limit dropped again and I managed it, idling past the loveliest historical million-dollar homes you ever did see, all done in tasteful stone or "appropriately" period colors, just so quaint and adorable that you can't help picturing it ready for Christmas with lights and garlands and maybe a few Victorian-era children singing on the corners.

He didn't fit here. Magic did not fit in my world. I had to get rid of this guy, and soon. "I don't know Notte. I don't know his children. I don't know any vampires at all. Get out of my car."

Bran smiled as if I'd said the opposite of those things and tucked the shell back into his pocket. "You mean you don't *know* you know a vampire. I'll come with you! We'll spot him together, and I'll get out of your hair. How's that?"

I pulled into the parking lot behind the two-story clapboard home Danner had converted to his offices. It's yellow, by the way—that particularly odd New England yellow that doesn't quite look like pee, but close enough.

The flurries had turned wet and nasty. It was a good thing I had a parking permit. Otherwise, well... historical towns do have their downsides, and lack of parking is always one of them.

I locked my car and faced him down. "Listen. To me. I don't. Know. A vampire. And even if I did, you didn't need to come to my house to see who I hang out with."

"Did you just give me permission to spy on you?" he said with a lazy smile anyone more susceptible would be writing about for pages, but not me. Nope. Just two sentences is all you get.

"No!" I shook my hands at him. "Are you crazy? No! I am not giving you permission to spy on me!"

"Then I had no choice but to ask for help, did I?"

"You didn't give *me* a choice in helping you! You just... showed up!"

And he looked confused! "I thought that was the better option. I'm not an expert in Ever-Dying protocol, Kate."

"Do not call me Kate."

9

"If you were still under your family's umbrella, I'd know the proper channels, but as it is—"

The North Church clock tower suddenly chimed the time.

"Dammit! I'm late!" I spun away from him, slipped wildly on ice and caught myself, and lunged for the door beside the discreet sign that said, *Danner and Danner, Attorneys at Law.*

Of course he followed me in. The stupid *clamshell* told him to.

I should've just called in sick and stayed home.

CHAPTER 2

A Little Knowledge...

I SHOULD TELL YOU about the Seven Peoples of the Earth before I continue.

Long ago, the folks in charge decided the sentient beings of the world needed to be categorized. Seven was and is a number of power; I honestly believe that's the only reason humans got included in this stupid little system.

The Darkness. The Fey. The Sun. The Guardians. The Dream. The Kin. The Ever-Dying. That's all of us, and we don't get along—and not only because only six out of seven are magical.

For one thing, *not getting along* is why we don't all live in the same world anymore.

Something like twenty thousand years ago, the great magical minds of the age figured out how to make parallel worlds, which could then be modified however their owners wanted. The Fey have one called the Silver Dawning, the Sun have one called Zenith, the Dream have one called The Dream (why not?), and the Darkness have Umbra—which legitimately has no light in it anywhere at all. Seriously. You can even bring a light in there if you want to, but it won't do a thing. They figured out a way to make a world that *bends light wrong*, turning it into something else, into its opposite. No, not shadow. It's *not light*. Forever.

So that's four "other" earths and one original, which the Ever-Dying, Kin, and few surviving Guardians share, but apparently, five worlds just aren't enough for everybody, so thousands of years ago, they figured out how to split off little designer worlds, too. They're pocket-dimensions; kind of like little casitas branching off the main building.

Bran has his own designer realm. He was king of it. I'm not sure what he rules there, but I know it has something called "bone collectors." Don't they sound fun?

His grandfather, on the other hand, rules *all of Umbra*. The whole thing. And you'd better believe the Raven King is a lot scarier than bone collectors.

Anyway, I said all that to make this point: there are rules for how magic folk interact with everybody else, and Bran was actually following them by trying to do this quietly.

The Ever-Dying humans *used* to be good for little more than servitude and slaughter. They were really quick to repopulate themselves— which, hey, was really handy—but they live such short lives that they weren't worth much. I mean, heck, just about anything can kill them (hence the name).

Ah, but that was then, and this is now. Now, with something like seven billion of them in the world, quantum technology, and nuclear devices, they're a threat. If some asshole got it into his head that there are ifrits and that maybe by nuking Ethiopia he could get rid of them, what do you think would happen?

Humans can be crazy when they're afraid of something. Even the Kin—and we're so closely related we can exchange blood—don't dare let on because the Ever-Dying would try to experiment on us or shoot us or fry us or worse. You know they would.

So—and I know you saw this coming—the rule is that humans can't know magic is real.

And yes, I choose to live among them. I think their brief, simple lives hold more grace than longer, convoluted ones. And I hate how we've used magic to twist everything. Life for humans is a lot simpler.

Where was I going with all this? Right here: none of my human coworkers could see or hear Bran as I walked into work that day.

So now you know. Tada! Don't you feel enlightened?

As I opened the door and spotted my pale coworker, Lisa, I came to a decision: I would invent a new game called *ignore the interloper*.

"Hey, Katie," said Lisa. "Don't look now, but you're in trouble."

"Are you kidding me?" I used the boot scraper before treading on the illustrious carpet of Danner and Danner. "The clock tower hasn't even finished chiming yet!"

"Doesn't matter. He was in early today, and he's saying later than him is late."

I sort of grunted (frustration plus winter-coat removal equals grunting; it just does) and hung up my things.

"He'll probably want to see you at lunch," Lisa considered, tucking back a strand of hair that had fallen out of her bun.

"Lovely." Great. A talking-to by the elderly Danner was never pleasant. He sprayed saliva when emphatic.

"You're more likely to keep your job than you think," she said, staring meaningfully at her monitor. "You're Asian. It's good for PR."

She seriously just did that? Yes. Yes, she did. The only reason I did not think, *could this day get any weirder?* was because I knew it damn well could, and was trying not to tempt fate.

I stared at her and decided not to validate *that* little opinion piece with a response. "Guess I'll have to buy lunch for us next time, huh?"

"They care that you're Asian?" Bran blurted, his entire face twisting.

"Yeah, that's fine," Lisa sighed. "I mean, I got the last one, but whatever, it's no big deal."

"They care you're Asian," Bran said again, stepping around me. "Are you serious? You're practically the same species."

I almost hit him, but punching the air would probably not be good for job retention. "Thanks, Lees. I owe you coffee." I pushed through the bar's hinged gate and headed back into the dusty, musty corridor of this house-cum-courtroom-cum-law-office.

"Asian," said Bran again, walking alongside me. "That's vague as hell."

"Go away, Bran."

He didn't go away, but, thankfully, he fell silent.

My job was so sweet; I got to sit in silence, ignoring the world, discovering long-lost lives through memories left like echoes in paper. Transcribing is easy since I can *feel* what the writers felt; digital scanning is the work of seconds. I preserve the past while getting paid. Marvelous!

I must have known it couldn't last.

"Two questions," he said.

"No."

"First, why is your arrival time a problem? Just make them forget you were late."

"No," I said again, and opened my door to a blast of warm dust and mold. A cough threatened my throat, tickling, teasing, making my eyes water.

"Second, *this* is where you work?"

My office was a windowless room about the size of three broom closets, filled with banker's boxes and filing cabinets and decades' worth of dust. I liked it, to be honest. It smelled like my uncle's ancient library, and the old records and journals that filled it were fascinating. My job: to read, transcribe, and scan them, preserving the whole lot. 'Digital Archivist' was my job title. Believe it or not, sometimes they even hired me out on a contracted basis. I was *that* good.

"Katie," said Bran, low. "You're a *Lin*. What the hell is this?"

"It's my job, and I like it. Will you just go away?"

"Your uncle would be ashamed."

I spun on him. "My uncle would be *proud*," I hissed, pointing my finger in his face. "I'm paying my own bills, I don't have to speak to anybody I don't want to, I don't have to make babies to 'preserve what remains,' and I get to decipher crinkly yellow paper filled with memories all day. I like it. I am staying in it. And my uncle is proud of me." How dare he. How dare he!

He touched his finger to my cheek.

"You're flushed," he said eagerly, and then, because that wasn't creepy enough, he leaned into near-kissing distance. "Do you need cheering up?"

I really hate magical people. Also, thanks *a ton* for telling everybody this kind of frightening behavior is sexy, Hollywood. "Bran."

"Yes?"

"Leave." I turned around—an act that took more courage than I like to admit—and opened a banker's box.

Dust everywhere. Clouds of it, blankets of it. I coughed, eyes watering again, as I took out my first assignment for the day.

Bran leaned against a filing cabinet, arms crossed. "When can we go looking for vampires?"

I smacked him with the box lid, getting dust all over his nice wool coat. Haha. "Find one on your own. You probably have more contacts than I do." The document in my hands practically sang. This was so much more than a simple deed for sale: hopes, dreams, sorrows—this was the note of sale for a house to a couple of former slaves who'd escaped on the Underground Railroad. Wow.

"I can't. It has to be a vampire connected to you," he said.

"Why? The clamshell told you so?"

"Yes," he said solemnly.

"I'm not in the habit of taking orders from mollusks." The couple who'd signed this old deed had so much hope when they bought property here, but this paper didn't tell me what became of them. I really wanted to know.

"It's not a mollusk. This is an echostone."

I turned slowly to face him. "An echostone. Really? Really? There are like six of those in existence."

"And I have two," he said, like that kind of voracious collecting was nothing. "This one holds the soul of Cassandra." He grinned. "*The* Cassandra."

I sighed. Maybe I wasn't tempting fate. Maybe fate wanted to be punched. "I don't care."

"You should. But naturally, some part of her curse probably still lingers, and that's why you don't believe her."

"No, I don't believe because that's a clamshell, you're crazy, and I want to get back to my job."

The door banged hard as someone knocked, and we both jumped. Both of us. The amazing Bran could be startled.

I'd have to lock that information away for later. "Yeah?"

"Package for you," Lisa called through the door, sounding about as thrilled to play messenger as she was doing anything else.

I hadn't ordered anything. Nobody knew I worked here. What was happening with this day? "Coming."

Bran smirked and opened his mouth to make some stupid comment.

I hit him with a stack of folders before he could, then left him there to choke on dust.

Oh.

Lisa failed to mention my package was delivered by the handsomest man I've seen in a long time.

"Hi," he said, his smile brilliant against his smooth black skin, his impeccably tailored suit the perfect shade of charcoal. And his tie, though solid red, showed hints of something unusual in the pattern. "We haven't met, but our bosses have been emailing for a while now."

"Oh." Not my best moment. Look; I don't get my breath taken away often. I really don't, so the fact that I was awed is part of what awed me.

"From Taylor, Taylor, and Lawrence, down in Boston?" he prompted.

"Oh! TTL! Right, I'm so sorry!" I shook his manicured hand (warm, strong, just rough enough that I know he does something with his hands besides office-stuff all day). "I thought you weren't due until next week." Timing! Timing! This was crazy!

"Yeah, sorry about that. I thought they'd sent an updated itinerary," he said, patting his enormous briefcase the way some people would a beloved dog.

I finally recognized the pattern on his tie: it was the silhouette of Marvin the Martian—in the same red as the rest of it, only obvious because of the different direction of the threads. This was an office-friendly tie with subtle playfulness. He won so many points with that tie.

I shook my head. "I didn't see it. I'm sorry. Not sure what happened, but you're here now, so let's do this."

"Here?" He smiled crookedly at my chairless, airless office.

I laughed. "No. We'll use the conference room instead. This way, please."

Bran crossed his arms as we passed him, scowling. Which I ignored.

"You've got a good reputation as a translator and digital archivist. Possibly the best on the East coast," Joshua said with a sidelong smile.

My cheeks flushed. "I doubt that. I'm just available due to tiny-town-syndrome."

He chuckled, a warm sound suited for firelight and fine wine. "Let's hope your reputation is correct. This is pretty important."

The conference room was a little drafty, but the long table should do. I rolled a couple of chairs aside, and he put his briefcase on the table. That's when I realized it had been handcuffed to him.

Yikes. What was in that thing?

Bran stepped in behind us and slammed the door hard.

Joshua startled. "Old building," he suggested after a moment.

Bran the Crow King was apparently five years old. It took everything I had not to make a face at him. "Something like that. So what exactly did you bring me, Mister Run? Danner kept the details to himself."

"Call me Joshua," he corrected, and pulled two pairs of latex gloves from his pocket. He handed one to me. "Ready?" And, gloves on, he took from his case several long, blocky shapes covered in cloth. "Pillaging ancestors grabbed these somehow from China, a long time ago. They're our client's family heirloom." Carefully, he folded back the cloth to show me something I really didn't expect to see: thin, wide strips of bamboo, perforated and held together with rotting silk to form a sort of awkward book. And on them...

Two sets of writing, one real, and one not. I was seeing double.

The fake, magical view: vertical lines of *xiàngxíng*—ancient Chinese pictographs—filling each strip from top to bottom, crowded, faded.

The real, hidden view: harsh, sharp lines, crossing each other to make diamonds and dissect them, to make triangles and bisect them, to form crude hourglass shapes and slash through.

Joshua could only see the *xiàngxíng*. And I had a headache.

I took a breath and held it for a moment. "Whoa."

"What is that?" said Bran, leaning right into Joshua's personal space.

Joshua shivered. He was probably telling himself he was feeling things and nothing was there. Let the record hold: if you feel like something is there, even if you can't see it, something probably is.

"They, ah. Told us you could read this," said Joshua hesitantly, probably afraid this was some kind of racial gaff. (Which I appreciated. *Lin's Chinese, I bet she can read it* had happened more than once).

"I can, but it's going to take me a little while." Gloves on, I touched the edge of one bamboo book.

Energy flushed up my arm like a cold shot of morphine, pleasurable, horrible, leaving an electrical, sour taste in my mouth. I took my hand away, clenching my fingers in my jacket pocket.

"I'm really glad to hear that, Ms. Lin," Joshua said, completely unaware that these things were cursed as hell.

My throat felt tight. On the other hand, he had really nice eyes. "Call me Katie. Please."

"Katie." He smiled.

I couldn't remember how to flirt. How did one flirt?

"Ahem!" Bran cleared his throat.

Not like that. "What's the timeline on this?" I said, finding it far easier to ignore Bran when someone I actually *wanted* to look at was in the room.

"Since they know there's research involved, they're saying three months. If you have to travel, we'll cover it."

I whistled. I knew my hourly rate for this kind of thing when contracted. Damn. They must really want these things. "Why do they need this translated and archived? Why not just go to a university or something? I can do this, sure, but... isn't this kind of a weird way to go about it?"

Joshua shrugged. "It's specified as part of an estate settlement: you can go to a university, but we can't give any of it to academia. It has to stay in our hands. I can't disclose more."

Sounded like one hell of a weird last will and testament, but who was I to tell some crazy rich person what to do with their things? "Okay, then. Let's get the paperwork taken care of, and I'll get right to work on these."

Bran threw his hands in the air and began pacing, but that made him even easier to ignore. The annoyance of others gives me strength, for lo, I am ridiculous.

Forty-three minutes and about five hundred signatures later, we were done. I swear applying for a mortgage would be less work; but then again, a mortgage wouldn't have me working with things that were insured for five million dollars, either.

You read that right. Five million, insured. Yikes.

"If you like, I can drop by and check on your progress in the coming weeks," said Joshua, as smooth as butter.

Five million dollars and cursed manuscripts. I almost missed what he said. "I'd like that."

"Maybe we could do lunch?"

"At least." I wriggled my eyebrows. How to flirt, by Katie Lin: just don't.

Miracle of miracles, he didn't run away. He chuckled again (I could get used to that) and handed me his card. "Let me know your schedule. We'll make it happen."

"Yes, sir." And I walked him out.

Five million dollars' worth of magical bamboo books waited behind us in the conference room.

Five million dollars of heavily charmed pieces, carefully spelled so humans would see gibberish (baloney like, "The flower that drinks the wine does sing the tune"—I mean, really? Really?) while hiding what it really said.

I recognized that other language, the hidden one. That was Anshan.

Anshan's users were all extinct.

They'd done it to themselves. Magic gone wrong, about as wrong as it can go.

And five "books" filled with that language were sitting in my conference room now, waiting to be read.

I should call the authorities. I should do something.

"This is Anshan," said Bran as soon as I got back into the room. He didn't look afraid, exactly, but he'd backed against the wall, away from the tables. "What the hell is some Ever-Dying doing with this?"

"I don't know." I'd call my uncle. He'd have advice. I carefully wrapped the books in their cloth, making zero contact with that bamboo. I didn't want to feel that again unless I had to.

"And you're just taking them?" Bran sputtered. "Just like that?"

"Gotta lock them away. I'm not leaving them out here for every Tom, Dick, and Harry to paw at."

He shook his head. "Leave it behind. Leave it behind, Katie. This isn't worth your life."

Of course, I didn't.

I took them into my little office and laid them carefully on my banker's-box-table, trying to calm my racing heart.

Today was weird, and that teeny little niggling instinct—magical in nature and never wrong—kept telling me it was going to get weirder.

"Katie," Bran said from the doorway, and I swear he was pleading.

That made twice today I'd seen the Crow King afraid. Bad omen? Yeah. Bad omen.

Well. At least I was going to get paid.

CHAPTER 3

The Manuscripts

THE ANSHAN LANGUAGE is something special. Even the Ever-Dying know about it, sort of, though they call it 'Proto-Elamite.' It belonged to a group of Iranian Zār—Fey—who, for quite some time, ruled part of Persia absolutely.

See, the Fey have a problem. Way back during the First War, someone created the Throne and the Scepter—two things that siphon all Fey magic away at birth, supposedly to use in case of emergency or defense or whatever. Practically speaking, it means the Fey are starving. Always. And they will do just about anything to refill their leaking buckets.

The Zār, like most, chose music to do so.

Music is amazing. It evokes emotion and thought; it can make people think they're in love or stir up desire for revenge. Emotion and music go hand-in-hand, and it's a handy way (pardon my pun) to refill those coffers, giving Fey their temporary magic back.

I had a picture book of fairy-tales from around the world when I was little. These fairy-tales, of course, were true, but aside from that, the Fey known as the Zār featured highly because they could make music so enchanting, so clever, that anyone who heard it just had to dance in response. It was joyful. It was sensual. It was overwhelming, and the Zār could keep it going until the dancers dropped dead from exhaustion. Which they did.

My storybook ended with some brave Kin princess dancing so self-lessly and perfectly that the Zār finally gave in and stopped her from dancing. For lo, She Was Just So Pure And Beautiful. You know, like all good girls should be.

Bleeeeh. Just for the record, magical ladies need feminism, too.

In real life, the Zār just made music until their chosen humans died, sacrificing all for the sake of the music, and the Zār absorbed all the energy and emotion from the whole experience.

Note: that's not why the Zār disappeared.

They were a fine hand (there I go again) with potions, too, creating and perfecting all manner of nasty-tasting juice to refill their rapidly dwindling powers. They say at least sixteen different varieties of plant went extinct thanks to their harvesting, which ticked off what re-mained of the Dream—who are really connected to plant life, like *wow connected*—and causing more than one skirmish between the Peoples.

But that's not why they went extinct, either. No, the Zār went ex-tinct because they invented a weapon.

The Daevas shared that part of the world, too—People of the Dark-ness, trapped here instead of in their own world of Umbra, probably banished or something. I don't really know. All I know is that like good neighbors, the Zār and the Daevas threw each other parties and cele-brations and made new laws and contracts on clay tablets and held huge get-togethers to prove how much they liked each other.

Except the people of the Darkness like to feed on the Fey. Any kind of Fey. The Zār were no exception, and they didn't enjoy it.

There's this crazy concept that you can only push a group of people so far before they start fighting back. And the surviving victors of that push-back are the ones who tell the stories, you get me? History is always written by the victors.

This was no exception. According to the Daevas, the Zār basically went hubris-gluttony-excess-hedonism-yatta-yatta and then they were dead.

In reality, the **Zār** and the Daevas lived in faux harmony for a while until one too many **Zār** disappeared one late night, and the **Zār** fought back. There might have been a black hole or some kind of really nasty portal involved. There sure as hell was soul-sucking civilization-ending absorption happening.

It was nasty. It was traitorous and rough, and the Daevas ended up leaving no **Zār** alive at all.

Funny thing is, I don't think the Daevas meant to kill them all, but you know what they say: once you pop, you just can't stop.

Reminds me of a dumb cartoon I watched a while ago, when I first stepped into the human world. In that cartoon, squid-headed aliens came to visit the Earth, decided they liked anchovies, and ended up eating them until they were gone. Oops. So Daevas-versus-**Zār** is kind of like that.

Ah, but here's where it gets interesting: before they died, the **Zār** supposedly discovered an ultimate weapon.

Legend says they actually figured out a way to steal energy *back*—to take it from the Daevas. No one has ever been able to take energy from the People of Darkness. In doing so, the **Zār** made themselves into the biggest target ever.

Remember the insane paranoia back when nuclear weapons were new and only one country had them? Now imagine if that country's biggest enemy thought they could wipe the nuke-owners out and prevent that weapon from being created. Now you understand the situation.

They say the day the country of Anshan died, a mountain made of shadow settled on the land over the capitol city. They say it ate everyone whole—heart, body, and soul—and that when it lifted off again, nothing would ever grow in that ground again.

But they *also* say that if the secrets the **Zār** uncovered ever went public, the Darkness would no longer have so much power. In fact, they'd finally have a fricking weakness.

See, the Darkness are wicked-hard to beat. (Like my New England slang there? I'm trying it out.) The people of the Sun keep them at bay, and they in turn keep the Sun at bay, and... well, it's the worst cold war ever.

Except that if the **Zār** myth were true, there could just be an end to it. Talk about a power upset.

You'd better believe people have tried to find that **Zār** secret over the years. They even got the Ever-Dying into it, taking advantage of that incredible nosiness and persistence that so marks the human soul. But so far, it's a bust. All archeology has found is clay tablets with boring information about grain and other shipments, payment due for furs or scented water or special silk from the Silver Dawning, and a lot of complaining that somebody's barrels of wine were late.

No spells.

No music (which is a sore spot among the Fey. Damn, they'd like to get their hands on musical spells that powerful.)

Certainly no secret weaknesses of the Darkness.

But along the way, anything from Anshan got sort of a... reputation.

Okay, remember those old Hollywood movies with mummies and Egypt, where the idea is Random White Guy disturbs the mighty dead, is cursed forever, and dies? Yeah, like that, except it happens.

Not with mummies, obviously. But worse things. Like maybe assassins from the Darkness taking out anyone who comes "too close." Or like horrible booby-trap spells—the kind that leaves a hell of a surprise for the next bloke to come along.

All of this means nobody in their right mind would mess with the Anshan language, any more than they'd hold a square-dancing contest on one of those fields riddled with mines in Mozambique.

Except, of course, that there are five books in the Anshan language lying on my makeshift desk right now. And I didn't back away slowly or run screaming.

I have lost my mind.

"Just tell your local magistrate," Bran suggested.

"No."

He was tired of hearing that word from me—or at least, his sigh said as much. "Do you even have a rational reason why not?"

"Because if I go to the authorities, I have to tell them that I'm here, and if they know I'm here, I have to register, and have a tracker put on my wand, and then my family will be able to find me, and everything I've worked for goes down the tube." I took a deep breath and added, "Duh," because it made me feel better.

He studied me. Studied me with a look that made my skin crawl, that made me feel like maybe I was naked but not in the fun way, more just in the *exposed* way.

"Cut it out," I said in my most grown-up voice.

"You'd do anything for freedom, wouldn't you?"

"Pff, no!" Like there was any safe answer to that.

"I think you would. I think we can work a deal." And he smiled dazzlingly, like an angel from on high. Or a former angel, anyway. "If you help me find Notte, then I'll make sure you get your freedom."

"Sure. Sure you would." I scanned in the land deed I was working on. There; now this old legal document was preserved in our system, and we could donate these pages to the museum, increasing community happiness and my boss' reputation.

"I can. I can give you money."

"I want to earn my money." I know how stupid that sounds. It's my life, okay?

"I can give you charms to keep people from suspecting you of witchcraft."

I had to laugh at that one. "Nobody does that anymore in this country, bub."

"Oh." He blinked. I guess the whole Salem mess wasn't too long ago for him. "Well, I can give you charms to avoid the kind of problem you ran into today. More favor with your boss—"

"I want to earn that, too."

"—and maybe even some charms to protect you on the roads," he said, ignoring me. "The Ever-Dying drive like they'll live forever."

I sighed. "The only thing I care about is what I have to do to make you go away."

In answer, he held out the clamshell again.

"The Lost Lin," it squeaked, "will lead you to the Blood King."

"This is such a weird conversation," I muttered, packing things in manila envelopes and pulling out new files.

"So it's settled. You'll help me."

"I don't even know how to help you."

"You will." He brandished the half clamshell at me like ladies used to wave handkerchiefs, then sat down on some boxes.

I did everything I could to ignore him and got back to work.

With the patience of a predator, he let me.

My haven lasted until four.

By that point, Lisa had clocked out (we officially close at three on Fridays), though I and several other paper-monkeys would be staying behind to do more work. I'd gotten through two whole banker's boxes of land deeds and court documents and was minding my own business when Bran sat up, staring at the door.

"Why is he here?" he hissed.

"Who?" I said, focusing on an old bill of sale, and then found out the hard way.

Magic poured under my office door like spiders. It crawled up my legs and into my bones, crusting my clothes with ice and burning my skin. My lungs froze, sharp and hard and useless.

My natural resistance didn't do squat. *This spell was designed to hurt Kin*, but before I could process that, Bran grabbed my arm and pulled. Ice held my shoes to the floor, but my feet came free. He stared at me for a moment, and then—

We moved. *He* moved, transforming the world to a dark blur, flying with a force like a train until we floated outside high above Danner's building.

My flash-frozen lungs struggled with New England winter air. "Wh-what's ha-happening?" I wheezed as quietly as I could. Whatever cast that spell didn't need to know where we were.

"My grandfather just attacked you," Bran said casually.

"What?" The spell fought me. Icy cold glued my eyes open and made my teeth clatter like a typewriter. Unless I was mistaken, I was going to be dead in a very short amount of time. I could feel my heart slowing. "W-why? I didn't d-d-o anything!"

"No idea. He's looking for you in your offices. You wouldn't have been able to get out but for me. I got the Anshan, too," Bran boasted, and held up a knapsack, which was presumably weighted down with five million dollars' worth of ancient books.

More ice cracked off my jacket; it burned my skin, seared my lips, made every heartbeat sharp and painful. I hate being a damsel in distress, but this was power way beyond me. I made one small sound.

Bran finally realized there was a problem. "Screw that," he said, and released a little bit of power. Just a little. But *dayum.* A black wave rushed out from him in a growing sphere, knocking the ice clean off me and snapping the spell like it was old, wet thread. I cried out— couldn't help it, that *hurt*—and gasped for air.

"We have to go," he said.

The Raven King was after me. The Raven King. What the hell was going on? "N-no Conflux," I managed. "I don't have the money, and the nearest one's in Epping."

He laughed—you know exactly the kind of laugh I mean, all devil-may-care and Hollywood-rogue. "I make my own way, Lost Lin," he said, right up close to my face, and then he ripped the air.

Ripped it. Stuck his hand through nothing and tore it open, like reality was painted on cheap canvas, and behind it was nothing but blackness. Not even stars.

Explosions sounded below in my workplace, muffled and terrifying. What choice did I have?

He pulled me through that rip in the sky, and everything turned upside down and inside out. *I* turned inside out, I'm pretty sure. We hit the ground—cold, rough concrete, some kind of sidewalk—and I threw up. The world kept spinning, that awful vertigo feel where everything is tilting left. I couldn't do anything but crouch there, my hose torn and my feet bare, gasping.

You see? You see why I hate magic? The people who have it just *do* stuff, assuming might makes right, assuming all kinds of things. This Raven King had no problem attacking me, and I had no idea why. He didn't even feel the need to tell me why he wanted me dead.

I don't have a lot of magic; I may have potential (hence why everybody wanted to make babies with me, oh joy and rapture forever), but I never developed it, and so am a middling magic-user at best. And my wand was in the trunk of my car. I had nothing to focus my power now, which meant I'd run out quickly if I tried to use it. Kin magic diffuses into the freaking air without a focus.

Even with a wand, I'd never had enough power to do what Bran just did. That dude just ripped reality to take us someplace else, tesseract-style. I love *A Wrinkle in Time*, but you know, L'Engle got that part wrong. Dimensional travel doesn't fold the universe neatly together. It's already folded. Real dimensional travel tears through the folds and comes out the other side like a bullet through a stack of towels.

Oh, I hurt. My stomach twisted, but there was nothing more to come up (it wasn't as if I'd eaten during my lunch hour). The world kept spinning, and I—with heavy head and heart already so done with this adventure—looked up.

"Welcome to New York City," said Bran with so much pride it's like he'd built the place.

New York. It was going to take hours to get home by train. I groaned and sank back down again, curled on my knees, face in my trembling hands.

And my mouth tasted like tea and vomit.

"The Lost Lin is closer to her goal," squeaked the clamshell.

"I knew it," said Bran.

"Screw you and your little shell too," I croaked.

CHAPTER 4

Predators and Portuguese

I GUESS THE ONE GOOD THING about New York City is they've seen just about everything, so nobody gave a damn that I looked like I'd been thrown through a wind-tunnel.

Baked chicken over yellow rice with salad and beans steamed in front of me, smelling like the best thing anyone ever smelled since creation. A Styrofoam cup with fountain-Coke and crushed ice made that pleasant little ticking-bubbles sound the really good sodas do. And across from me sat Bran, who'd just shown off by speaking great Portuguese and producing cash from nowhere to buy me some food to make up for the partially-digested breakfast I'd lost. I would have paid for myself, but my purse was, naturally, back at Danner and Danner's.

This wasn't the awkwardest meal I'd ever had. What the hell; I ate it all. Who knew when I'd get another one?

Of course, Bran sat across from me grinning the whole time, having apparently impressed himself. Weirdo.

His fingers tapped the table. "Once you're fed—and you're not throwing up anymore—we can go and find the vampire."

"I don't know a vampire." Napkin. Don't spray, Katie.

"You must. Cassandra is never wrong. It's part of her curse, you know."

"I know. Will you just let me eat?" I was so ungracious; my mother would have been livid.

I calculated while we sat there and I chewed. Penn Station wasn't far, which meant I could potentially be in my home state in a few hours, but nowhere near my car, which would suck. My phone was in my purse... which was back in my office and therefore useless to me right now.

And I'd have to beg Bran for a ticket. Ugh. "Next time, hero, grab a lady's purse, not just the cursed manuscripts, okay?" I saluted him with my Coke.

He laughed.

I was working really hard to avoid thinking about the fact that the Raven King tried to kill me. Yeah, that internal conversation was going to wait until I had a glass of wine and lots of safety spells and maybe a good night's sleep. "Anyway, like I said, I don't know a vampire. I'm sorry."

"If you don't know one yet, you will." He shrugged.

"I thought blind faith was the territory of fairies." My Styrofoam container was empty. I sat back, just over the edge of comfortably full, and sighed. "Man, that's good."

"Not a lot of Portuguese cuisine in Wales?" he suggested.

"Sure there is, but it doesn't taste like New York City's." I was calming down a bit, which probably wasn't good. A girl needs a good dose of frantic to get through something like this, and I didn't have it. Maybe I was out of adrenaline. "Let me see those books."

"What? We're in public. No." He put one arm protectively around the knapsack.

I held out my hand. "Gimme. Or I will help you not."

The Yoda quote went right over his head, of course, but at least he obeyed.

The moment I opened the knapsack, strange and sinister vibes rose like flies. Those books felt horrible, buzzing, whispering (they hadn't

done *that* before), caressing my hands with invisible tendrils—
"Whoooop," I said, zipping it right the hell back up again. "I've
changed my mind. You're right. We need to turn this in. I'll just not
tell authorities who I am. That'll go over splendidly." By which I meant
it wouldn't work at all.

"What about your job?" he said.

He was right.

I couldn't just lose these books. I was responsible for them. So basically, my choice was give the books up and lose my job, or turn them
over to the authorities and lose my freedom. Either way wrecked the
life I'd worked so hard to build. Neither addressed the Raven King's
out-of-nowhere attack.

No, I was *not* going to cry. Crying could wait for that glass of wine
later. Later.

"Hey, don't do that," said Bran. "We could erase their memory of
you receiving these manuscripts easily enough."

I laughed, bitter as an old sailor. My job was screwed. I was
screwed. Memory alterations? Really? That would not work at all.
Sure, I could zap my co-workers and even the charming Joshua Run,
but what about the folks in Boston who'd sent him up to me? What
about all the email correspondence, secreted away on servers who
knew where? What about people who'd had conversations, or paper
trails that I had no way of tracking down?

There's no such thing as an easy magic-erase problem-solver. It
would come back to bite me in time, but more than that, it would bite
all the people involved. I wasn't looking to get anyone fired because
they couldn't remember a conversation I stole from their minds. I'm
not an ass, thank you very much. No, the only decent option I had was
to get rid of the books, change my identity, and get a new job somewhere else. My old identity would just be on the run from the law forever. No big.

I rubbed my face, suddenly tired. "No. No, it's okay. I guess I can
start over." I sounded a *lot* cheerier than I was. "Get new ID from my
uncle. Move someplace. Do something else."

"You sound miserable," Bran said brightly, and bussed our table.

Non-humans found Kin emotion funny sometimes. Why? Damned if I know.

The knapsack wasn't heavy; magic does have its benefits, including nifty weight re-distribution. I slung it over my shoulder, grateful that whatever material he'd made it from, it dampened the whispering texts inside. "Guess we might as well get going."

One thing for sure: I was losing the business skirt and the heels.

I knew a few spells I didn't need a wand for, and I used one as I passed beneath the lintel of this hole-in-the-wall and out onto the dirty, snow-clogged sidewalk: boom, fancy clothes *gone*.

I traded them out for practical things, for water-proof boots and thick jeans, a way more comfortable brassiere, and several layers of shirt, sweater, and coat.

I loved that spell. It's called an *amnewid*, and essentially, it's a trade of materials you can set up beforehand—which is why I didn't need a wand. The spell was already focused: I just let it go (sort of like lifting one end of a stretched rubber band off a hook and letting it fly), to instantly trade whatever I was wearing.

Yes, even panties. Since you asked.

Happily, I had it all mapped out, so my socks didn't end up on my hands, or something stupid like that. And it was quick. Really quick. No flash of skin.

"Nice," Bran purred as if he'd seen something when I damn well know he did not.

"You're making me use up my emergency spells. This is not okay." I still didn't have my purse; I had no way to fetch that, no pre-prepped spells for purse-fetching. I'd have to consider it for the future. If the past year was any indication, I couldn't hope this would be the last weird incident. Magic seemed doomed to follow me, to seek me out, no matter where I went. What was I supposed to do, go to the moon and live in a hole? "Damn moon rats would eat my books," I muttered.

"Where are we going?" he said, ignoring my mutters.

"The trolls in Central Park. They'll be the best bet for bribing to take the books off our hands without giving my identity away."

"I wouldn't give those books to trolls if I were you," he said with rare caution.

He was probably right. I didn't care. I was kind of done.

At least my feet were finally warm. I moved at a quick pace up the street, heading north toward the Upper West Side where I'd seen trolls when I was younger. My family had once taken a vacation in the States, which was fantastic in spite of being micromanaged by my mother. I liked the trolls. They seemed nice... if a little opportunistic. Trolls and capitalism went together like fish and chips. Like cawl and beer. Like *pice ar y maen*—lovely little spiced cakes—and butter.

How the heck had delicious Portuguese food made me miss Welsh cuisine? Eh, I just wouldn't be satisfied today, that was all, and also, I still wasn't thinking about the Raven King because I had no solution for that.

I could be relentlessly cheerful. What else was I going to do? I wasn't going to cry in front of *him*.

Bran strode beside me, one wide step for every two or so of mine, hands in his pockets and increasingly smug with every appreciative side-glance people gave him.

Then he stopped dead as though he'd been hit with a door and gripped my shoulder. The cool tingle of one of his subtler spells fell over us like a veil.

There are no coincidences, *capisci*? But spotting Joshua Run across the street still rocked me to my core.

What. Was he. Doing here?

Joshua hadn't seen us. He looked relaxed, his tailored suit traded for leather jacket and jeans, the twists in his hair short enough to be professional but lively enough to be un-boring—kind of like the Marvin the Martian tie. And he was smiling like the moon at the gorgeous lady by his side.

Wow. What was up with this day and beautiful people?

She was on the short side, but I promise you, nobody cared. I had no idea just what ethnicity she was; black hair, terracotta skin, high cheekbones and full lips. Maybe Saudi? Maybe Hindi? Maybe mixed—her eyes were a brilliant green that put traffic lights to shame.

Wait. I knew that green.

She hung off his arm, smiling up at him, and yet she controlled the direction and speed of their walk, wherever they were going. Joshua was stricken, entranced, and I couldn't blame him one bit: that was a vampire or I was a hairy-assed baboon.

This couldn't be happening.

"A Child of the Blood!" Bran hissed, gripping my shoulder.

Okay, I told myself. Joshua should be fine. There were rules for vampires, everyone knew that; it wasn't like the movies where they ran around killing people or pretending to be high-school students or strangely androgynous drug addicts. They had rules about eating people, and Joshua should be just fine.

Every instinct I had screamed that he was not.

"A vampire, Kate!" Bran repeated, his breath tickling my ear. "There! Right there!"

"I don't know her! And don't call me Kate!" I breathed back, but screaming, screaming, my instincts were screaming, *something was wrong*, something here was terribly wrong, I couldn't put my finger on it, I didn't know—

The vampire looked up and smiled straight in our direction.

Bran went really still.

"So I guess your spell is rubbish," I said, shivering like the green of her eyes was somehow pressing into the front of my skull like radiation.

"That's not possible," he whispered to himself.

Apparently it was, and my screaming instincts gave up and went into full-blown panic. "Let go. Let go!" I tried to pull away from him.

Bran yanked me against his chest. "Don't. Run."

Screw him, I was running! We were prey, right now, I knew it, he knew it, screw the rules, something was *so very wrong*.

She turned toward to Joshua and said something, he nodded, and the two of them walked across the street toward us.

Joshua still couldn't see us, of course.

I was about to scream. It was rising in my throat, unstoppable, like the pressure from a fire hydrant.

"Steady," Bran said.

She walked like a lioness through tall grass, and everything I knew about everything went right out the window. This was it, the end, and I lost my mind. I tried to run. I elbowed him, tried to bite his arm, but it didn't change a thing. Bran held me tight, feet off the ground, very still, and I stopped struggling when they came to a stop in front of us.

Joshua looked around, unseeing, inches away, and he didn't hear the tiny sounds of panic slipping from my throat.

"Among the Mythos, I am of the Blood, called Ravena," she said, and her voice...

I'm not *that* weak, okay? This shouldn't have done what it did—frissons of pleasure, drug-like and soothing, and my vision blurred as I went limp in Bran's arms and waited for whatever she wanted to do.

"Stop that," said Bran.

"How rude," she said, and smiled. "That's all right. I know who you are, prince of the Darkness, called Bran, and your friend is Kin, called Katherine Aelwyn—sometimes also called the Lost Lin."

My blood froze. I couldn't place her accent, but it was perfect, just like the rest of her, and wasn't that a nice observation to have right before I was going to die?

Joshua stirred like waking from a dream. "Katie?"

"Run," I whispered.

"I think you have something interesting there," said Ravena, and pointed at the knapsack I'd forgotten, dangling off my shoulder. "I'd like very much to see it, you rude children, you."

Bran shuddered.

"Give that to me," she said, and her will washed over us both like the tide.

I'm pretty sure we would have obeyed if all hell hadn't broken loose.

No coincidences. None. When the bar down the street suddenly blew up and a wash of horrible, broken magic followed it like shrapnel, I acted as fast as I've ever moved in my entire life.

Three beats:

Boom went the corner at the end of the block, cement and glass and heat suddenly everywhere, enough to make all four of us scream and duck and stop whatever we'd been doing.

Whoosh went the magic, ugly and broken and somehow putrid, snapping the spell she'd woven and waking us all up. Joshua suddenly staggered to the side, gasping.

"*Bran!*" I shouted in command, hoping he'd understand, hoping he'd do the right thing and forget his stupid clamshell and prophecies and all the rest, and I gripped his hand with my right and grabbed Joshua's with my left.

And for one second, I saw the monster behind this Ravena's green eyes, saw the mad beast about to be denied, and I opened my mouth to scream because she opened hers *way too wide* and her fang-teeth were thick and sharp and made for rending—

And Bran actually did it. He ripped the world and jumped through, pulling me, Joshua, and the knapsack with him.

Everything spun again and Joshua yelled. Ravena disappeared, Manhattan disappeared, and we all crashed together through some inconvenient trees into a pile of crisp, dead leaves.

We lay there like discarded dolls, breathing.

The leaves were bright. Golden sunlight poured between the bare branches, warm and perfect. Wherever the hell we'd just gone, it was still autumn, a lovely golden fall.

"Dammit!" Bran screamed, and slammed his fist into the leaves (which was probably less satisfying than hitting something solid would be). "Why did I do that? She was right there!"

"That can't have been the vampire you needed. Cannot." I didn't even recognize my own voice, thick and hoarse as if I'd been strangled. "She was gonna kill me, Bran." It was true. Twice in one day, someone I did not know had tried to kill me. Why? Why? What the hell was going on?

"I know," he said, confirming without fanfare.

"What the hell is this? Where are we?" Joshua cried, struggling to free himself from us, crunching through leaves and flailing over roots as he tried to get to his feet.

Then he threw up.

I didn't blame him. That was a rough trip. I'd probably join him in another few seconds. "Bran," I said, shivering. "What the hell is going on?"

"Something bad," Bran said softly.

Joshua panted, wiping his mouth on his sleeve. He didn't say anything yet.

That was okay; it was my turn to throw up now, so I wouldn't be answering anything for at least the next thirty seconds.

For the record, the Portuguese wasn't nearly as good coming up as it was going down.

CHAPTER 5

The Silver Dawning

THROWING UP TOGETHER is such a bonding experience.

"Gross," said Bran cheerfully.

I burped, and it tasted bad. I wanted to die. "Can we... maybe not jump this far next time?"

"'Oh, thank you, Crow King, Echelon of Darkness, Heir to the Darkseed,'" Bran said in a terrible falsetto. "'However can I repay you? My womb awaits—perhaps that will go some way toward paying you back for all you've done for me today!'" And he tossed me the knapsack.

I caught it. I caught it while *glaring the ever-loving hell at him.*

I know I'm not brave. My bravado and my sarcasm are my defenses, sort of like a tiny bird that fluffs its feathers, hoping things will think it's big and strong. I'm not big and strong. I'm not brave. But now, I was mad.

Joshua stared at him. "What'd you just say, man?"

"Hey!" I yelled, and threw a handful of crumbly leaves in Bran's direction. "Grateful? Grateful? You *did* this to me in the first place! If you hadn't dragged me into this, you wouldn't have had to save my life, and I'll tell you something else, *bucko*, as of this afternoon, *you owe me!*" I leveled my finger at him, breathing hard. "I am ninety percent sure your grandfather attacked me because of *you.* You just wrecked *my entire life,* and unlike you, it wasn't freaking handed to me. I earned it. You ruined it. Do not talk to me about owing, or I swear on Merlin's ass, *I will end you!*"

I might have been screaming.

Both men stared at me.

"Whoa. Whoa, now," said Joshua, hands up, looking at us like we were both crazy.

Bran threw back his head and laughed. Laughed, and then clapped his hands like this was the best thing he'd ever seen in all his days.

"Whatever. I'm done with this." My cheeks felt hot, anyway, which was a sure sign it was time to get out of here. "Come on. There has to be a road around here somewhere." And off I went, crunching through the autumn leaves like I was out for an afternoon stroll.

Joshua walked beside me for a long moment before saying anything. "Mint?"

Of course he had breath mints with him. "Thanks."

"I'm not a wealthy man," he said slowly, "but I would give every penny I own to know what the hell is going on."

I hunched, fuming, not quite calm enough to give him a considerate answer. "Magic is real. We just went through a magical portal. Your date was a vampire." I jerked my thumb at Bran. "He's not human. We're all in trouble."

"Okay," Joshua said, much more calm than I wanted him to be. "So when can we go home?"

"Did you hear me? Magic is real."

"Okay."

"We can't go home yet, Joshua. That woman was a vampire. She has your scent. She'll hunt you."

"Okay."

"Okay?" I threw my hands in the air. "What's that mean, 'okay?'"

He glanced at me. "Not your enemy, Katie. Chill."

How dare he be so rational in the middle of this? "Sorry. Just... what do you mean, 'okay?' You're fine with all of this?"

He sighed slowly, cheeks puffing out. "No, I'm not fine. Did you notice there are two suns?" He pointed up. "Two of them."

"Yeah." I sighed, too. "The Silver Dawning has two suns. We're not in the human world anymore."

"Okay."

"Don't say that again."

He smiled weakly. "All right. Here's what I'll say instead. No, I'm not fine with all this. I'm pissed. I'm scared. I'm doubting my senses. But what else am I supposed to do? Freak out? Sit down and have a good cry?"

"I kind of feel like I could use one," I muttered.

He shook his head. "I don't think you're right."

"What?"

He lowered his voice and looked at me through his thick, black lashes. "I'm a student of history, and in history, funky crap goes down all the time, right? Until somebody figures it out, it's called magic. Once they do figure it out, it's science, and then we build things out of it. So. This." He swung his arm around, including everything. "Whatever's happening, there's a rational explanation for all of this, and I'm going to act like I already know what it is until it comes clear so I don't mess anything up. So, in sum, 'okay.'"

He *was* being too rational about this. Boy, was he in for a shock or three. "Please promise when reality hits and you do freak out, you won't take it out on me. I've just decided you'd make a terrifying serial killer." That last part just slipped out. See, this is why I don't talk to people.

The skin around his eyes crinkled in a smile. "And I'm a lawyer, so I'd know how to defend myself in court."

"Dangerous."

"Calm under pressure. Determined to save the day. Sounds about right." And he winked.

Was he *flirting*? Really? Now? "I'm glad one of us is." I smiled. He earned it.

"We can't go home."

"We can't. For real. If we send you back, she'll hurt you. I'm sure of it."

"Ravena?"

So that was her name. "Yeah. She's a monster. She's a vampire. Literally a vampire."

He didn't seem to believe me. "And the other dude?"

"Bran. The Crow King."

He raised his eyebrow. "The bird king just harassed you."

"It wasn't that bad," I said, not looking at him.

"Lady, it was downright rapey."

"Rapey. Is that the legal term?" My voice shook a little.

"No. But it's the right one." He looked at me again. "Just for the record, if you want help, I'll give it. You don't want it, I'll back off."

Oh. Oh, I liked him. Oh, this was going to go so bad when he realized it was real. "Thanks. I appreciate that."

And then we fell silent, and became just two young people walking through a glorious autumn wood in perfect sweater-weather with golden sunlight dancing through the branches. In any other circumstance, it'd be wonderful, but monsters were after us. We were in a semi-friendly world, but it was hard to predict how Fey would react to a member of the Lin family. We didn't have a good reputation.

Bran passed us. "Follow me. I know where we are."

"You dropped us here. It's good to know you know where you put us," I snapped.

He looked back at me.

I swallowed the rest of my words. The Bran I'd first met months ago was here: the prince of the People of the Darkness, whose steady gaze held terrifying weight, and whose authority filled the air like heat. This kind of command could not be learned. It was born, not made.

"Where you taking us, man?" Joshua said respectfully after a long moment.

"A waterfall. Then a desert." Bran resumed walking.

"That's creative," said Joshua, trying very hard to retain his self-confidence in the shadow of that authority. "A waterfall, then a desert? How do they keep the ecological zones separated?"

"Don't encourage him," I muttered.

"I'm going to do the nice thing and drop you two off with someone who can help you," Bran said, enunciating slowly. "Then I am going back to find that vampire. And if keeping you two alive means I lost the vampire, I am going to come back here and skin you both."

He didn't sound like he was joking. So naturally, I mouthed off. "How do you know that was *the* vampire, huh? I mean, after all, I'd never have seen her if you hadn't brought me to New York. Maybe it was a vampire back in Portsmouth, working at Starbucks or something, and we missed it because you jumped the gun."

Poor Bran. For a moment, he looked rocked. "No," he said. "No. Can't be."

"Can." I pointed up at nothing. "So far, everything that's happened has happened because of you, not me. Cassandra could've just told you to go to New York. If that was it, what do you even need me for?"

"You are messing with my head, and it makes me want to kiss you," said Bran.

"No." How the hell had that backfired?

"Too bad. I want to."

"The lady said no," Joshua rumbled, arms tensing, not realizing that his impressive height and build meant precisely nothing.

Bran ignored him and glanced back at me, his expression weirdly softened. "I'll win you yet," he said.

"This is not happening," I moaned.

"This is harassment," Joshua started.

"Do not come between me and my choice," Bran warned.

"The lady. Said. No," repeated Joshua.

The lady. Was being. Ignored. "Hey, guys. Remember *Twilight*?" I interjected. "With all the stupid infighting? It's aimed at teenage girls and there are none of those here, so let's not act it out here in the woods of a strange world, okay?"

They just glowered like a couple of morons.

Was I the only sane person here? Joshua would die. Bran didn't know how to hold back. His people never did. "Hey!" I said brightly. "Here's another idea! Just show us where to go. We can go do that, and you can go do whatever you have to do, and everybody's happy."

"I can't risk that," said Bran. "As you just pointed out, that might not be the vampire, in which case, I'd need you again. Thanks for pointing that out, by the way."

So many curse words flashed behind my eyes that I temporarily went blind.

Slow breaths. Slow. Think it through, Katie. This was the Silver Dawning—the parallel world created by the Fey, for the Fey—and we Kin weren't always welcome. "Who are you thinking of turning us over to?"

"Jaden, probably."

Spit-take time! "What?"

"He owes me a favor," said Bran as if talking about a lover and not the freaking king of the Seelie Fey.

Jaden held the Scepter. *The Scepter.* He quite literally controlled half the magic of all living Fey. And possibly dead ones, too, if the rumors were true. "He owes you?"

"I rescued his nephew from a sticky situation," Bran rumbled. "Come, now, both of you! There's nothing to fear. I will see you treated well." And the smile he tacked onto that little line could freeze the blood of a woolly mammoth.

There are times when Bran's non-humanness leaked through, no matter what glamor he put on himself. This was one of those times.

Joshua gulped. I heard him.

"Right," I said, my voice scratchy. "Lead on, MacDuff."

He led on.

"I don't like this, Katie," said Joshua.

"I know. I'm sorry. I promise you, there are good reasons."

I swear I could hear Cassandra squeaking away in Bran's jacket, probably giving him more ways to ruin my life.

There are a few things you should know about the Seelie and Unseelie courts. See, they're global superpowers, and they do it by robbing their own people.

As far back as anyone can remember, the Throne and the Scepter have been the most valuable and dangerous weapons among the Mythos. All among the Mythos produce magic; we just create it, like exhaling carbon dioxide. Well, from birth, every Fey's magic is leeched away from them and channeled into either the Throne or the Scepter.

It leaves the Fey starving, like trying to breathe in a room without oxygen. They find ways around this—supplementing with magic they gather from the world around them, from people's emotions, from sex, from fire. But it still sucks. Really sucks.

What sucks even more is it's not limited to the Seelie and Unseelie Fey, but *all* Fey, all over the world.

That includes the **Zār**. The Xana. The Ciguapa. The Diwata and Anito, the Dökkálfar and Ljósálfar, the Huldra, the Sirens. More. All of their magic is taken from them at birth. No choice. No way to stop it.

In case you ever thought Sirens were the bad guys, they can't help it. They're starving.

Anyway, all this is basic. Nobody's been able to circumvent, turn off, destroy, or hijack the Throne and the Scepter. They're terrifying. Powerful. Some people say they're even alive.

My uncle told me once that the two creators of the Throne and Scepter somehow sublimated themselves into them. Sank themselves in somehow, sacrificed themselves, something. Whoever went into the Scepter is gone, or so says my uncle; that guy did it wrong, and whoever wields the Scepter now runs the risk of being absorbed, too.

But Mab still lives in the Throne. She's completely in control of herself, her people, and all that power, or so I'm told.

I was kind of glad we were not going to the Unseelie court. That's hers. Instead, for whatever lucky reason, we were going to the high court of the Seelie Fey. Jaden was the current ruler there—wise, tightly wound, a very serious and very reasonable king. However, he has no sense of humor. Which makes this "nephew" thing really interesting. See, I *have* met his nephew.

I almost got giggled into bed with his nephew.

Aiden is....

How can anyone describe Aiden? He's shorter than most Fey, more cute than pretty; silly as the silliest thing you ever met, laughs at everything and gets you laughing, too.

He's adorable.

He's the embodiment of joy.

And he's the most voraciously pan-sexual being I've ever met in my life.

My history of bed-hopping is none of your business, but I can tell you this: Aiden nearly talked me into it just by making it seem like so much fun.

This was going to be interesting.

The waterfall was a sight to behold: tall as Niagara and graceful as Angel Falls, sending rainbows in all directions with no regard for the position of the suns. Beyond it stretched a blindingly bright desert, as brilliant as if it had been made from polished gold dust. The Fey sure did know how to show off.

"This can't be real," Joshua muttered. He said it again as we stepped onto the crystalline sled that waited at one edge of the fall, ready to float us smoothly across the chasm and over the golden sand.

"Focus. If you do this wrong, you're in trouble, and then I'll mouth off, and I'll be in trouble, too. Come on, Joshua." I waved my hand in front of his face.

He stared at me, color gone slightly ashen.

I sighed. "Please. I need you to focus. Rule number one?"

"Don't talk unless I'm directly questioned," he muttered, much more willing to listen to my rules since we'd stepped aboard our impossible transport. Beneath our feet, the falls churned in clear water, granting glimpses of the smooth, multi-colored stones that lined the riverbed.

"Yes. Rule two?"

He shook his head like rule two tasted bad. "Humans are called Ever-Dying. I still don't get—"

"Questions later. I promise, I'll tell you everything." The breeze blew my hair into my face, and I tried without much success to tuck it behind my ear.

"Everything. Sure." He looked around. "There's an explanation for this."

"Yes. It's called a levitation spell. Focus. Rule number three?"

He sighed. "Don't say anything three times in a row, or it's constituted as a legally binding oath."

A magically binding one, too, but I wasn't going to tell him that. "Good. Rule number four?"

"Don't go off with anyone or eat anything offered unless you give the okay. It's like we're going into the Underworld."

"I'm pretty sure they won't serve pomegranates. And the last rule?"

He rubbed his forehead. "I'm not a child. Is this necessary?"

"It is. I'm trying to save your life. We're heading into a completely different culture here, and they're ready to take offense. Too ready."

He sighed. "All right. Rule five is to keep my opinions to myself."

I smiled weakly. "Not so easy, I know."

"You're asking this of a guy who's paid to give his opinions and back them up."

"I know. I'm sorry. Just pretend we're in a different country instead of a different world, and maybe it'll sit better."

"None of this will sit better until I get some real answers, but fine. I'll go along with it. And in another hour, the camera guys will jump out and tell me which friend paid to 'punk' me so hard, and I'll punch my ex-friend out, and everything will be good again."

"Sure. That's what's going to happen. Right."

He managed to give me a smile. I counted it as a win.

Bran ignored us both, arms crossed, looking out over the golden hills as though calculating their worth. He was preparing for this meet-up, no question; dark power sifted off him like sand from the top of those dunes. I could see it. Joshua couldn't, but he could feel it, and it made him shiver.

The sand suddenly became a city, with no warning at all.

I know I have to correct some imagery you have in your heads. Fey are not woodsy. They're deep into tech; they love it, and they're really good at it. In fact, you'd be surprised how many really important inventions were inspired by Fey who got sick of feeling like a visit to Earth was a visit to the Dark Ages.

Tall, curved towers sported intricate glass and ebony ornamentation, somehow organic and Gothic and sleek all at once. Statues, flowers, and entire histories played out in hints of shadow and silhouette. There were no fuel-run vehicles here; lots of animals—plenty of them flying, big enough to carry a couple people at a time—and all over, everywhere, a mishmash of Fey and plenty of other Peoples of the Earth on foot.

The Fey need other people to take magic from, so commerce was always welcome. The sled we rode flew low enough to give me a glimpse of Naga and Naiads, of large, red-skinned Shadow's Breath (the same species as Bran, though he didn't deign to look their direction), kelpies and wulvers and a couple of dragons. Trolls, gorgons, things I couldn't even identify—fish-headed things and large, shy octopus-creatures who moved slowly and nervously through crowds of much smaller shoppers.

And of course, the Fey. In this wildly varied population, they still shone.

None of them bothered looking human here. Skin and hair gleamed in all colors, makeup drawing attention to eyes, lips, and those pointed ears—ears as long as their forearms and so thin that the double suns shone through them, making them glow. Steam-punk kimonos seemed to be the "in" style right now, along with what I might call Han Solo boots. And of course, there was the walk.

You've never seen allure until you've seen Fey in their element.

Magic sparked off their fingers and long hair, glimmered on skin and lips. They were mesmerizing, like firecrackers in a field of nightwheat. And the music they made....

Not all of them made it, of course. It was mostly small groups here and there, every other city block corner, but every song they played complemented the rest. No matter where you turned, it all seemed like one great symphony, unending, connected, an ouroboros of sound.

There were guards, too, lots of them. These Fey didn't smile; their long hair was braided back, and they wore slim metal guards to protect their paper-thin ears.

The sled landed smoothly, perfectly, with nary a bump, though Joshua nearly stumbled off. Gee, I wonder why he was a little distracted?

"Easy, there," I murmured, taking his arm. "Stand up. We can't hide that you're new to the place, but you can at least look like you're not terrified."

"I'm not imagining this," he whispered hoarsely. "This is real."

"Yeah." I patted his arm. "Remember your promise. I'm spared in your mad serial killer purge."

He laughed weakly. "Yeah, yeah. Sure thing. But I didn't promise three times."

"Ooh, you got me there." Soothing, I could do, even though it felt like bugs were crawling through my flesh. I hated this; I was a Lin, and Fey didn't like Lins in general.

Bran, fortunately, was taking charge. He raised his hand and summoned one of the guards over like a flame calls a moth. "We will see Jaden," he announced.

Every word carried weight, magical and otherwise. Two minutes later saw us on another sled—this one solid black—and on the way to the palace.

The Seelie palace rose from the center of the Silvermoon City in a pyramid, towering over everything, polished and shiny as black glass. Unlike every other edifice here, it caught the light and threw it back painfully, intentionally blinding. The magic emanating from it was dark purple and so thick it twisted the air, even in broad daylight. Nobody was storming this place anytime soon.

Bran's casual clothes suddenly transformed into form-fitting black armor like fish scales from head to toe. Sleek, dangerous, strong. "You two don't look the part," he said with a smirk, and waved his hand.

We both yelped. Instantly, our practical, familiar clothes changed to the current style of steam-punk kimono, trousers, and boots.

Okay, I admit it: we looked damn good. Bran had chosen orange and white for Joshua, really bringing out the warmth of his ebony skin, while he'd given me soft blue colors—some of my favorites, if I were going to admit it.

I wasn't going to admit it. If he thought giving me things would win my heart, he'd never stop. "You'd better give my clothes back at the end of this," I warned.

"In a pile on my bedroom floor," he said.

I smacked my own forehead. This. This was why I didn't like talking to people.

Joshua touched my arm.

I gave him the *I'm okay* nod, though I wasn't.

"Don't suppose you could give my wallet back, man," he said to Bran.

Bran looked at him—through him, completely dismissing those words—then turned away.

"I'll make sure you're taken care of," I promised, though I had no idea how I was going to manage that. And then I panicked. "The knapsack!"

"Stored," said Bran. "Safe. You wouldn't want to bring that into this place, anyway."

My heart pounded. He was right, but I didn't care. Those had been my responsibility. Stored where? I had no idea, but asking now would be bad.

We had eavesdroppers. The guards said nothing as the sleigh rose up toward the top of the black pyramid.

It was blinding, double suns reflecting off the glass-smooth sides like knives into our eyes, and so I was squinting when we reached the top. A clever design; it looked pointed from below, but the top had been sheared flat. Pillars rose seemingly at random, carved, ornate, curved and somehow terrible to behold.

Curses. There were curses all over those pillars. I decided it was a good idea not to try to read them.

"Follow me, please," said the guard ahead of us, a freckled red-headed Fey who would not look out of place on the cover of a magazine. But then, none of them would.

There was precisely one way into this place: a single dark stairwell in the center of the roof.

Bran smiled. "At last, some decent shade." And he disappeared down that hole almost at once.

Deep breaths, Katie. No panicking. I went next.

The circular black stairs seemed to be floating in the center of the world. Around us, the pyramid opened up into enormous space. Blue things like ghosts glided past—even though there *are* no ghosts—smiling and singing and almost recognizable as their former selves. Glints of red, green, and blue appeared and disappeared in the air, glimmering, and one of them flew close enough to show us a jewel-colored moth, pulsing with life of its own.

I should mention every step took us hundreds of feet down.

It was dizzying, but I wasn't about to complain. We'd be walking forever if they hadn't.

Joshua had a death-grip on the railing. "This is messed up."

"We're almost at the bottom." I was pretty sure I could see Bran down there. "Almost there."

"I'm gonna kiss the ground when we get down there," Joshua promised.

"Sure you will. And I'll watch."

We saved the rest of our breath for walking and trying not to fall. Do you want to know how many steps down we went? Thirty-two. Each of those was several hundred feet. You do the math. My head spun, and vertigo threatened to pull me down. We were far below the city by the time we reached the ground level.

A pretty Fey doge waited there. I was pretty sure I knew who this was: he wore a kimono, but a real one—a wedding one, weirdly enough, a glorious orange-red with white phoenixes—and his makeup was on point.

No lipstick could help lips pressed that tightly together, though. This had to be Quinn. Behind his back, they called him the Ice Queen, and the Bitch. To his face, it was most definitely *sir*. He swept forward the moment we both reached the ground. "Among the Mythos, I am Quinn, Seelie Fey, vice-regent, bearer of the Silver Seal, at your service." He bowed to Bran. "Lord of Crows, Echelon of Darkness, Heir to the Darkseed, you are welcome here. Our lord Jaden awaits your presence with great eagerness."

Quinn spared one glance for me and Joshua, that was all: we were nothing here. Less than nothing. A gum wrapper on the bottom of someone's shoe.

I was *completely* fine with this. Being nothing meant no attention.

"Good. I do not intend to wait," said Bran. "These two need help, and I have places to go."

Wow. In this society, that was rude on a level I could barely comprehend, and I stared at him.

Quinn's perfectly shaped left eyebrow twitched once. "As you wish, great one. Please follow me." He swept off. His kimono was so long we couldn't see his feet, and he made no sound; dude might as well have been on skates.

Those ghost-like things continued to sing hauntingly all around us.

"I'm not looking," Joshua said randomly.

"That's probably a good idea," I said back.

We walked until the darkness suddenly narrowed to a warm hall, beautiful in rich wood with gold scrolls. Thick, red carpet muffled sound all the way to the doors to the throne room.

Naturally, the doors were huge. Evidently pure gold, raised bas-relief detailed some crazy battle with giants and many-armed beasts and Fey in pointy helmets. Quinn ran his fingers over certain figures—a chariot driver here, a winged horse there, one long, strangely gleaming spear—and the doors opened.

The music.

Previous exposure is no protection. Even magic spells are no protection. I thought I'd been mentally prepared for this, but I was wrong.

Sweet strains on tenor flutes and plucked strings caressed my body, penetrating my skin and lighting up my nerve endings. Lush percussion like heartbeats on hide bodhráns took control of the pace of my breath and every step of my feet.

I wanted to lean against a wall and listen forever, floating up with the notes to dissipate with them in the darkness. I wanted to be touched, intimately, right now, even though I didn't really want those things at all. It was the audible equivalent of a date-rape drug. And people wonder why I ran away from the magical world.

The throne room had no ceiling I could see, but all around the walls hung enormous portraits of painted Fey throughout the ages, doing grand things—riding dragons, kneeling before piles of jewels, playing enormous and elaborate harps. Beneath them, living Fey stood here and there in steampunk chic, talking quietly and acting like they *weren't* steadily sucking power from the servants around the room.

The servants were all human.

They looked happy. Sure, they did; well-fed, cared for, probably wealthy beyond their wildest dreams, and happy to laugh at stupid jokes or carry trays of food or just stand by, looking pretty.

And their emotions fed the people in this room. It's a parasitic relationship, technically harmless enough; no one was dying. No one was going to die. But I didn't really care. It was creepy and tempting and terrifying *because* it was tempting, so I fixed my gaze on Bran's back and followed him, trying to seem boring as possible.

I almost forgot about Joshua.

To my amazement, he kept up with me. Desire dilated his pupils and quickened his breath, but he kept himself in control. Kudos; that was absolutely no small feat.

Quinn kept up a quick pace, but we could see where he led. Jaden was impossible to miss.

The throne he sat on was golden, spreading up and out like sun-rays, each stair of its dais a different color of the rainbow and polished like jewels and *just* muted enough to be classy.

And Jaden was the icing on that classy, muted, wealthy cake.

He looked young, like all Fey do; they don't age like humans, but they grow hard until their deaths—when they turn to stone. But Jaden wasn't ready to calcify yet; his long black hair fell past his shoulders to pool around his hips, and his gray eyes missed nothing that went on here or anywhere in his world. Strange orange glints shown through those gray eyes, as though he were internally on fire. He wore no makeup; he also wore no smile. And across his lap rested a thick, heavy scepter of gold tipped with a large, black ball.

It looked heavier than I was. It looked simple, if not simplistic. And it radiated so much power—tendrils of it, reaching out to vanish in the air like a spider-web too big to see—I could barely even look in its direction.

And then, like a nightmare, Jaden stood, raised that scepter, and pointed it straight at me. I froze. "The Lost Lin," he said in a surprisingly young voice.

Everyone went still. The music stopped. Bran turned to stare at me in surprise, along with pretty much everybody else.

My stomach did backflips. I tried to say something. It came out like a choked frog.

"Katie!" came a sudden cry, and Aiden burst through the gathering like a sunbeam in a dark barn, bouncing over to me and flinging him-self into my arms. He was shorter than I am, which is really short for Fey, but he made up for it in pure elastic energy. I staggered under his weight, and he nuzzled me, blue eyes bright and mischievous, and kissed me on the cheek.

Quinn pulled him off. "Un! Acceptable! Behavior!" he hissed.

"No, I like her!" Aiden cried, flailing and drawing attention to himself and away from me.

He knew I hated attention. That was... so sweet. If useless.

"Miss Lin, you are welcome here," Jaden boomed in the silence, though the way the guards gripped their shiny black spears made me think he might not mean those words. "Take them to the Beryl Suite."

And with that, we were hustled off, through a side-door I hadn't spotted, down a normal-sized hall with plush carpets and weird wallpaper, and into a round foyer with five doors.

The guards left us there, alone.

My companions eyed me.

"Spotlight thief," Bran teased, as if I'd wanted any of this.

"The Lost Lin?" Joshua said.

"Me. That's me. I ran away. I'm not lost. Dammit." I was shaking.

"He's not having you," said Bran. "I saw you first."

He was taking this way too calmly. "You're not helping." I turned away. "Think he'll be awhile before showing up and doing whatever he's going to do?"

"What's he going to do?" Joshua demanded. "What just happened?"

"Hell if I know." Why were they looking at me? I didn't have any answers. "You know what we should do? Sleep. No, not together," I snapped at Bran, and opened a door. "Look. Guest rooms. A bath. Beds. We should sleep, guys. All of us. It's been a horrible day."

"There's fruit in here. Cheese. Bread," said Joshua, checking another. He glanced back toward the foyer door.

"It'll be guarded, and you might have noticed there are no windows. We've got to be a mile underground or something." I rubbed my face. "Let's get some sleep. We're powerless until then."

"I'm not," said Bran. "I only let them bring me here to make sure you were all right."

"Then go. You have a vampire to track down, don't you?"

"You're right. I do," he said, and handed the clamshell to me.

I stared at him for a long moment before taking it. "Why are you giving me Cassandra?"

He grinned. "Because I want you to know I'll be back for you." Then he transformed into a shadow and sank right through the solid floor.

"What the *hell*?" demanded Joshua.

"Greetings, Lost Lin," said the clamshell.

I was ready to scream. "Not one more word before I sleep, or I swear I'll smash you!" I said.

The shell went quiet.

"Where'd he go?" Joshua said, spinning in a circle.

"Back to New York."

"He left us here?"

Yes, he'd left us here. In plushy custody. "Yeah," I said carefully. "He knows he won't lose track of us this way. Look, we've been welcomed as guests. We're safe. We can't leave, but we're safe." Sort of, but I didn't want to panic him, so. "And Bran will definitely be back. This shell is one of the most valuable treasures in the world. It's a guarantee he'll come back."

"Great. So when do we go home?"

"We... we can't. For now."

He clenched his fists, but said nothing.

Yeah, he'd probably lose his job. The police could be called, his family would be worried.... "I'm sorry," I whispered. "I know this is a mess."

He just shook his head.

Nothing like ruining someone's life to cap off a wonderful day.

I led him into his chosen bedroom and took off his boots. "Get some rest, okay?"

He said nothing. When I closed the door, he was sitting on the bed, staring at the sleeve of his kimono, looking utterly lost.

I felt him on that. Lost Lin? I'd never been more lost than since all this started happening. Something huge was happening here, and it was all converging on me. I had no idea why.

But right now, it was time to regroup.

I took a hot bath.

I drank some wine and some water.

I ate a bunch of grapes.

Then I went to bed, and by some crazy stroke of luck, I did not dream.

CHAPTER 6

The Lost Lin's Prophecy

THE DAMN CLAMSHELL WOKE ME.

Weird, nasal singing broke its way into my sleeping mind, filling it like a train whistle fills a cavern. It pulled me awake, though I really did not want to be awake, and when I finally got there, I had one hell of a headache.

"Shut up," I commanded into my pillow.

"Lost Lin, awake! Destiny waits," said the damn clamshell.

"Ugh," I said.

"Answers beckon. Lingering thoughts pursue; choices are many, but paths are few!"

Well, that was informative.

I sighed and rolled onto my back, sleep-sweat gluing my white t-shirt and boxers to my skin.

"Turmoil rages, and the words unspake!"

"'Unspake' is not a word," I said.

"The dark seed cannot hold the light, and yet must lest the shadow o'ertake him!"

"What the hell does that even mean?" I groaned and rolled over, rummaging in the little nightstand for paper and pen.

"The word you bring contains the end. To stopper death, the bright soul must be given in exchange."

"Uh-huh," I muttered, scribbling what would hopefully be readable when I could open *both* eyes.

"Beware! Beware! Beware! Three times doom: beware the orange eyes. Beware the pointed tongue. Beware the teeth that drop. Beware! Beware! Beware!" The little clamshell rattled, evidently moved by its own impressiveness.

Not that it looked impressive. It was just half a clamshell, *sans* mother-of-pearl, ridges worn smooth by many fingers and much sweaty, desperate hope.

There was a soul in there. Cassandra. That girl went through so much in her brief and miserable life, and now she was stuck like this. You know what? That sucked. "I'm sorry you're trapped in there. I don't suppose there's a genie-with-three-wishes kind of deal where a kind owner could set you free?"

The shell was silent for a long moment. "I know not of such a cure."

Geez. "That sucks, Cassandra."

Someone knocked on my door.

I padded over barefoot and was surprised to find Joshua standing there.

He wore an outfit just like mine, perfect for sleeping—a light white tank-top and boxers—but unlike me, he didn't look rested. Okay, one side of his hair was a little flatter than the other. But he looked gray. Gray and kind of tired.

"Hey," I said after a moment.

"So you're one of them, too?" he said.

Oh, boy. "Come on in. I won't bite, unlike your last date. Haha... sorry, that wasn't funny."

He quirked a smile, though, as he came in. "Yeah, it kinda was."

"Not really, but at least I *know* my jokes are stupid." I sat down on the bed and patted a spot beside me.

He hesitated this time.

I just looked at him, as dry as I could. "Really?"

"Sorry. I... sorry." He sat down—maybe not right next to me, but close enough.

So he'd figured out I wasn't human. I'd wondered how long it would take. "I'll bet you've got questions."

"What are you?"

And there we go. "Kin. I'm part-human."

He swallowed hard, and a moment of silence passed. "She wasn't a vampire." He stumbled over the word.

"She was. And something was really wrong with her. They've got rules they follow, and she wasn't following them. She attacked us. She was some kind of rogue."

He rubbed his face. "I don't believe it."

I said nothing.

"I didn't ask for any of this," he said, a little desperately.

I snorted. "Neither did I, bub." It was all too much. Monsters, magic, alternate worlds. He was crying a little. I was, too, to be honest. Both our lives had been blown to bits.

"Aiden said you came from a mixed family," he said, wiping his eyes.

I blinked. "Aiden talked to you?"

"Yeah. Brought me some kind of sweet tea. It helped."

Go, Aiden. "Yeah. Kin are mixed by nature, and I'm doubly *blessed* because there's both Welsh and Chinese in my blood."

"I'm mixed, too. Jamaican and Lebanese." He looked at his hands and took a slow, calming breath. "Guess we've got a lot in common."

"Yeah, bonding over culture-clash is definitely my idea of a good time."

He looked at me, startled, and then he laughed. It wasn't a good laugh (nor was it a good joke). It was shaky, and uneven, but it was real. I laughed with him.

I made us some hot chocolate in the silence that followed. "We good?" I asked, warming my hands on my mug.

"Yeah. We're good." He sipped. It probably burned him, but he didn't seem to care. The gray had left his face, replaced with a sort of dark determination. "So what about the bird king?"

Sigh. "Bran? He'll be back. When he does come back, I intend to use those Anshan manuscripts as leverage to find out what the hell is going on. The 'Lost Lin,' indeed."

"The *what* manuscripts?"

I told him.

He gaped at me, mouth working. "Let me get this straight. I was carting around cursed manuscripts?"

"Yeah."

"And I didn't know it."

"Yeah."

"I could've died."

Another sigh. "Yeah. I'm sorry. Somebody was a real jerk."

"What else don't I know? Wait. No. I'm already on overload. Don't want to hear it right now." He rubbed his forehead and we both just breathed, processing.

I didn't know what else to tell him. Sorry? Watch out for wooden nickels?

His lips quirked. "'Lost Lin' does have a ring to it, anyway."

Nice segue. "Bleh." That's my summation of the whole situation."

"I get we can't go home. I get it. But what do we do now?"

I looked at him long and hard. He was still saying 'we.' Even after establishing I wasn't quite the same species, and that he was only in this mess because of me, he still said 'we.' I appreciated that more than I could put into words, so I didn't try. "I guess we wait. It's not like we can leave. Besides—"

"Even if we did, that whole 'Lost Lin' thing seems like it's going to follow you," he said.

"Yeah." He'd hit the nail on the head.

"That sucks."

"Yup." I sipped more chocolate.

"What did the clamshell say again?" he asked.

I handed him the notebook.

"Huh. Well, if I stepped back and looked at all this—and maybe pretended we were on *The Outer Limits*—I could see some of this made sense," he said. "The 'word' containing the end might mean those manuscripts I brought you. The 'bright soul' could be the prophesying clamshell over there."

Hey, he was good at this. "Or it could be my soul, if we're just that lucky," I inferred.

He ignored that. "The dark seed's gotta be Bran."

"Probably. After all, he's in danger from the Raven King."

"Who?"

"His grandfather. It's complicated."

"Oh, just a little."

I wrinkled my nose. "Sorry. Grumpy."

"Understandable. But the rest of this doesn't make sense yet. What I want to know is what started this," he said.

I admit, I was impressed. These were good questions to ask. "Bran came to me, asking for help, because this clamshell told him to. Why, you think they're connected?"

"Gotta be. I got a strong feeling coincidence is even rarer than real magic."

He had a point. And then came another knock at the door. Would this day never end?

"Grand Central Station!" I said as I opened it.

Aiden bounced on his toes in the foyer, wearing a smile so wicked it could make nuns blush and flowers bloom. "Katie," he said, and skipped inside.

Joshua smiled. "Hey, little buddy."

Aiden winked at him.

"Glad you two have been introduced." I sat on the bed again, bouncing. "I don't suppose you know what's going on."

Aiden wriggled back and forth, looking guilty and eager all at once. "Aye."

I stared at him. "Aye, what?"

"All the prophets. All the seers. All the dice and feathers and teas. All fortunes are telling to look for you."

So it was worse than I'd thought by a significant portion. My voice came out really squeaky. "Me?"

"You. The 'Lost Lin.'" He made air quotes. "Ah, but the reason is always different, never the same! One is promised gold, and another longer life. Uncle Jay-Jay was promised control over the Scepter so's it don't eats him up whole." And he made a horrible sound, inhaling and flapping his tongue, like the worst soup-slurper ever.

"That's horri... did you just call him *Jay-Jay*?"

"He thinks you can extend his life. Mmm, I think that's not so directly true," said Aiden, skipping in a tiny circle. He smiled again. "What's *your* little seer promised?"

How did he know she existed? "Do... do you mean Cassandra? Okay. She told Bran I'd somehow introduce him to Notte and save his life from the Raven King."

Aiden laughed. At least somebody saw this as ridiculous as I did.

"To me, she didn't promise anything," I added. "She made some noise about dark holding light things and the end and... I dunno. Nonsense."

"Not exactly," said Joshua, and read off what I'd told him.

Thanks. I think.

Aiden looked thoughtful. "Maybe everybody's looking for you because you have to be in position."

A beat. "Position for what, pray tell? I'm not very powerful. I'm nobody. This is silly."

"Very silly, but nobody knows that but you—" He touched his finger to my nose. "Him." A finger to Joshua's nose (Joshua blinked). "And me." And Aiden touched his own nose. "They all talk of you. All of them."

What. The hell. Was going on.

If he was right and every bloody fortune-telling thing from here to Tortuga was telling people to look for me, it explained a whole lot. The Raven King showing up at my workplace. The weird rogue vampire in Manhattan. Even Jaden. "But what the hell for?" I demanded, even though I know there wasn't an answer. "Hey! Hey, you!" I stalked over and grabbed the clamshell, then shook it like an idiot. "You! What's this all about? Tell me, dammit, or so help me, I'll find something unpleasant to do to you, and then, by gum, I'll do it!"

And the clamshell laughed at me.

I suppose it's not that shocking. I'm tiny. Threats from me don't hold a lot of water. I'm just not mean enough to carry them out, appearances aside. Still. A girl's got her dignity to protect. "Stop that," I muttered.

"I have told you the steps you need," she squeaked at me. "For now."

"Steps? You haven't told me any steps! You hear her?" I made spooky fingers. "For now, she says. Ooh."

"I can't imagine how frustrating this is," said Joshua. "I'm sorry."

His empathy pulled me up short. "Thanks. I appreciate that."

"Might want to get dressed," said Aiden, suddenly not bouncy or perky or anything else. "Jaden is coming."

"Damn," I said, and lunged for the closet.

By the time I'd chosen something, Joshua had left the room, likely to choose his own borrowed finery. I found myself hoping he'd let Aiden pick for him. The little guy had taste. And also, it'd be funny.

I was *almost* composed when my door opened without warning and Quinn swept in.

He was just more outrageous than everybody, all the time, no matter what the style; I swear his white-blond hair had some kind of silvery streaks in it, artfully done and anything but natural. In this small, sedate room, he felt like an insult to all five senses. "The great lord Jaden, wielder of the Scepter, scion of the Orkney Isles, king of all the Seelie Fey, comes!" He didn't *say* 'bow, you puny mortal,' but he managed to communicate it, nonetheless.

Ugh. Well, I knew my manners. I bowed at the waist and waited. Three. Two. One—

Jaden stepped into the room in total silence.

He wasn't that tall. A young face—all Fey had young faces—but his gray eyes were old, and now that he'd come this close, I could see lines in the irises of some other color—something flickering and red, a color that didn't belong there.

It was like something inside him was burning up or cracking apart. Great.

Armed with that comforting thought, I bowed a little deeper. "Your lordship is gracious to visit his servant," I said, trying not to make a face over words that were so blatantly untrue.

He said nothing, looking at me.

Okay. He was supposed to say *something*. I peeked.

"You don't look like much," he said, approaching me.

How nice! And he had the leisure of ignoring etiquette, but I did not. "Thank you, my lord."

"That was not a compliment."

Apparently, sarcasm went the way of humor: over his head and out the door. "Of course, my lord."

He stopped in front of me. The silk brocade of his simple robe was seriously ornate; gray on gray, silver threads with darker charcoal whorled and shaped into an orchestra of visuals, telling some story I didn't know and probably wrapping him in power. "You're Kin," he said.

"Yes, my lord."

"A descendant of Myrddhin."

"Yes, my lord." My uncle—well, many-times-over grandfather, but whatever—Merlin was known all over these parts.

"We do not always have much to say to you and your family," he said, applying the "royal we" without a trace of irony, "but today, we are merciful. Rise, lady, and give us your kiss." He held out his hand.

Whee! Isn't the magical world *fun*?

I bent over his hand to kiss it. There was no ring. There was, however, a hardness to the skin; the very ends of his fingers had gone dark like granite stone. He was aging.

Fey age that way. They turn to stone. It freaks me the hell out.

"My lord, you are gracious," I said, ingratiating enough to make even my own mother proud.

"The niceties have been seen to and are done," he said dismissively. "Where is the book?"

Okay. Book?

I'm so glad Aiden warned me. This must have something to do with whatever Jaden's seers promised. "What book, Your Eminence?"

"The book of Dark Things. It is written in Anshan; my dreamers have told me it is or was in your possession. Where have you hidden it?"

Uh-oh. "I don't have it." I wasn't about to tell him there were five.

"That is not what I asked, child." Softly pretty, he was, with black hair and pale skin, his stone-gray eyes flecked with... something red, and no laugh lines in evidence. But he was already hard as stone, wasn't he?

"The Crow King took them and hid them away. I genuinely don't know where they are."

His eyes widened, and the red lines in his gray irises flashed. "Bran?"

"Yes, your lordship." Try and take 'em, why don'tcha. I mean, Jaden probably *could*, but it'd be seriously messy. It would be an incursion of one People upon another—and the Darkness and the Fey already have a pretty ragged-rough history. He'd start a war.

"Will he return?"

"Probably? I'm sorry. I don't know anything else. I'm not trying to be unhelpful, sir. I genuinely don't know." I would have shrugged, but who knew how he'd take it?

The red lines in his irises flickered, flickered like fire burning within. "Very well; it cannot be helped. The Dark Prince is... whimsical, at best, and capricious at worst; this, we personally know."

I didn't want to know how he personally knew.

"You will remain here as my guest until he returns," he said casually. "Which I suspect he will. He's not one to leave his toys behind."

Oh, he did *not* just say that.

Quinn swooped beside him as if by magic, and I saw—just for a second—shock and concern there before it was erased by customary smugness. "I will see to finer lodgings than this... paltry temporary stay," he said, as though it'd been my idea to march in here in the first place.

"And my companion?" I swallowed. This was bold of me, speaking out of turn.

For once, Quinn seemed uncomfortable. "What is he to you?"

Careful, Katie. "A friend."

They glanced at each other, communicating who knew what. "He will be seen to," said Quinn.

"He's human." I couldn't let this go. If I was going to manage even one goal today, it would be taking care of that poor guy. "And he's under my protection."

I actually said it.

Those words are never spoken lightly. I'd sure as hell never said them before. It was almost a magical contract. It made me responsible for him in a way he couldn't possibly understand.

If Joshua screwed up, I'd be doomed.

But if I screwed up, so would he.

I was tying our fates together and I wasn't even asking his permission. Dammit. I was just as bad as the rest of the Mythos, wasn't I?

I wondered if Joshua could feel me doing this to his life. Probably not.

Quinn and Jaden looked at each other again, communicating more things I couldn't read.

"As you wish," said Quinn finally, and he floated over to open the door.

Jaden—thousands of years old, supreme ruler of the Seelie Fey and legitimately one of the most powerful beings on earth—looked at me with his weird eyes, and suddenly, I knew he was in pain.

The Scepter in his hands didn't look like much. It was kind of ugly; simple. But not so simple. Fully half all Fey magic flowed through that thing, and it wasn't channeling it right. Jaden was in pain.

Did he mean to let me see that?

"Goodnight, Katie Lin," he said, turned, and left.

Quinn sniffed at me—the way only really snooty people can—and swooped after him, closing the door behind.

"What the hell did I just do?" I said out loud, then flopped onto the bed and sprawled, face in the pillow. "Uuuugh."

"The dark seed will cradle the light," squeaked the clamshell.

I didn't bother answering. I'd probably just egg her on.

CHAPTER 7

Operation *Katie Saves Her Own Damn Self*

YOU KNOW, THERE ARE A LOT of terrible literary tropes out there.

Seriously. You run into them in movies, in songs, in books, on television. Pretty much any medium that tells a story has the ability to elevate its characters above stereotype and boring, or to leave them in the mud, forcing them into shapes leftover from the corpses of bad stories past.

I've got lots of tropes I hate (Bran pisses me off for the "alpha-male is always sexy" one), but the one I personally hate the most is "damsel in distress."

Damsel in distress, *my ass*. Are you a damsel? Have you been in distress? Let me tell you, it is *not* like the damned fairy tales want you to believe. Know what it's really like to be a female in trouble? Oh, I'll tell you.

One, you aren't waiting and hoping for your prince to swoop out of the sky. You know better by now; princes come with baggage, and romance has poisoned barbs. You're not looking for a romantic savior.

You may take advantage of one to get out, but you don't really think he's Mister Perfect.

Two, you don't really want to be saved; you want to save yourself. But see, that's the problem—sometimes, you can't. And that makes you feel helpless. Is there a worse feeling than helplessness? Maybe shame, but that's about it.

Three, if you see a way out, you might take it, you might not. See, you're desperate. That's what being a damsel in distress feels like. You are *so desperate* that some people might mistake it for weakness, but it isn't weakness. It's not at all. Even though sometimes you feel like it—helpless, drowning, and weak—you're not. And deep down, when push comes to shove, you know that, which is why I come to number four.

Four: *You are dangerous.*

Desperation and limited options tend to make people that way. It's why unarmed men will stand up to tanks. It's why abused children with no resources will run away.

It's why damsels in distress become black widows.

I lay there, ignoring the clamshell, guilty over Joshua's life being destroyed, angry over my own life being smashed to pieces, and I just... had it.

I wasn't going to take this anymore. They needed me, did they? Something about prophecies and whatever the hell that was all about? Ha! The Lost Lin was about to live up to her nickname, *bucko*, because I was *out of here.*

It was a worthwhile risk. They weren't gonna kill me if they caught me. They might lock me up, but they'd be really careful about that, too—the Lins were the most powerful family among the Kin, and while we couldn't stand up to full Fey power, we had enough connections to make trouble if this got out.

And it would get out. I was sure of that. Aiden, at least, would make it known, and Bran was hopefully selfish enough to make a fuss.

I was leaving. Done. Gone. Splitsville. But I couldn't fight my way out. I'd have to sneak. *With dignity.*

I just had to get Joshua home first. Pfft, how hard could that be?

I changed my clothes. Bran had stolen my jeans and comfy bra and all that, but I could still dress in layers. My own magic is pretty limited (it's the only reason my family let me run away, seriously), so I couldn't do much, but I sure as heck could modify the already-magical clothes in the closet.

I took a dark-blue kimono and legging combo and concentrated hard, focusing on stitching, on fit, on shape, until I'd turned them into something a little more like a body-suit—not a cat-suit, because hello, not practical, but a one-piece dark thing that fit me fairly well. This was good for sneaking (with dignity).

The boots I couldn't do a lot with; they were charmed to prevent wear, which made them wicked-tough. So I went with that, and poured my magic into making them tougher—sort of more like army boots than fancy Han Solo knock-offs. My final touch was comfortable, practical underclothes (including warm socks) and a good bra, because Bran hadn't given me one, and I might need to run.

I needed a few minutes after that to catch my breath. I wasn't even working against Kin magic here; this was Fey, and it was really well-done.

I put it all on. Then I put on a fancy gold and red ridiculous kimono over top of it, hiding my little escape-uniform.

The mirror told me the results were pretty okay. Kind of bulky, but eh; this would be good enough in case of watching eyes. Then it was time for a test: I walked out into the round foyer and over to Joshua's room.

This was brave. Really brave. The moment I stepped outside in my double-costume, I took a risk. There was no turning back, not now.

Damsel in distress, my ass. This little adventure was just about over, or my name wasn't Katherine Aelwyn Lin.

Joshua looked tired. This wasn't "lack of sleep" tired. This was "whole world just turned inside-out and no longer makes sense" tired.

His lovely dark skin was gray, and that just made me sure this was the right decision.

"Hey," he said.

I closed the door. Took a breath. "I'm sending you home."

He blinked at me with no comprehension and sat on the edge of his bed—a carbon-copy of the one in my room. "Home?"

"Home. No arguing."

"Okay." His brow knit, and I was suddenly hit with the desire to sculpt in clay again. I haven't done it in years, but his face—his whole form—just begged to be immortalized.

"I can't get your wallet back right now," I said. "I'm sorry. I think I'll be able to in time, but not now. You'll have to call your credit card company."

"Wait," he said. "You talk like it's just me leaving. What about you?"

No use lying. Honesty may seem like trouble in the moment, but boy, is it easier to maintain than deceit. "I don't know what I'm doing yet. I'll figure it out as I go."

"I'm not leaving you alone in this," he said.

"There's nothing you can do to help me here. I'm sorry, but there isn't."

"Because I'm human." He sounded bitter.

"Because you can't do magic." I tried to sound gentle.

"This is bull," he muttered, but that wasn't a refusal. "So how are you doing this? Before, you said you couldn't."

"Fortunately for you, I've got favors to trade. That's currency among the Mythos. I'm going to trade stuff for getting you home."

Now he looked concerned. Smart guy. "Katie..."

"It's okay." No, it wasn't, though I liked the way he said my name. "I've been playing this game all my life, and I know how to do it. So: I'm willing to bet that Aiden left you a calling card. Right?"

Joshua blinked at my non-sequitur, but pulled a green gem the size of a raspberry from his pocket. "He gave me this. He said if I rubbed it with my thumb and said his name, he'd, uh." He cleared his throat.

I laughed. "Yeah, you don't need to tell me. I know. Booty-call emeralds; what a world, am I right?"

He laughed, too. "I guess I'm flattered?"

"You should be. So do it. Summon him in."

He did.

I don't need to go into the details. Aiden showed up, adorable and bouncy and wriggly, but his little-kid act disappeared the moment I explained what I wanted.

I guess it's a testament to how important friendship is that he agreed. What I promised in exchange (not what you're thinking) seemed easy enough to provide once I got out.

"I'm not okay with this," said Joshua.

"I know. Too bad." I could play tough when I needed.

And then Joshua hugged me. "I hope you're still up for coffee."

Wow. I hadn't expected that. A hug; body-contact. I took a slow breath. "I hope so, too."

Aiden winked, blew me a kiss, wrapped himself around Joshua's arm, and vanished with him.

I took a deep breath. Joshua was safe. Operation *Katie Saves Her Own Damn Self* was officially on.

That doesn't mean I left right away. See, I've escaped from the magical world before. Just in case you ever have to do something like it, let me give you a piece of advice: know what's expected of you, and most of the time, do it.

There's incredible power in toeing the line. See, the less you look and sound like a rebel, the less your owners or masters or parents or whoever look at you closely. That gives you power because it grants one all-important chance to do the unexpected.

Of course, the unexpected only works once. But that *once* is usually all you need.

So I toed the line. I waited politely in my room, and when guards showed up, I answered with wide-eyed shock that I had no idea where Joshua had gone (technically true; I didn't know where he lived). I played the innocent, obedient female all the way. Then I dressed for dinner and went submissively with my guard-escort to the royal ball room.

This weird underground palace just got more mind-blowing the more I saw of it. Here was a ballroom that had to be hundreds of feet high and twice that wide, made of the same material as the black pyramid that sat on top of it. It had almost no lights—the blue and purple torches and candles reflected eerily off floors, walls, and distant buttresses.

I smiled. I didn't speak when not spoken to. I laughed at jokes, no matter how terrible, and ducked my eyes humbly when asked questions. I picked politely at each of the eight courses, and bowed deeply toward the distant head seat when I left.

I toed the damn line. And when I went back to my room, there were no extra guards or security. Joshua had disappeared, but nobody really cared about him, anyway. In fact, my guards were content to stand outside the foyer, giving me complete privacy.

I bathed. I went to bed. I counted five thousand seconds in the dark—just over an hour—and then I made my move.

I can't really blame magical communities for using plumbing. Constant water production would be a serious drain on magical resources, but really—what can top a hot bath, I ask you? Not much, and so all five of the rooms in this foyer had a full bathroom.

I had just enough magic to pull off one fancy bit of transfiguration. Bwahaha.

Fifteen minutes later, I screamed as water "mysteriously" filled my room right over the top of my bed—along with the other rooms, and the foyer.

The guards were quick, I'll give them that; they opened the doors to let the water rush out in a flood, spilling into the throne room, and carried me to safety as quickly as possible.

Water poured from all five bathrooms, and there was a hell of a lot of it. Magical alarms went off. Fey in orange jumpsuits ran past me, magic sparking at their fingertips, ready to repair whatever the heck had gone wrong. Guards searched each room, trying to find whoever did this; one of them put a warm, thick towel around the hysterical girl (me) and told her to take deep breaths.

When I quieted, he paid me no more attention. All the bathroom plumbing had just opened up full force, faucets gone, sinks missing, toilets vanished, and the pressure flooded the rooms as quickly as they could be emptied.

They'd figure it out in a few minutes.

Before they did, I had my one chance.

I abandoned my soaking-wet finery with sneaky (yet dignified) fumbles, then made my way into the terrifyingly dark throne room.

I had no choice about where I was going. The foyer led to the hall which led to the throne room; there were no other exits, no alternative ways out.

The throne room was completely dark and empty; Jaden wasn't here. No one was here. It was sleepy-time for fancy Fey powers.

I hurried, hugging the wall and hunching down. Water splashed around my feet, but there was enough noise from the guest quarters that I wasn't worried about noise; I was worried about being seen. And here was the next challenge: I had no way of opening the throne-room doors, so I hunched behind a suit of armor and tried to be invisible.

I waited.

Guards ran by. Handy-Fey ran by. Nobody came through the doors, not yet. I didn't want to risk getting lost in this palace; I only knew one way out, and I was willing to wait to take it. But that meant crouching in cold water in my dark clothes, shivering, pretty much out of personal magic for the time being. The downside of Kin magic: without a wand, my efforts left me spent.

I don't know how long I waited. It felt like years. If I were wrong, and everyone lived on this side of the doors, I was dead, so dead, so dead—

The doors swung open and vice regent Quinn came zipping past me at such a speed he created rills of water on either side of him, though somehow, he did not splash. Hair up in a gloriously messy bun, *sans* makeup, he looked young. Younger than I expected, but that didn't matter to me now. He sailed past me toward the hall, and I slipped behind him and through those closing doors.

Quinn would certainly remember to look for me. The countdown was seriously on.

I wanted to run. I wanted to tear down that hall toward the ridiculous stairway, gearing myself up to climb stairs for the next twelve gajillion years, but I had to be careful. I had no guarantee I wouldn't run into a phalanx of guards or something. I had to sneak.

There may be nothing more nerve-wracking than creeping around a strange place when you have no way of anticipating who is around the corner. Was the hall this long on the way in? Had I taken a wrong turn? On and on I crept, shivering and terrified, and it was still dark, still only that polished black stone without end, still claustrophobic in spite of its size and nearly utterly lightless. In fact, the sourceless light barely let me see anything... and it struck me suddenly how very strange that was.

Fey needed light. They needed *natural* light, in fact, not just torches and light bulbs. Put Fey in a land without natural light, and they fade pretty quickly.

So what the hell was the deal with this place? Natural light was nowhere to be found. When had Jaden last seen the sun? I'd seen Quinn look worriedly toward his king, and those red cracks in Jaden's gray eyes—

Wait. Red? Or were they orange?

Were *those* the orange eyes the stupid clamshell warned me about? Oh, hell. If he was one of the three "dooms" Cassandra mentioned, then I'd just pissed the first one off.

My heart pounded in my chest, and I had trouble catching my breath. I needed to slow down, think, calm myself. Operation *Katie Saves Her Own Damn Self* was still in swing. I just needed to go a little further, push a little harder, and then I could climb that forever-long stair and get out. It'd be great. What could possibly go wrong?

My creeping was pointless. For reasons unknown, there were no guards here.

Okay, that made no sense. There should have been something, someone. By now, Quinn had surely raised the alarm, but no one came running down this walkway after me.

All too easy, I thought in my worst Darth Vader impression, and that's when I saw Jaden, wielder of the Scepter, scion of the Orkney Isles, king of all the Seelie Fey, waiting for me at the foot of the stairs.

Operation *Katie Saves Her Own Damn Self* exploded in my face.

He sat there, holding the Scepter, completely alone, looking directly at me. He'd magically hidden himself until I was practically right on top of him and there was nowhere to go.

I stopped and sort of choked, frozen like a scared rabbit, looking from the Scepter to his eyes, which, in this gloom, glowed like cracks of lava in dark earth. "You're leaving," he said calmly, and stroked the Scepter's shaft, because *that* wasn't creepy at all.

I had to swallow twice before I could speak. Where were his guards? What was going on? Was he going to blow me up or something? "Yes."

He nodded. Or no, he didn't; he looked down at the Scepter and stroked the shaft again. "I see. So you are unwilling to help us."

"I *can't* help you." The words tumbled out, so small in this cavernous place thousands of feet below ground. "I know the seers said something crazy about the Lost Lin giving you whatever you need, but none of it's true. Bran's seer told him I could introduce him to Notte. Some crazy vampire attacked me in New York, and the Raven King tried to freeze me to death just this morning. It's all nonsense. I can't help you, sir."

At Notte's name Jaden's eyes widened a little, but he didn't comment on the rest. He tilted his head. "Truly?"

"Truly." Yes, dammit! "I'm sorry."

His left eye twitched.

I took a deep, slow breath, and so did he.

I shook. My sopping wet ninja uniform felt like the worst idea in the world right now, and I wondered if I'd end up sick.

"We had wondered," Jaden said, and his voice broke. He swallowed, hard, and began trembling himself. His head bowed as though heavy, and his long, thin ears angled back and down. "*I* had wondered how a simple woman of the Kin, no matter how high-born, could help me with this."

He'd dropped the royal "we." This conversation had just become far more intimate than I was prepared for. "I would if I knew how," I said quietly. "I'm not sure what's going on at all. I'm sorry."

"I believe you." He looked up; the red in his eyes had dimmed, and even in this near-dark, I could see that the gray of his irises was the color of old granite. "I appreciate that you did not insult me by attempting to lie."

Lying is never worth it among the Mythos. They can always tell. "Yes, sir."

"I cannot..." he hesitated.

"Please let me go." I know I sounded desperate. "Please. I just want to leave. I don't know what's going on, but I just need to go."

"Owe me." He looked up. "One favor, unspecified, to be fulfilled when there is need."

I stared at him. "Forgive my bluntness, your majesty, but that's horrifically vague." And it was. That could mean anything. Murders. Babies. Licentiousness or slavery. A favor, unspecified, could mean anything at all.

"Yes, it is vague. It is also my condition."

Oh, dear hell. "What could I ever offer you that you'd find worthwhile?"

"Perhaps we will find out." He was back to *we*, and in that moment, my possibilities narrowed to one.

Screw it. "Fine. Okay. Yes. I owe you a favor. Now please let me go." I was going to owe everybody in the world when this was over.

Jaden stood and moved away from the stairs.

He really wasn't tall, compared to most. Slim, like he'd been eaten away. So tired, so weary; Fey don't show age the way Kin do, but I knew for a fact that Lord Jaden was a thousand years old if he was a day. But he could pass for twelve; at least, right now, he could.

"Thank you." I climbed onto the stairs, shaking. "Thank you."

"Hurry." He turned and walked away, a slow, measured step. "If you are caught, I will not defend you."

Yeah, I didn't think he would. So owing big favors and owning nothing but the sopping wet clothes on my back, I took my chance.

The stairway curved above me into the dark, its top invisible. This was going to take a while. Steeling myself for a long, long climb, I started up those stairs.

CHAPTER 8

Escape

NOBODY TELLS YOU THIS, but escapes are usually as dignified as diaper-changes.

I made it out. And I think I climbed for fifty-eight years.

Okay, that's an exaggeration. It probably wasn't longer than a decade.

Stairs are no one's friend, I think, except health-nuts and people exceptionally good at fooling themselves. These stairs were horrible; my quads burned, and my lungs weren't working right. We were miles underground, and while automated magic sped my trip up slightly, I know a human couldn't have pulled this off. That little extra *something* in my blood makes me a little bit hardier, a little bit quicker, a little bit stronger. *Just a little* was enough to get me the hell out.

The stairs were still a bitch to climb.

I sweated and gasped, quads burning, cursing when I tripped a stair-edge (why had I made the boots sturdier? Was I out of my damn mind?), and occasionally freezing in a panic because I thought I'd heard something.

There *wasn't* anything. There was nothing but me, because nobody came after me.

No one shone spotlights along the stairway. No flying guardians swooped through the air in search of a lone, gasping woman. No one even lobbed a tracking spell. I would have known if they had. Being high-born Kin has some advantages, and feeling when magic is lobbed at you is one of them.

But nobody came.

This made no damn sense. What did Jaden get out of letting me leave? A favor from someone so comparatively insignificant in power that it was pointless to ask? He didn't even have reason to believe my word over whatever prophesying pool or frog-eyed bird or singing cupcake had told him I was the key to his troubles.

I'd be fooling myself to think I'd gotten away scot-free. He was having me followed, that's what. Of course, that meant wherever I led them, I could end up endangering someone else.

My instinct was to call my uncle Merlin, who was strong enough to protect me, wise enough to interpret whatever was going on around me, and clever enough to make me smile in the direst of circumstances—but there were two very good reasons not to.

One, if I called him now, I could be bringing freaking *Jaden and the Scepter* into a clash with my uncle. Merlin is the most powerful of all Kin, anywhere. He might even be powerful enough to fend off the Scepter, but at what cost? If this blew up, thousands of lives could be lost.

Two, my uncle is a seer. He sees the future, though he calls it "pretty good guessing," and I had no choice but to believe he already knew I was in trouble... and he hadn't reached out.

Why?

Logically, he was receiving the same weird messages about me and the future that all the rest of the seers were—but that didn't mean he believed them. He'd *earned* my trust, earned it and kept it, so I had to hope he had good reason to leave me alone to flounder.

It still hurt.

Unfortunately, I didn't have any one else to call. I'd been out of the magic game for a while, and the normal currency of favors was distinctly low in my personal account.

I was on my own, and Operation *Katie Saves Her Own Damn Self* had taken a serious blow.

I had to shake whoever or whatever was chasing me. How? Not a clue.

I climbed.

The top of the pyramid was surprisingly peaceful in spite of the big, black columns that sparked malignant power from their deep-carved grooves. I could barely hear the rest of the city up here, but oh, it was beautiful.

Silvermoon spread out in all directions, filled with lights and colors and beauty that could make me forget my cares, if I let them. Hey, if you think the Fey are remarkable in daylight, let me tell you—you are not prepared for them at night.

In starlight, they glimmer.

By moonlight, they shine.

At night, in the soft seas of natural light, the Fey come into their own. They move with such grace that a simple wave leaves afterimages of sigh-worthy beauty in your mind. They smile with perfect, dangerous teeth, and add so much loveliness that the whole world seems brighter because of them.

Sirens have nothing on Fey in their element. Don't misunderstand: it's not some crazy sexual thing. It's just beauty, plain and simple; beauty that takes the breath, steals the attention, quiets the thoughts.

And they use it. Of course they do; their own magic is stolen, re-member? They have to refill it however they can, and weaving fresh magic from emotion is the simplest way.

Of course, that means all that star-born prettiness gets aimed at *you*, and if you listen to it, you'll have a really good time, probably not remember everything that happened, and never be quite sure the next morning why you feel so tired and the world so gray.

Look, nobody gets hurt, technically. Everyone recovers. What the Fey are doing isn't *evil* the way most define evil. That didn't mean I had to like it.

Regardless, I needed to be careful right now—I was tired, and tired meant vulnerable. I was being followed and spied on, and *that* meant paranoia, which led to mistakes. *Katie Rescues her Own Damn Self* was still in swing. I just had to think carefully about my next move.

Again: that didn't mean I had to like it.

Crap. I wasn't alone anymore. Bright-sharp laughter danced like ice cubes in a crystal decanter, approaching from below the pyramid's edge, and I hid behind a pillar just as one of those glass-like sleds came floating into view. This one was manned like a gondola, one single bored-looking Fey poling listlessly while his finely-attired passengers toasted one another and shed light-sprinkles with every movement, generally acting like he didn't exist.

A taxi? Sure looked like it. Someone in the pyramid was throwing a party. Oops. Hopefully, that party wasn't in the flooded throne room.

The passengers hopped off, creating their own light, focusing on one another as they headed toward the pyramid's entryway (officially my least favorite hole in existence right now). None of them saw me as I leaped for the sled.

"Wha?" said the pole-wielder, gripping his big stick like a weapon.

My clothes were wrinkled like I'd balled them up and stored them under a bush. I stank. I was clearly neither Fey nor where I belonged. "Please get me out of here," I whispered. "I'll give you magic if you do."

His pupils dilated and his ears went back so far they almost hid in his honey-brown hair. He glanced away from me and all around, but Jaden's people were too good, and he couldn't spot them. (Neither had I, to be fair.) "I don't know what you're talking about," he said, just a little too loudly, and pushed off.

The sled was heading down. Down. I could see the ground. We'd be there in a few seconds.

"I don't traffic in the trade of, uh, illegal... what are you selling?" he said.

"Nothing. I don't sell anything."

He looked me up and down, taking in the whole sweaty mess. "I think that's a good decision?"

I glared.

He smiled sweetly.

Ugh. Fey.

We reached the bottom without issue, and a small queue of flashy-clothed Fey waited a few feet away, politely pretending not to notice me.

"A kiss?" he said hopefully.

"This is business, not romance." You had to be stern with these people. If I let him kiss me on the mouth, I might lose myself until next Tuesday. Or I might not, but I wasn't going to risk it. I was too tired.

He pouted. "Just the hand, then." He took my offered hand and brushed his lips across the back.

Something like sparkling blue-purple mist passed between us, a brief puff you'd miss if you blinked.

I swayed on my feet. I had been tired; now I was *bone*-tired, soul-tired, slightly dizzy, ready to sleep. But there was no time for that. "Thanks."

"No, thank *you*," he said, his eyes a brighter green than they'd been two minutes ago, his skin shining a little. "Ah, but that was too high a payment for a simple ride, not that I'm complaining. It's a pity I won't be home for a few hours to enjoy it. I wouldn't even know if someone showed up at East TerraStar Street, number fourteen, and walked in through the front door which I've somehow left unlocked. Also the shower is hot."

Translation: my magic tasted really good (of course it did; it's Lin), and he didn't want to owe me. Also, even Fey aren't totally heartless. "I'll take you up on that," I warned.

"On what?" He made a shooing motion and turned to the waiting Fey. "Come one, come all! The smoothest ride to the Duel Ball you'll ever feel! One blink and you're there, like you never even moved!"

He might be exaggerating slightly about the ride, but he hadn't been about the offer. I could see hints of my own power playing in his aura if I concentrated, like tiny blue-purple fireworks all around him.

Well, at least someone was happy. I wandered off into the city, all but a zombie, and tried to figure out where the hell East TerraStar Street could be.

Silvermoon City sprawled around the royal pyramid in all directions. I saw not a single person down on their luck, not a being or creature any less than coiffed and curled to perfection. I didn't fit in. At all. Still, nobody chased after me. It was assumed that I had permission to be there. If I didn't, I wouldn't have been allowed, right?

When people trust the system, they don't 'see something and say something.' It's just fact.

I staggered through the streets, smelly and sweaty and a serious wrinkled mess (my ninja uniform had *not* stood the test of time). All the foot-traffic, music, and shopping crowds had lessened not a bit since I'd been here last, though the crowd content itself had changed. Diurnal beings had made their way to fancy hotels or wherever they were staying, whereas the more nocturnal Fey had only upped their game. I saw trolls, sylph, numerous members of Shadow's Breath, shape-shifters from various Peoples, a few Ekeks, a phalanx of teen-aged Yaoguai out to sow their wild oats, and quite a few Kin.

None of the Kin were my family, so that's all I cared about.

In spite of my condition, hungry Fey are hungry Fey. Several would-be Romeos or whatever actually did try to greet me, if you can believe it. My well-executed growl sent them packing every time, though hardly afraid; they chuckled as they backed off, hands in the air, as if to say, *Well, we can already see you had a rough night, so you just go on and engage in some self-care.*

Ugh.

I was never going to find the street I needed by wandering around. I needed to ask someone, but everyone around me seemed to be occupied—talking, dancing, seducing. At least they kept the results behind closed doors, for crying out loud.

Ah, ha! There was one Fey on his own in the square, seated on a stone bench, quiet and focused on his book. He seemed safe. I could do with safe. "Excuse me," I said to him. "Where is East TerraStar Street?"

He didn't look up for so many seconds that I momentarily thought he was deaf. When he did, it came with a series of sharp cracks, and flakes of stone fell away from his neck to catch in his robe and tumble to the ground.

Eek. This guy was *old*.

"East TerraStar?" he said in a voice as young as mine. Slow, slow, slow raising of his hand, more cracks and stone flakes popping, he pointed. "Down that way. When you reach All Abandon, take a left. Follow it to the end; residential area... quiet... you'll find." And he stopped moving completely.

Holy crap.

Had he just *died?* "I'm so sorry. You can go back to reading now," I tried in a rush, hoping he could be prompted, but he didn't move.

A breeze blew my hair into my face, but his didn't move at all.

No. Way.

He'd been quietly aging to stone in a position to read. Now he just stared down the street as if memorizing all the life he'd never have again. The color faded as I watched, turning gray and smooth. I held my hands in front of his face and chest, searching for life, however faint, but it wasn't there. This nice old man—however young he looked—was gone.

And I found myself crying on a strange street in Silvermoon, crying for some guy I'd never met before, whose last pleasant seconds I'd stolen away with a dumb question I could have asked anybody. What the hell should I do? Call someone? Scream and point? What the hell should I do?

His book tumbled from his stiff fingers and landed on my feet.

I don't know what morbid curiosity made me pick it up. You didn't just go around grabbing magical people's stuff, but I picked it up anyway, and found a lovingly hand-written and hand-bound journal with the calligraphied words of *The Charge of the Light Brigade*, by Alfred Lord Tennyson.

This was really personal, and I felt like I'd stolen it from him.

The partying continued around me, loud and happy and mercilessly alive, which might be in response to this old one's passing.

I had no emotional juice left to give right now. I couldn't do any good here anyway without possibly getting myself arrested, or something.

"I'm sorry," I said, touching the old Fey's outstretched finger, and leaving the book on his lap, followed the direction he'd given with his very last breath.

The pole-wielder was as good as his word. His door was unlocked, his shower was hot, and though he hadn't mentioned it, his towels were also clean.

I knew the worth of what I'd given, so after showering, I nipped into some food and found a set of clothes that almost fit me: jeans, a button-down plaid shirt, and a jean jacket clearly meant for Earth-visits.

And also made me feel like I'd returned to the 90s. Or possibly Seattle.

I didn't really feel better about the Fey who'd died an hour ago, but I still didn't know what I could have done about it. He'd chosen to respond to me. I couldn't have done anything to prevent what happened. So said logic.

The guilt in my gut clearly didn't care. And I still had to hurry.

I took some more food, then in exchange (see how careful this balance of owing and being owed is?), I left him my stupid ninja outfit, which was actually a damn good trade. See, my "transformations" aren't really transformations. If I were powerful enough to make true transformation spells, I could also control portals, and I wouldn't be stuck in Silvermoon. My changes to the kimono were similar to changing an outcome by observing it: the effectiveness depended on my will. Undoing my spells was as easy as pulling one end of a Highwayman's Hitch. The kimono melted, reformed, remembered what it was, and reverted to its former gaudy glory. Everything remembers what it is in the end.

Of course, it *really* needed to be cleaned, but the worth of that outfit would more than cover that. I doubted this pole-wielding taxi-driver had ever even touched something so fine.

And I needed to go. I also needed a nap, but I didn't dare sleep there lest he return and find me, making things awkward. I'd nap in a park or something. It'd be great.

That was sarcasm.

Happily, Cassandra fit perfectly in the breast-pocket of the jacket I'd snagged. The shoes were only a little too big (he wasn't large, the pole-wielder), and I left his house by the front door, looking as much as I could like I belonged there.

The feeling of being watched had not lessened at all. In fact, it had gotten oddly stronger. I may not have had much adrenaline left at that point, but instinct still tried sluggishly to push me into flight.

I needed help. I knew that. But I didn't want to owe anybody else. Who the hell could I call?

Being watched. Being followed. Being stalked.

I took slow, careful breaths as I walked the streets of Silvermoon, hoping for a portal, hoping for signs pointing to something I could use for help. This wasn't my normal low-key fear; it overwhelmed me like noise in a wind-tunnel. I stopped and looked behind me like an idiot, but of course, there was nothing obvious there: just revelers wrapped in wild clothes and perfect beauty, bringing joy and taking life from the people they entertained. And yes, the ones taken from knew what was happening. No harm done, right? All consensual!

I had to get out of here.

Wait. Was that... *whispering?*

I was going crazy. Had to be, crazy from tired and running and stress and fear. Because above all the ruckus, above the constant music and laughing and conversation and dancing and vehicles and animals and bizarreness and bellows and hoots, I heard whispering. From all around me. Not left, not right, not up or down.

I wasn't crazy. It was getting louder. Sibilant, painful in my ears.

I turned and started walking, but I trembled with the need to run.

There were sheath-eared guards here and there in the street, as ubiquitous as ordinary police officers, but if I went to them, I'd end up back in that damn pyramid. There were Fey revelers all around me, but they didn't seem to hear anything strange, which meant this whispering was targeting me.

I had so little left to trade.

There were visiting beings from all seven Peoples mingling among the crowd, but they were here on vacation and half-intoxicated. They were not likely to help me without putting me in a far worse situation. Aiden's warnings echoed: seers and prophets had all been talking about me. How many of these beings had heard some crazy crap about the Lost Lin, and might just prefer absconding with me instead of playing Good Samaritan?

In spite of all I knew, I was panicking now, freaking out as if I couldn't get enough air. It had been so long since I'd given magic away that I'd forgotten how bad it was, how gaspingly desperate it left me, and I paused to lean beside a bookstore window and try to catch my mental breath.

Calm down, Katie, I told myself. *It's just Jaden and his cronies.*

I knew it wasn't just them.

Shut up, I told myself.

Hello, beautiful.

That wasn't my inner voice.

It came from nowhere, from everywhere. I shook, wiped sweat from my forehead onto my jacket sleeve, looked myself in the eye in my windowed reflection and fought to stay calm.

What are you doing here? This isn't a place for you! You're a lamb among wolves, a little bird in the nest of a snake.

Yeah, and every inch of my body screamed I needed to run.

This wasn't natural panic at all. This was being pushed into me, added to my natural airlessness after the events of today. The nerve!

I did not run. I would not run! I was Katherine Aelwyn Lin, dammit, and *I would not run!*

I see the twinkling power in your aura, unaccessed, untouched, as virginal as I suspect you may be. I see your gaze canvas the world, seeing everything, missing me. Oh, you poor, pretty thing. Shall I help you go home?

"You can go to hell, is what you can do," I breathed.

The world swam. Was I going to faint? Oh, *hell,* no, I wasn't, not even if it meant I had to go screaming into the middle of the street and get carted back to Jaden's palace—

Don't worry, precious. I'm here.

Warm breath touched the back of my neck, and my courage broke. I swung around with a shout to punch the hell out of whatever stood right behind me.

And I socked Bran in the face.

He let me. I mean, it's not like I hurt him.

I curled around my hand. "Ow!"

"Shh!" he yanked me right against his chest, and I heard something then I never imagined: three hearts, pounding away, making a weird counterpoint rhythm that I somehow knew was faster than his normal. "He's here."

"What? Who's here? What's happening?"

"You've got a tail. I followed them. You got out on your own? That's so good for Kin!"

If he hadn't dragged me around the corner into an alley between the bookstore and the little tea cafe next to it, I'd have hit him again. Maybe in the groin. I'm pretty sure he'd have felt *that.*

"My grandfather is here," he hissed at me.

And then I knew. "Oh."

"I don't think he's found us yet, but he's close. Really close."

Yeah. He'd found us, all right. And the sourceless chuckle that echoed off the alley walls didn't really need to confirm it. "Um."

"We've got to move. Jaden's fools are likely leading them right to us."

Sigh. "Bran. I've got really bad news."

But I didn't get to deliver it.

The darkness that swept out of the shadows at the alley's end was solid as the sea and about as irresistible. It knocked us both off our feet, and I didn't even get the chance to inhale before I couldn't breathe at all.

Bran struck out—I think—but whatever power he wielded was subsumed in the Raven King's spell, and *I couldn't breathe*, and the world was going darker than dark, darker than shadow, darker than the mere absence of light.

Bran was fighting. I could tell. Massive power, clashing, conflict.

Ice ate my muscles, my organs, my spine and my skull and my eyeballs. Everything went sharp, hard, cold.

I. Couldn't. Breathe.

"Beware," I thought I heard the clamshell squeak, but I might have dreamed that.

Screw this. Screw all of this. If I'd had air in my lungs, I'd have laughed. As the darkness took me, my last, petty thought was, *I'm dying! Then they'll be sorry!*

As famous last moments go, that could have been worse.

CHAPTER 9

Umbra

I WOKE AND MY FIRST THOUGHT WAS, *I better not be naked.*

You know the drill. Lady gets knocked out for whatever reason, wakes up sans clothing (or possibly in someone else's clothes—a white shift, or a random ball gown, or something), and it just gets weirder from there.

The bed was soft, anyway.

To be honest, I was surprised to find myself alive. I lay still and listened, but if anyone was here, I couldn't hear them. To hell with this; I sat up.

Well, I wasn't naked. Unfortunately, I'd been removed from the clothes I stole—ahem, traded for—and placed in a blue silk slip.

Great. This was going to be fun.

The room had no windows. The air... how can I possibly describe air that's never tasted sunlight? That's never known moon or stars, that's never known any kind of natural light at all?

It's *different*, strange, not something that makes a person think "poison," but after a while, it makes the breath taste weird, leaves something strange and old on the tongue, and irritates the nostrils. If

I stayed here too long, I'd cough, eventually bleed out through my pores, and die—though that would take a couple of years.

I don't know why that happens to us mere mortals here. I just know what Umbra feels like, tastes like, and smells like. I was in the world of the Darkness—the Raven King's home—and the only reason I could see was he wanted to show me something.

So I wasn't naked, and I wasn't dead. Two points in my favor, but that was all I'd get.

The bed was the only thing in this room; the rest of it was strange, dark stone, probably dug from the depths of this strange, dark world, and I hated the way it felt on my cold feet. I was really tempted to make a toga or something out of the sheet, but it would give someone more to grab if I got in a tousle. Besides—my clothes were gone. My captors had seen the goods already.

I really hate magical politics.

Yes, this was political. I was taken from a world not my own without a legal passport of any kind, which put my kidnapper legally in the clear—I had no rights. Worse, the only people I could call for help wouldn't be able to do much without breaking world laws themselves.

Just finding the place would be a problem. Umbra is a parallel world that's never had natural light, so you tell me: where the hell is it? There's sky; it's not in the center of the planet, or something. It's supposed to be an alternate Earth, but that doesn't make a lot of sense, does it?

There are all kinds of debates. After all, you can't *walk* to any of the parallel worlds. Portals are required, and nobody really seems to know how they work. Kind of like how primitive humans could use fire, but had no idea why it burned.

I'm getting off-topic. I guess you can't blame me. I woke up wearing someone else's clothes in a room without windows and no idea what to do next.

And Bran...

I couldn't afford think about Bran right now, but chances were good he was dead. I'd have to cry about that later. No time now. No time, dammit.

I tried the door—thick, old wood, clearly brought from someplace with trees—by pulling on the enormous darkiron ring it had as a handle. Nope, it wouldn't open.

Trapped. In a slinky slip. I realized right about then that I was breathing too quickly and making myself light-headed.

And Bran...

Focus, Katie.

Why was I here? Why had I been taken? What stupid prophecy had been given about me this time?

The door opened.

I jumped backwards, hands covering my tiddly bits because this stupid thin silk showed everything, desperately wishing I had something to put between me and whoever was coming.

A man stood there. A man who looked absolutely nothing like Bran, who in fact was rocking a silver-haired-and-bearded Jeff Bridges look. What?

"Hello, Miss Lin," he said, closing the door behind him, because that wasn't a terrifying thing for him to do *at all*.

This was all psychological. It's magical bullying 101. If he actually wanted to hurt me, I'd be hurt. Badly. *This* baloney was messing with my head; it was making me vulnerable, using body-language and every other trick to terrify.

It worked.

"What?" I said. "What do you want from me? Is it so hard to leave me alone for five freaking minutes?"

He took my outburst well. "Among the Mythos, I am Kanon of the Shadow's Breath. Sometimes, I'm called the Raven King." And he smiled as if that was just silly. "I'm sure you have questions."

"Yeah. Like where are my clothes?"

"They weren't your clothes." He waggled his finger at me, never blinking.

And my old co-worker Lees wondered why our very human boss in Portsmouth didn't intimidate me. She had no idea.

Kanon was pretending to be amiable (I knew the reputation; this was all a lie), so I might as well play along. "I paid for those clothes, sir."

"You'd think so, wouldn't you?" He walked past me—ignoring the way I flinched back—and sat on the bed, studying me as though I were a really intriguing puzzle.

The whole Jeff Bridges thing was unnerving. "Sir. I don't belong here. I'd like to go home."

He said nothing.

See, this right here. This kind of crap is why I left the magical world. This crap happens *all the time.* "Sir, maybe I can clear a few things up. There are apparently some confused seers running around claiming I can give people things, and it's just not true."

He said nothing.

"It's not even logical. Everybody's been promised something, and all the somethings are different. Ergo, it's baloney."

He said nothing. Did nothing. Not a blink. Not a centimeter's change in that thoughtful perusal.

Screw this. "Where's Bran?"

"My grandson is none of your concern," he said.

Is, not *was?* He might be alive! I clenched my jaw. "I owe him my life, sir, so if you don't mind, I think I need to make it my concern."

He laughed. "Almost as brave as the ignorant Ever-Dying! All right, I'll give you something to make you wise again. Do you know how old I am, little girl?"

Yes, that *little girl* sounded just as condescending as you imagine. "No, sir."

"I'm coming up on my sixteenth millennium. What do you think of that?"

I choked a little. Sixteen thousand years? Baloney! "Um. That's... must be nice for you," I said instead.

He smiled like a shark. A Jeff Bridges shark. "Try again."

Right. Lying doesn't work, no matter how good you are. "I think it sounds like craziness?"

"Of course it does. No one of the Shadow's Breath could possibly live that long, right?"

"As far as I know, nobody does, period."

"Notte does," he said with his teeth bared.

And my head did a funny little spin.

Remember what got me into this in the first place? Bran's clamshell predicted I could somehow bring him to someone who could take him to Notte, hadn't she? That's what started this. And now here I was, talking to someone who... what, knew the guy? What the hell, Cassandra? "You know Notte?" I blurted.

"Well," he said, tilting his head back and forth, "I know him a little. We used to 'hang' back in the day."

I swear you could hear the quotation marks.

When nervous, I blurt things. "So what's Notte like?" I blurted.

Kanon ignored that question. "Normally, you'd be right. No one lives that long—but a few of us know some tricks. We know the secret to true long life."

Sounded like Jeff Bridges, too. Trippy. In spite of all the terror, I had to know: "Sorry to interrupt, but what's with the Hollywood actor thing?"

"I like it." Shrug.

Well. Okay. I shrugged back.

"I'm sorry about all this," he said, gesturing at my slip. "I had to see what you'd do. Response is indicative of essence."

"Okay." No, I don't know what he was looking for, either.

"Bran has come to the end of his life," Kanon said suddenly. "I always give my progeny one last request, and he's requested you."

"Me? What? End of his... *what*?"

"My guess is he's trying to extend his life by doing the thing he was supposed to do years ago." He shook his head, smiling. "As if that would work! He should have made an heir by now. This really makes things complicated. Now, I'll have to do it for him."

I just stared at him. I may have squeaked.

Shark-smile. "Try again."

"An heir?"

96

Kanon laughed. "No, I wouldn't touch you! You're far too weak. Unbelievable, though, isn't it? You'd think he would have been more responsible."

I can safely say my head was spinning. "Why kill him? What did he do?"

Kanon's blue eyes widened. "No, no no—he's not being punished for anything. You've got it all wrong. What nonsense did he tell you, anyway?"

"Nothing. Just that you were after him."

For a moment, the mask cracked.

That was madness, *that* was rage, *that* was features twisting into something inhumanly insane and immeasurably furious, and he stood and turned away from me to face the wall, breathing hard. The light was sourceless, but as if his anger had broken it, he suddenly cast a shadow that showed the truth of him: two feet taller, horned, strangely angular as if his flesh was jagged, cracked, gullied. Which it was. "His death is for the good of the breed," he breathed. "Do you understand?"

Something in his tone had changed. I didn't feel safe asking things anymore. "Not entirely, your lordship," I said, nearly a whisper.

Kanon's hands clenched behind his back. "Their death gives me life. Death brings life. It always brings life. It always needs death to give life! Do you understand *now*?" He whirled, and Jeff Bridge's face had deep cracks in it, canyons, like glimpses into some other world, and the flickering inside them seemed too far away to be just in his body.

I deemed it wise to say nothing and cower against the wall like a proper prisoner.

The Raven King took deep breaths, the tight kind that made his shoulders rise and fall. "He gives his essence to me. This is the sacrifice and the... *purpose*... of his entire line. It's why he *exists*. He gives it to me, all of it to me, and then he doesn't have to age and fade away, but he serves his *purpose*, he fulfills his *reason*, he DOES EXACTLY WHAT HE'S SUPPOSED TO DO!"

Could I crawl under the bed? He might not notice; he was yelling, but he wasn't seeing me. He was seeing generations, I think, of stubborn progeny not wanting to give up *their life essence* to him, and suddenly I knew how he'd lived so many years. He'd done it by eating his children.

Was that Notte's secret, too?

Bile rose in my throat, but it didn't spew out because my throat was also choked with horror.

"I'm sorry. I must be boring you," Kanon said, suddenly calm. "Family drama is no business of yours, of course."

I didn't want Bran to die.

I couldn't save him. Could I?

I had to try. "He... is it really time to harvest him? I mean, he'll get more powerful as he ages, right?" What was I even saying?

He sighed. "That is true, Miss Lin, but that isn't the problem." He ran his hand through his longish hair, and it glinted like spun silver in the sourceless light. "Cassandra—you know about her, right? Well, Cassandra seems to think that if I use Bran to fulfill his purpose, then I won't be able to get what I need from you. She's frustratingly vague on the details. I don't suppose you know what she means?"

I didn't even know what she'd promised him. She might have extended Bran's life. Cassandra, you crazy clamshell; I didn't know whether to curse her out or praise her name. Funny—although she'd been doomed in life so no one would believe her, it seemed everybody believed her now that she was dead.

"No. I'm afraid I don't know what she means," I said.

He sighed. "Then we'll have to do this the hard way." And he grabbed me.

There is little as undignified as being carried over some guy's shoulder while wearing nothing but a slip.

"Could you please at least give me some real clothes?" I said, just kind of bouncing on his back.

"You're clothed well enough for this," said evil Jeff Bridges.

"Well, screw you, then." I was done, so done, and no longer gave a damn if he thought I was rude. I mean, what was he going to do, torture and kill me? He was probably going to do that anyway!

Besides, I had to save my strength. I couldn't even scratch him. I couldn't so much as make him sneeze, and needed to save what resources I had left for my big finale—whatever that turned out to be.

Oh, and just to up the nightmare factor, all of this was taking place in complete and total darkness.

Outside that room, Kanon hadn't bothered with any light. I could see nothing. Even if I'd had a flashlight, it wouldn't have helped. This was truedark, not the simple absence of light but an actual thing, a measurable substance like light itself, and required a special kind of magic to pierce. I know the spell for it, but I don't have that much power. I don't think I ever did.

He walked straight for some time, and I heard things on either side breathing and chittering. Once, we passed something like a big, echoing hall filled with conversation and laughter but not so much as a cigarette butt to light it. A phalanx of something with hooves trotted past us in marching time. Water flowed to the left and anvils clanged to the right. Through it all, I could see absolutely nothing.

I'd never find my way out of here. I couldn't ask for help (and even if I did, so many people might die on my account that I just couldn't consider it). I was not okay. I was screwed. That's what I was. There really wasn't another word.

We started down some stairs—that's what it felt like—and suddenly, the only thing I could hear was the distant, cold air that exhales from deep stone tunnels.

"Here we go," said Kanon, and opened a creaky door.

The sudden light from a gargantuan forge burned my eyes; it wasn't bright, but after so long without light, it shocked my system. Kanon put me down on a warm stone floor, and I blinked, eyes watering, until I could see.

I couldn't tell if it was a lab or a temple, but either way, it was bad news for Bran.

The prince of the Darkness lay strapped to an altar in the center of this cavernous room. Corkscrew tentacles snaked down from the ceiling and into his flesh, wriggling as though trying to burrow into him. His disguise was gone. He lay there, nude, the bright red of brick ovens, deep cracks all over him hinting at impossible darkness and distant flickers. Enormous black horns curled up and away from his head; muscles contoured that craggy, hairless skin, which stretched as he gasped and trembled. None of that was unnatural. He was Shadow's Breath in the prime of health, naked, inhuman, beautiful and terrible as scorpions and sun-bleached stone.

Pain rose off him in waves like heat.

"Bran," said Kanon, walking over and jiggling the few tentacles that weren't wriggling so they started to writhe. "How are you holding up? It seems you were right, for the record: you aren't fully developed yet. The question is whether that remaining growth is worth the wait. Oh, and she's here."

Bran turned his head slowly with the sound of stretching ropes ready to snap. "Tell him," he rasped.

Tell him? Tell him *what*?

Kanon moved around Bran's supine form, squeezing and jiggling the curlicue tentacles as if checking their ripeness. His back was to me.

I mouthed at Bran: *What?*

Bran's over-large blue eyes widened.

I gave him the universal two-hand gesture for *What the hell, man?*

"I'm still waiting," said Kanon, though he didn't seem to be waiting at all.

It was my moment—maybe one that mattered more than any other tonight. "He's right." I drew myself up to my full five-foot-one and raised my chin. "If you take his life, you won't get what you want from me."

"'It,' Miss Lin?" Evil Jeff Bridges leaned in to study one corkscrew tentacle that seemed slightly more purple than the rest.

I had no idea what 'it' was, but my ignorance didn't matter. In for a penny, in for a pound. "If you kill Bran, I will not cooperate with you. I will not give anything to you. It's pretty damn obvious that whatever you were promised has to come from me by choice, or you would have just taken it, so don't pretend my opinion doesn't matter."

"So what you're saying," Kanon murmured as he pinched a pinkish tentacle, "is that your price is my grandson."

That is not what I had in mind. His phrasing could mean anything, absolutely anything.

Kanon yanked on a bluish tentacle, making Bran cry out. "No," Kanon said.

"Then you're out of luck, aren't you?" I had one bargaining chip, and I didn't even know what the hell it was, but I was still all-in.

"I have ways of extracting what I need." Kanon yanked again, maybe just to make Bran shout.

"Not this, or you'd already have done it." Logic, don't fail me now.

Kanon stopped and looked at me over Bran's quivering, craggy form. His eyes were still blue, but they were not the blue of human eyes. Silver-blue circles gleamed like polished metal set in solid black, his pupils like dark matter, and in spite of all my resolve, I trembled.

But I did not look away. I did not back down.

"'Twas half the night, when all affright, the 'buncle you did take," squeaked through the cavern at a high and grating pitch, and all three of us jumped.

"Cassandra!" Kanon warned in a rising snarl.

The half clamshell sat on a small table on the altar's other side, and I hadn't even seen her. "Return to the wall lest all shall fall, both day and night to break!" she sing-songed with great cheer. She also rhymed now, apparently, though she still made no sense to me.

She made sense to Kanon, though.

"How dare you!" he roared, and snatched the shell high as though to smash it to the ground.

"Wait!" I shouted, not even sure what I was doing.

Kanon roared again and spun with frightening speed to rip the tentacles out of Bran's body in one thick, squirming handful.

Bran screamed. Blackish-red blood flew everywhere, sizzling and steaming where it hit, freezing and then shattering anything resembling glass in the vicinity. One drop hit my stupid slip and burned a hole in it, then in my skin, somehow freezing and burning all at once, and I screamed and fell backwards. I tried pulling the fabric away from my skin, only barely retaining the sense to avoid touching the blood and burning my fingers, too.

"You think you know so much? Then *go!*" Kanon bellowed, and somehow, Bran rolled off that altar-thing, and somehow, he grabbed me around my waist (the hole burned *so badly*), and somehow, he pounded for the door.

In total darkness, he ripped a portal in the air with what had to be his last magical reserves and leaped through.

The burning seemed to pierce my gut, my spine, my soul. It put acid in the back of my throat, fog in front of my eyes, and sobs I *had not authorized* in my mouth.

"It's okay. It's okay. I've... damn, we'll fix this," Bran said, but I was shivering, curled around a white-hot poker of pain that punched right through me, and barely heard the other voices that joined his.

Warm voices. Bright light, too, bright enough that it seared right through my eyelids.

Warm, strong hands took me from Bran's arms and pressed me against the firm chest of a bronze-colored centaur. Light like I'd never seen shone around him, around me, beyond heavenly, beyond healing, and I almost forgot about the horrible pain as I gaped at his long, somewhat horsey face.

No. Bran couldn't have done what I thought he did. Was he crazy? He wouldn't be welcomed here.

"Welcome to Zenith," the centaur said.

That confirmed it. Bran had taken me to the home-world of his people's longest, angriest enemies: the People of the Sun. Bran, the Crow King, Prince of the Darkness, had lost his ever-loving mind.

CHAPTER 10

Zenith

THEN BRAN DISAPPEARED, and I was left alone with centaurs and an overly helpful sylph.

Someone licked me, but it was not sexytimes. I cannot tell you how much this was not sexytimes.

"She's crashing!"

"Internal bleeding. And it's still eating through her—what is this?"

It was Bran's blood, but I was in no condition to tell them.

I don't blame Bran for running. He wasn't welcome—the Sun and the Darkness have never been friends. Also, I was naked (the slip had just been in the way), and these folks—the People of the Sun, who *prided* themselves on healing—were failing to keep me alive.

Awkward!

Then there was the sun itself. Have you ever known a day when the sun is so bright and so hot that that it feels like actual weight, like it's melting your bones and cooking, drying, dehydrating you into a mummy? That's Zenith. All the time. It's worse than Phoenix.

"Romus! Get her heart steady!"

"I'm trying! Her damned Kin magic is resisting me!"

I also don't blame them for cursing out the Kin. Look, we're mixtures of different magical races; we're a pain to treat, but these people were sure gonna try.

"Her heart's stuttering!"

"Transfusion?"

"We can't. Kin. Purify!"

Fire poured through my veins, or at least, that's what it felt like. So instead of dwelling on the fact that I lay there screaming until my throat bled, I'm going to tell you a little more about the Seven Peoples.

You may have noticed that among the Mythos, there are a lot of strange bedfellows.

It's tempting to think of a People as one *kind* of being, but that's not how it works. Sort of like "China" isn't really "Chinese," but actually the Han and Dai and Lisu and Tu and Jingpo and at least fifty more groups. It'd be insane trying to keep track of all the Mythos that way, so thousands of years ago, they came up with two criteria to divvy us all up: one, how natural lifespan comes to an end, and two, primary instinct or ability.

People of the Sun, for example, generally live about a thousand years; but so do some Fey, and so do certain members of the Darkness. The Sun, however, also have a drive and power to heal, and nobody else has that.

There are phoenixes here. And seraphs. And numerous fairies, and talking warthogs, and folks with animal heads and human hands. Root Whisperers, the Life (buffalo-headed people), a phalanx of fairies, centaurs, and more. All of them have a variety of powers and completely different cultures, but all can—and have a knack for—healing.

It's a matter of pride, too. So my persistence in dying was a *real* blow. They wouldn't be putting it in the brochures, I can tell you.

"I'm losing her!"

"Energy! Quickly! Energy!"

I really wanted to stick around, but sometimes, these things are just taken out of our hands.

I'm fairly sure dying is a whole big adventure, different from anything else, and maybe it's even the great release some people say. Well, I'm here to tell you that *half*-dying sucks.

I plunged straight down. Down, out of my body and through hot, cold, and scraping earth. Down, down, away from sound, away from light, until I landed hard in what looked like some kind of cave made of deep blue stone.

It hurt. Knocked the breath out of me. Which wasn't, I was pretty sure, supposed to happen when you were dead.

Also, there was what felt like a large cargo hook through my center, tugging straight up through that rock and into... what? My body? A giant fisherman? God? I had no idea.

It hurt.

I curled around myself, shuddering. The stone was so cold. I couldn't smell anything—and you never realize how much scent there is until it's all gone. I felt weirdly blind with no scent, nothing, anywhere.

"So have you decided?" said a woman's voice, and it somehow managed to be husky, sensual, and as terrifying as a sudden fall.

Slowly, I looked up.

I had never seen this woman before in my life—but that didn't matter. I knew her.

It's weird, knowing someone when you've never seen them, never known them, never even thought of them beyond basic textbook studies. But I did. I did. "Death?" I squawked.

"No. Just his little sister. You can call me Dis." She moved toward me, her skin dark blue like the cavern, her hair a deeper blue with moving glints in it like it was actually spun from the universe.

Galaxy-hair. I couldn't look at her hair without getting dizzy. Oh, oh, this was not good.

She knelt by me, and her wrap-dress was made of some material blacker than black; looking at it just made me dizzier. There wasn't anywhere to look but her face. Those irises were purple, violently purple, like the color of chilled flesh. "I'm not going to hurt you. I just wanted a look at you without all that pesky flesh in the way." Casually, she took my chin and tilted my face from side to side. "Interesting. Untapped talent. Virgin. Stubborn. Scared—my, my, you're scared." She *tsked*. "You know, if you just settled down and had some babies, you'd feel better in general."

"I doubt it, but thanks for that, Miz Traditional," I found myself saying, and you do not know horror until you find your satisfying but deeply secret sarcasm tumbling from your lips without permission.

She laughed.

"I didn't mean to say that," I said to this being of terror and weird domesticity.

"Why don't you call me Nephthys instead?" she said, and her face—which I could never have described to you a moment before—suddenly narrowed, took on sharper contours and fuller lips, and became a dark-skinned beauty with heavily painted eyes.

Her irises were still cold-meat-purple, though.

"Sure, why not?" I blurted. "Nephthys, sure, because Egyptian gods always hang out in basements. Okay, what's wrong with me? I can't stop talking."

"You're temporarily not in your body," she said as if that explained everything, and raised her left hand—not a good thing coming from an apparently Egyptian deity—to show me the dark blue rope she held. Like fiber optics, it sparkled in rows, little lights zipping along it faster than I could follow.

And it was connected to me. The cargo hook attached to my center and pulled toward the ceiling, but I could not feel the tiny fishhook she'd used to pierce my left ankle. That looked like it should hurt. It didn't. But hey, was the room tilting?

"Careful," she said, sitting me upright again. "I can't keep you here long, obviously—"

"*Obviously*?" I said.

"—but I just had to see you first. Before you made your decision."

"What. Decision." Had the gods been lied to by crazy seers, too? I mean, I know, there *were* no gods, as all enlightened Kin knew, because hey, we could do magic just as well as they could, and you didn't see *us* getting worshiped, but that was beside the point.

"You're funny when you ramble," she said.

I tried to ignore that. Thinking too hard about what I was thinking would throw me off my game.

"So have you decided?" she pressed.

The tug in my center jerked me once, twice, really hard, and I felt like my heart was going to rip right out of my... not my body, but whatever this was.

"Careful," she said again, placing one hand over my chest and keeping me literally grounded. "I'm sorry. Your moorings won't break, but a few might be stretched out. I forgot how fragile you mortals are."

Okay, now would be a good time to start screaming.

"Don't scream, please. It's horribly loud in here. Just tell me: what did you decide?"

"About WHAT?" I bellowed, finally speaking by choice.

She was right; the echo was dreadful.

She waited for the sound to die down again before responding. "The future or the past?"

"Huh?" Future or past? What? What? You know, maybe none of this was happening. Maybe I was really sitting in a nice, happy room in Wales, painted with my favorite colors, dreaming all of this.

I knew I wasn't dreaming. It all hurt too much.

Her eyes widened, and her long, straight hair swung over her shoulder and gave me a pretty good glimpse of a nebula as she drew back. "You mean you don't *know*?"

I was beginning to understand how people can go nuts and just start stabbing things. "No. I don't know. Future or past? I have no idea what you're saying. I haven't known what's going on since this madness started. Do you have an expla—" The invisible hook in my chest yanked again, and I lost a couple of seconds; it felt my soul was getting the wind knocked out of it.

"Careful," she said again—pointlessly, I thought, because I wasn't doing anything, careful or dangerous.

I continued. "DO you have an explanation? Because I'd pay good money for one right now."

"It's simple," she said, gleeful as though she relished telling me this. "There is a will beyond our own, a force of fate beyond that chooses people. You, Katherine Aelwyn Lin, have been chosen for a Cross-road."

Hearing my name from someone related to Death felt like a fist in my chest, hitting with every syllable. And no, none of what she said made sense to me, either. "What does that mean?"

"It means you have a decision ahead of you with great personal cost, and the repercussions of your choice will determine the course of the entire world. It's all about repercussions, you see," she said.

"What choice? I haven't been given any choices. I've just been kid-napped, shot at, and maybe killed!"

"Do you miss your father?" she said suddenly, low and bile-bitter

I gaped at her. Even my thoughts went silent.

"You could have him back, you know," she said, and her face changed again, broadened, bloomed intricate tattoos from her bottom lip to her throat as if she'd bitten her own tongue and bled ink. "Fathers are important. I should know. I bit mine in half." She smiled, and her teeth were sharp, obsidian-black.

And there was a strange, stone-on-stone chomping sound from be-tween her legs, from somewhere definitely *not* her mouth, gratefully hidden by her dress, and I really didn't want to know how she'd bitten him in half. I was pretty sure I knew, anyway. "Obsidian curtains match the carpet?" I said, only half-regretting it because *really*.

She shook her head. "You're out of time. I just wanted to know. Good luck, Katherine Aelwyn Lin."

Okay. That was that? Was I supposed to say something? Thanks? Bye? Please don't bite me with your obsidian-nether-places?

I didn't have a chance for a parting shot. She took her little hook out of my ankle and I shot upwards like a cork in water, scraping through hot rock and cold rock and hot again, and I landed back in my own body so suddenly that it felt like hitting a brick wall.

My eyeballs ached.

"She's breathing!" shouted the centaur, and everybody cheered.

"Yaaaay," I croaked, and then I passed out.

CHAPTER 11

Curse-Eaters

ONG STORY SHORT: I recovered. The People of the Sun did what was expected of them and healed me. Unfortunately, my "inside voice" failed to come back for a couple of days, so everything got awkward.

The People of the Sun had questions, of course. I kept my answer careful and brief: Bran had saved me from someone in Umbra and wasn't at fault. I did not try to implicate Kanon. There'd be no point.

They didn't really care that much, anyway. Healing is the People of the Sun's primary thing, but they also excel at rules, strictness, and stiff propriety, along with know-it-all egos. They're very grand and powerful, the People of the Sun, but most of them know it a little too well.

I'm not ungrateful. Far from it. But the fact remains that the moment I was declared "well," they gave me three days to clear out.

At least I didn't have to pay them.

I didn't mind leaving. This place was too hot, too bright, and too formal. Use the wrong fork at dinner and you'll get *the look* for the next four hours (you know the one). The thing is, I wasn't sure where to go. Home was right out; until I got this resolved, I'd be a sitting duck. I didn't have enough money to just go hiding in the human world, anyway, and I didn't want to hide in the magical one—my family would eventually get wind of where I was and show up with a handful of marriage proposals, promises of reward for child-bearing, and threats of disinheritance if I didn't comply. And no, there is no lack of Lins in the world. No, there is no lack of Kin, either. We're more numerous than *anybody* because magical people just can't keep it in their pants.

"Well, I never," huffed a sylph at breakfast, and flounced away.

Stupid inside voice.

I had questions for Bran, that's for sure. Cassandra's weird words to Kanon kept bothering me: something about stealing a "'buncle" (a carbuncle? Maybe?) and returning it to a wall. Weird. It made Kanon lose his ever-loving mind, so it had to be important.

"I wouldn't know," said a phoenix, puffing little bits of ash into the air along with his opinion.

I decided to keep quiet until I could actually keep quiet for good.

My last night, a centaur brought me an outfit to wear.

"Thanks," I said. "Are you sure Bran didn't give any idea where he was going?"

He gave me a look that clearly said *good girls don't nag*. Funny, coming from a guy who was half horse. "You're better off staying away from him," the centaur said, stomping one hoof as he crossed his arms.

I think they still thought he'd been the one to hurt me, and I was a battered girlfriend or something. Whatever. "Please. Any clue. Anything at all."

"He did leave something for us to give to you. We didn't feel comfortable with that, and I still do not," he said, implying arguments about me behind my back. "It shouldn't be trusted to"—a pause—"a loner."

Thanks for that. "What is it?"

"One of the six remaining echostones, priceless beyond measure, bearing the soul of doomed prophetess Cassandra herself!" The way he said it, you'd never guess he was talking about half of a clamshell. "She insists she's supposed to go with you," he said stiffly, and abruptly produced her from his little waist-sack.

Seriously? Had he just been trotting around with her in his 'murse?'

The shell squeaked. "Beware! Beware! Beware! Three times doom: beware the orange eyes. Beware the pointed tongue. Beware the teeth that drop. Beware! Beware! Beware!"

"Hello, Cassandra." We were back to that again, and I still had no answers. Was Jaden orange-eyes? Was Kanon pointed-tongue? Maybe the vampire was the dropping-teeth thing. How should I know?

"She won't prophesy to anyone else," said the centaur in wonder, wrinkling his long nose. "How? How are you getting her to do that?"

"Damned if I know." I took her gently and studied her in my palm.

Just an ordinary half of a clamshell. No mother-of-pearl or pretty places. I wondered if she would feel it if I tickled her.

The centaur cleared his throat and indicated my exit-uniform. "This is acceptable?"

At least it was utilitarian and designed for the Western-hemisphere human world: jeans, sneakers, a thick down coat, and a men's t-shirt emblazoned with a mustachioed Spiderman ("With great power comes great facial hair").

No underwear. I didn't care at this point. Gratitude was all I had to pay with. "Thank you."

"You are welcome." The centaur turned to go. "Oh—you should know that Sylvia, who is of the Dream, says your moorings are a little out of shape. She thinks they'll heal in time, but right now, you need to be careful. You could die easily." And he just trotted away.

That was horrible. Moorings are the things that keep your soul attached to your body. Suffice it to say this was *bad news*. Well, it wasn't something I could fix, so like most of my life, I put it behind me to deal with on another day. "How's it hanging, Cassandra?"

"*Hine-nui-te-pō* has been unwise," said Cassandra.

Okay. I guess now I knew who chompy-bits lady was. Why the Egyptian thing? Who knows? Maybe she thought I'd find it familiar. So-called deities were weird that way. "Why was she unwise? For pulling me out of my body? Or saying what she did?"

Cassandra said nothing, which was to be expected. She wasn't all that helpful.

I was just zipping the coat when Cassandra apparently changed her mind. "Bran is in the Emblazoned dimension," she said, "trying to return what Kanon stole."

Hello, information! "What did he steal?"

"If he succeeds, the world will end," she said instead of answering.

Holy crap. "That's not good," I said.

"If he fails, time will rewind."

"Rewind? What?" This was beginning to feel like coming into a movie halfway through. "What do you mean, 'rewind?' What are you talking about?"

"The one who rewinds will feed the three," Cassandra squeaked, and suddenly, the top of her shell cracked. Tiny pieces of periostracum shot off like little knives, and she wobbled on the desk as if struck.

"No!" I grabbed her up, panicking, cupping her gently as if my very touch could possibly keep her in one piece.

She wasn't really gasping—I mean, she was a seashell. She had no lungs. But somehow, she was gasping.

I swallowed. Magical objects are precise creations, and if she'd been bound to this thing the way I thought she had, then she could probably only speak in weird prophecies at peril of her remaining life. "This is because you answered me directly, isn't it?" I said.

She didn't reply.

Why had she done that just now? For me? To commit suicide by verbage? What the hell?

For a moment, it was all too much. It felt like everything I did hurt someone else lately: Joshua Run; my coworkers, possibly; Bran; now Cassandra.

All I could do was try. "Can I... help you, somehow? Don't hurt yourself by answering if there's nothing."

No answer.

The shell looked so fragile now, but somehow, it hadn't broken apart. It just looked like someone had begun to step on it but pulled back at the last moment. Damn it. Would glue work on a magical half-shell?

I could not deal with this on my own. Bran might have chosen to leave me here, but I had choices, too, and letting him walk off after getting me into this mess was not one of them.

"Here's what's happening," I said. "We're going to Emblazoned and we're tracking his ass down. Besides, he has my Anshan manuscripts."

She made a small sound that might have been a chuckle.

Figured.

Well, it's laugh or cry. Anybody who's *survived* knows that. "Come on, Cassandra," I said. "We're going Crow-hunting."

I know. This feels like some weird Tour of the Worlds, but it really isn't. The magical universe is big, huge, multi-faceted, and magnificently interconnected because we figured out a long time ago a global community was needed to survive.

Through proper channels, it's normal to jump from world to world to conduct business, find pleasure, acquire schooling, whatever. It's also exhausting. Look, there's a reason I moved to a tiny little New England state. It was so nice to stay in one world, to explore one landscape, to face such small distances between things that I could just *drive* where I wanted to go.

I've already decided I'm getting that back, by the way. Somehow. But first, Awful Adventures with Katie and Bran had to come to an end.

Leaving Zenith wasn't hard. I found a Sunspot (you've seen them before—they're the dancing sparkles on water in bright, bright sunlight) who was willing to make me a portal for free, so off I went.

She thought I was crazy to go to Emblazoned. I had no money. Nothing to trade. And I was dressed *really* wrong.

Emblazoned is a pocket dimension, not really a full parallel world. Worlds take a hell of a lot more to make, which is why there are only four of them. Pocket dimensions are more like extra rooms in a house, tacked on to someplace that already exists, siphoning power and weather and water and whatever.

Emblazoned just happened to be built by a group of Ren Faire rejects.

Okay, that's not quite right, but it might as well be. You know how Renaissance Faires are geeky, pretty, and largely innocent if occasionally bawdy fun? In other words, not at all what life was really like for the Ever-Dying in the era being aped?

That's what Emblazoned is. A group of folks from among the Mythos liked many of the trappings of the Middle Ages but not so much all the dirt and death and poor people, so they made this place.

It's a 24-7 carnival of knighthood (not remotely historical), performing gryphons (because even gryphons need a job), and an elected king and queen who rule for a year in a flurry of brocade and velvet and jousting and feasts.

Eh. Why not? They weren't hurting anybody.

I got some funny looks walking down the street, lemme tell ya. Vintage 21st century meets Ren Faire! Total chance of blending in: zero percent.

Fortunately for me, pocket dimensions are never really big. This place had a lot of forested land and hills and lakes (because what's real period-drama without a little hunting) but only one real town, so if Bran was still here, I could find him.

Children with varying shades of skin and numbers of eyes ran past me, dressed for the period and playing silly games with wooden swords and weird dolls. The adults danced, laughed, drank too much, and slipped into darkened doorways for cheerful little trysts in semi-private. I saw Fey, ogres, one troll, a pod of merlions playing in a fountain and making an awful mess, and fairies just... everywhere. Everywhere. Everybody was in character and having a wonderful time.

It was all weirdly innocent, if Euro-centric. Sure, I was on a mission. Sure, I'd nearly died, but you know what? This was fun. I almost wished I'd come here to play,

But I hadn't, and in the third pub I tried, I found him.

It was appropriately dark—the spooky, dramatic kind of dark that says *dark deeds afoot here*, which is perfect for a place built on what is essentially role-play. Even with that, Bran was easy to spot.

He was back in his human guise, visibly healed, and I confess that was a relief. He hunched over his rough wooden table, strong shoulders and dark scowl, sharp and beautiful and dangerous. Oh, and light leaked through his fingers.

I had no idea what *that* was about, but it didn't matter. Beside him, at his feet, was that knapsack he'd conjured all the way back in New York City. He still had the manuscripts. Maybe my job and my life weren't over yet. I slid onto the bench across from him.

Bran stared at me. "What are you doing here?"

"Yep, I did find you, and yes, they healed me, and oh yeah, you should be impressed," I said.

"I left you safe," he moaned. "Get out of here. Are you crazy? My contact will see you!"

"Did you see how I'm dressed? Your contact could see me from space. Besides, those are *my* manuscripts at your side."

"I'm trading them," he said.

I gawked. "What? Why? You can't do that!"

"Can."

"You are going to get me fired. And arrested." Pink slips and police cuffs danced before my eyes. "Look, whatever. Are you okay? Last time I saw you..."

He sighed and leaned back against the wall, and I had a moment of jealousy for just how well his rough linen shirt fit him. It was illusion (I reminded myself firmly), but a very good one. "I'm all right. He didn't take much."

"Take much what? What was that about, anyway?"

"It's how he sustains his life. He takes it from his children."

"I got that part, but seriously?" I gestured at him. "Is *that* why you wanted to make a baby with me? Knowing he'd eventually *eat* the child? What was our kid supposed to be, an offering?"

"No, no, you've got it wrong," he said, eyes widening. "I knew you'd say no."

Wait.

What.

So all of that with my uncle and exploding birds had been... what, for show? I stared at him. Shook my head and my hands, momentarily bereft of words. "What the *hell*, Bran?"

"The longer I put it off, the longer he'll wait," he said. "Only his bloodline can give him what he needs. I don't know what he thought he was doing when he grabbed me. He'd never feed himself again if I died before doing that."

This is so messed up. "He said he'd make his own."

"He can't."

Ouch. "So you two are at an impasse," I murmured.

He nodded and signaled a buxom, one-eyed waitress. "Could we both have some red wine, please? Something good. Modern, if you have it."

Her eye communicated all levels of *Do you, like, not know where you are?* before she sashayed off.

I sighed. "So why do you need *my* manuscripts? What are we even doing here?"

"You need to see what he stole." Bran opened his hands.

A gem? No. Coal-shaped light? Sort of. A rugged opal? Maybe. If you could put so much depth into it that falling face-first onto the thing would surely send you spinning into the next galaxy. It was a rough, uncut shape, unevenly faceted all over as if it had just been broken out of a piece of larger rock. Every single one of those facets—concave, convex, all different shapes—seemed to draw me into a different distant universe, spinning and expanding and heating and exploding and creating forever.

I swayed in my seat as I looked away. "Whoa."

"Yeah," he said. "This is part of the wall of time."

Nope, he didn't say that. Baloney.

He read my face. "Yes, it's real. I know it's real because my damn fool of a grandfather found it and chiseled out a piece."

"That... sounds bad," I said slowly. "Isn't that wall holding in a bunch of excess time, or something?"

"Supposed to be. I'm betting if I don't put this back, something bad is going to happen."

Bran's a hero now? Or maybe just covering his own hide? No, this was pretty heroic. "Where is the wall of time, which I still don't quite believe exists, but that thing in your hands is blowing my mind so it must?"

He smiled a little. "You're cute when you ramble."

"No flirting. Answers."

"He wouldn't tell me where it was." Bran shrugged. "I've been searching for months using clues I stole from his place."

Ah, so there was more than the usual tension between them. "Go on."

"I know where it is *now*. And the people I'm trading with are going to give me the map to it."

Well, this was great news, wasn't it? Maybe? "Why would your grandfather do this in the first place?"

"I think he thought he could use it to fix his own clock, or something. I don't know." Bran rubbed his face. I'd never seen him look so tired.

"How do you know you're getting a map to the wall of time? If it exists."

"Because they don't know what it's a map to. They just have it and don't care about it at all."

My head hurt. I glanced at his hands, cupped over the light again. "How... How does it feel?"

"Terrible. Wonderful. My hands ache. My bones thrum with pleasure. I've never known anything so good, and if I closed my eyes, I might forget there was anything else in the world."

Wow. I decided to look at the wall and not his face after that.

The wall of time. We had officially entered la-la land.

This is like finding out Santa Claus was real, only instead of a flying guy with presents, it was a wall built from the bones of Guardians to contain a power that couldn't be dispersed or undone, and if it got loose, might just destroy everything.

I can't explain it fully. Nobody knows more than rumors, legends. All I know is that during the First War, no one could manage proper genocide while the Guardians were running around; they kept defending people and messing up objectives, getting in the way of all-out conflict.

So they—whoever "they" were—found a way to siphon time and try to take out the Guardians with that.

You wouldn't think time is a thing that could be siphoned, would you? Surprise! Turns out it can be, like light or sound. Nobody's ever figured out how to do it again, mind you, but this is what they say around campfires in hushed tones: the siphoned time was so powerful that a spilled drop of it aged part of Earth so badly that nothing will ever grow there again. There's one long, narrow, dead scar straight to the center of the planet—utterly dead, as if just that chunk has been circling the sun for a billion billion years.

They also say it didn't work. The Guardians stopped it somehow, but the time couldn't just be returned, so the Guardians sacrificed themselves. They trapped the siphoned time somehow within the wall made from their own broken bodies and wings, protecting all the world from it for all eternity.

That's all I know, and this is seriously not history. This is nonsense, kid's stories, meant to be told with jazz-hands and spooky voices. And if I hadn't seen that impossible rock between his palms right now, I'd still believe that.

"Bran, I have to know," I whispered. "Why did Cassandra drag me into all this? What do I have to do with this mess?"

"Nothing," he said, looking surprised. "You're going to help me get in touch with Notte, somehow, who's the only one strong enough to fight my grandfather. It's pretty simple."

"It's pretty far from 'simple,' bub," I started, but then two large men slid onto my bench, one on each side of me.

They towered; they were huge, hot, breathing like bulls in shiny gray suits, and some weird-smelling oil slicked back their black hair from their pock-marked faces. They leaned in, beefy arms pressing me in from both sides.

Okay. Here was one of those fun moments I could never have predicted. Don't you love the magical world?

"Bran!" said a third man expansively. He was big, too, but with cleverer eyes; that yellow smile said he'd seen all the games, played every one, and walked away from most the winner. "So good to see you! Can I buy you a drink?"

The one-eyed waitress brought us our wine just then.

"Wonderful! I've got this covered," said the third man expansively, handing a folded bill of some kind to her as he slid next to Bran.

"Hey, Gerard," said Bran. "You got my spell?"

Gerard? Never had there been a more inappropriately-named person.

"You know that's not how this works," said Gerard.

Bran grinned. "I know lots of things," he said, and held up the knapsack.

I had no idea who these people were, or why they were playing-pretend as Hollywood mafia, but at the sight of that bag, they stared, visibly salivating. Gerard licked his lips with a long, pointed tongue, striped like some kind of lizard. "Fresh?"

"If by 'fresh' you mean ancient, sure," said Bran.

Oh, hell, I knew what these guys were now. They were freaking curse-eaters. It was a weird-ass cult that focused on *eating* artefacts of power. Why? I don't know why! Were they going to *eat* my five-million-dollar-insured manuscripts? Was this really happening?

I must have looked like I was going to say something. Bran kicked me under the table. "So," he said. "Payment?"

"Hm? Oh, sure, sure," said Gerard, whose eagerness to chow down on horrifyingly dark magic parchment made his illusion slip a little; his skin went more green than brown, and his cheeks seemed to sag. He reached into his shiny suit (which held a gun in a holster because why not?) and handed Bran a small, ordinary piece of printer paper.

Okay, that made a little more sense. The curse-eater cult figured out a long time ago that copying down the information from ancient documents *before* eating them was a good way to bring in revenue. And Bran was right: they never really cared about what they had, just whether it could get them money. Lucky us.

"Gimme," Gerard said, reaching for the knapsack.

"Bran," I whined.

"I'll take care of it," said Bran. He was doing it again: that overly-confident, uber-male baloney that I saw every day of my life and usually wanted to smack until it stopped.

But not this time.

I'd gotten too many glimpses of the real Bran over the last week to be fooled anymore. Yes, part of him was precisely that kind of annoying, and I was under no delusions about it. But he was vulnerable, too. He was scared. And funny. And occasionally heroic. My uncle Merlin was right: Bran wasn't a bad guy, and with a shock, I suddenly knew I trusted him.

I trusted the Crow King, Prince of the Darkness. What had my life become?

Gerard opened the knapsack and inhaled what I could only presume was yummy ancient evil because he groaned. "We're done here. Boys? Always a pleasure, Crow King."

"Same." Bran saluted him playfully, and all three yobbos got up and shambled away. Just like that.

"Bran," I said again.

"Trust me." He opened the paper, glanced over it, and smiled. "I was right. We finally got a break."

My manuscripts were gone. My life was over. I sighed. "I'm not sure I appreciate the word 'break' in a good sense right now."

"This time, you do. You know what this is? It's instructions for a portal."

"Okaaay."

Bran looked ready to explode from pure inflating smuggery. "It's a portal to the lost world of the Guardians."

And for the second time in an hour, I found myself speechless. "There is no lost world of the Guardians."

"Yes, there is. There are only four parallel worlds now, but there used to be five. And that's where it is."

I gulped. "The wall of time?"

"It'll be there. We can go to my home, create the portal, and find the wall. We'll replace the carbuncle, fix the problems my grandfather created, and then he'll owe me. He'll owe me big—big enough that he has to leave me alone for a while."

I'm glad his faith in his plan was so strong because mine most certainly was not.

There was no sixth world. Really. Everyone knows there are five, the original Earth and four parallel worlds: the Silver Dawning for the Fey, the Dream for the Dream, Umbra for the Darkness, and Zenith for the Sun. There was no sixth world.

Apparently, I was all kinds of wrong today. That's not a good feeling.

You know what else was not a good feeling? The Anshan manuscripts were gone, possibly masticated, and so was my job.

I put my face in my hands.

"Drink your wine," he said.

I did.

Then I finished off his.

"Screw it," I said while he blinked at me, my cheeks burning and my stomach wonderfully warm. "I'm going with you." And I slammed my glass onto the table in emphasis.

"Of course you are," he said with patented Bran Certainty™. "You're part of my future. Cassandra is never wrong." He held out his hand. "Let's go."

Take his hand or don't take his hand?

I could always stay here and get a job as a not-very-buxom wench instead.

Haha. Kidding.

"Let's do this," I said, and because it felt really good to make at least one decision about my own fate, I *decisively* took Bran's hand.

CHAPTER 12

Bran's Tower

I BET YOU THOUGHT I'D FORGOTTEN that weird goddess' comment about my father. Nope. I was just choosing not to think about it. But we'll talk about that another time.

Bran's home was a place I'd visited before, albeit under duress. There had been this whole *thing* with my uncle and a baby dragon and kidnapping and weirdness, and it ended with exploding taxidermy. This tower wasn't a place I ever thought I'd go back to.

Bran's home was a pocket dimension in northern Wales. Well. Sort of in Wales. If you stepped outside it, you could see a lovely little Welsh town at the bottom of the hill and what looks like a wrecked Iron Age hillfort.

But take too many steps toward that hillfort—assuming you're magic—and you suddenly find yourself slipping out of the human world and into someplace else. Someplace of complete darkness, except for his tower—which was visible for no clear reason. Tall, black, and phallic, it glinted with tiny red pinpoints like thousands of eyes.

And there was no light. None. I could see, but it wasn't because of light. Only my magical blood gave me visual access. I can't imagine what a true non-magical Ever-Dying would do in this place. (Panic? Panic.)

Bran's castle stood exactly where an old Ever-Dying castle once had. Our parallel worlds often piggyback on one another in terms of building-placement. Last time I'd been here, something I could sense but not see stampeded by in the dark. "Bone-collectors, right?" I murmured, following Bran down his entry hall and trying not to be creeped out by the wriggling patterns on the rug under my feet, or the blue stones glowing in sconces in place of anything reasonable like torches, or the odor of sawdust and feathers.

That last one was kind of my fault. I blew up his collection of stuffed birds last time I was here. Long story.

"They're just vermin," said Bran, turning his head so that I could see the sharp line of his jaw and a hint of his full profile.

Dismissive. Authoritarian. Kingly.

My sarcasm makes it hard to see, but Bran was nothing to laugh at. He felt like a king with real authority, born and not made. I was nobody, comparatively. I could ignore that most of the time; I *had* to ignore it most of the time so it wouldn't mess with my head.

I couldn't ignore it here.

Reality seemed to warp where he walked, even though he just looked like a handsome guy in jeans and a t-shirt and bare feet, walking across the dark stone hall of his very own castle.

But he wasn't that. He was the prince of the Shadow's Breath, hero to the whole People of the Darkness, and his grandfather was some kind of insane cannibalistic monster, and I couldn't ignore any of it here.

"They were too big for vermin," I said.

"'Big' is relative," he added.

We passed doors now, and just like before, escaping beneath each was a confusing plethora of sounds, smells, and weirdly dancing shadows. Burning scents, flowery scents, something that might be screams or operas for mice or ancient, recorded laughter being played backwards and at a high rate of speed—

"Still creepy," I muttered.

He turned and gave me a full-on Bran smile. "You love it."

"No. I really don't." I hugged myself. "Do we have to be here to do the thing?"

"Yes. We have to be here to do the thing. I can't guarantee control of this portal anywhere else."

"What's stopping your grandfather or someone else from just waltzing in here and interfering?"

"I am."

And the way he said those words....

I was, I realized at that moment, in very big trouble.

Bran was still intimidating, controlling, full of himself and power and darkness and smarmy good looks. But—and this is the important part—he wasn't frightening to me anymore.

That was bad. Fright was a really good wall of protection.

I knew I didn't want to be in any kind of relationship with *anybody*, so that was that. But that didn't mean I wasn't fully capable of breaking my own heart. Damn him for getting me into this.

He pushed open a heavy wooden door, the one I was pretty sure led to his sort of dining room/stuffed aviary. "Have a seat," he said, snapping his fingers. The fireplace—so to speak—lit at once, blue stones flickering in its depths, giving off heat and some kind of light, but without flame.

"The birds are all gone," I said, and yes, I felt a little sad about it.

"I haven't had time to collect again," he said, not looking at me at all.

They were one of his hobbies. He collected things, Bran, and his collection of stuffed birds was apparently well-known all around the world for its rare and extinct stuffed fowls.

Was. Like I said, I'd... um. Blown most of it up. "I'm sorry about all that."

"No, I understand." He still wasn't looking at me, though. "Merlin explained."

Oh, goody. This guy goes and kidnaps my uncle, who then makes excuses to me about Bran, and then makes excuses to Bran about me, like *I* was the weirdo in all this. "Glad to know it."

"He told me you're a scared little virgin who wishes she was Ever-Dying," he said.

"If I stab you in the back of the head, will you die?" I said sweetly.

"Kidding. He told me you're the best thing to come along in his family for about a thousand years, and he's proud of you. Then he told me to keep my dick away from you. So. There's that."

Well. "Good. You should take his advice."

"I am. We're just friends." And he did that sideways smirk, the one where he peeked over his shoulder and practically smoldered at me.

Yeah, you know what? We were *both* in trouble. After this was done, I was hiding in the human world *so* hard.

Without warning, he suddenly caged me in between his arms, leaning on the door behind me.

I went stiff as a board. Oh, we were *not* doing this. "Bran, *no.*"

But he didn't look amorous. So close I could feel his body heat, he inhaled slowly, then whispered, "Why is there death-residue on you?"

He could *tell*? "Because I nearly died?"

"Not that. You've been touched by someone close to Death. What happened?"

Why did he care?

If I moved, I'd lose. Not that I knew the rules of this game. "Death's little sister showed up. You know, no big. She said I have some big choice to make. Oh, and she also said my moorings are loose."

That got the response I wanted: Bran jerked back, staring at me, his eyes wide and dark in the flickering blue light. "Death's little sister? *Dis?* Your *moorings* are loose?"

"That's what she said?" I tried a smile.

"Damn those match-heads! They were supposed to keep you alive!" he snarled.

"I'm fine." I raised my hands, placating.

"No, you're not. You can't go," he announced.

I sighed. "Haven't you been paying attention? I leave here, I get eaten by something, or kidnapped, or held hostage until I do whatever it is the prophets of the world think I can do—which has not been resolved, by the way."

"Then stay here. I'll take care of this. It has nothing to do with you, anyway."

"Really." I gave him the driest look I could. "So you think it's an accident that I got assigned to 'translate' Anshan manuscripts, which *just happen* to be the perfect trade for portal information to a place that doesn't exist?"

He paused.

Gotcha. "Not bloody likely, is it?" It wasn't, but saying it out loud made it feel so much worse. What the hell were we mixed up in?

"No," he sighed. "It's not likely. None of this is, I guess."

"You guess? All the prophets saying I can solve the world's problems isn't weird to you? We're being set up, and it's being set up around me. I'm not sure if you were supposed to be involved. I mean, if you hadn't shown up when you did..."

Bran suddenly went very still.

It was one of those moments when his inhumanness was impossible to ignore. No human being can be that still, that solid, that terrifyingly angry like growls in the dark. He was beyond simmering; something like heat rose from him in waves, but it was cold and dark and terrifying.

I froze. "You okay there?"

"It was a setup." He bared his teeth. "My grandfather was aimed at you like a gun. He was supposed to get there and find you with the manuscripts."

I could feel my face lose color. "And then what?"

"*He would use them.* One of the reasons I traded with these guys specifically was so those spells would be gone for good. I even made the curse-eaters swear a three-times oath that they wouldn't copy the information first." He turned to face the blue-stone fire. "I took a look at those manuscripts; it's what the **Zār** said they'd made: a portal to nowhere, to nothing, to a place that doesn't exist. They'd have won against the Daevas if they used it." He looked up. "Do you even want to imagine what my grandfather would do with that? He was willing to rip a hole in the *wall of time*. This, in his hands..."

I could imagine. "But why was he coming for me? Who sent him there? Who sent me the manuscripts?"

"I don't know yet, but I think Cassandra does."

"No way. When she tries to answer questions, it hurts her."

He snorted—yes, like a bull—and held out his hand.

Suspiciously, I handed her over, and to my absolute amazement, he began to sing.

You're going to have to imagine this is Greek, okay? "I bid you, shell, to tell your tale, and sing me safe to sleep. Now free your song! Your curse is gone; your words, my soul will keep."

The shell wriggled in his hand. "The end is near, my lovely lord, and seeing fear is great. Together we have mapped the way, to use the greed and fear and hate, to force the doorway in. And then, her choice. And then, her choice. Her choice will set paths straight."

Bran looked at me meaningfully.

I wanted to scream. "That. Doesn't. Mean. *Anything.*"

"Yes, it does." He handed her back to me.

"No, it doesn't."

"Does. And you're right about one thing," he said. "I can't just leave you here. Who knows what you'll get into? An empty world is a safer idea."

"Safe with the wall of time," I deadpanned.

"And me."

He meant that with every ounce of arrogance, every ounce of certainty, every ounce of self-defined strength he has. I wanted to strangle him. I wanted to thank him. I wanted to kiss his cheek. I wanted to run away forever. Clearly, I was losing my mind. "So what does it mean, then, if you're so smart?"

He ticked off his fingers. "One, whatever is coming scared the seers witless. Two, they seem to have figured out a way around it using you. My guess is whoever sent the manuscripts was tricked into doing it. The seers are up to something, and it involves you. Whatever choice you have to make, Katie, it must be a doozy." He smiled like this was just a happy puzzle he'd figured out.

The choice had something to do with my father, according to Death's little sister. I wasn't ready to tell Bran that part. "So what are we waiting for?"

"That's the spirit." He looked at the paper in his hand, silently mouthing the words, then turned his back to me.

The magic that took place then is something I could barely comprehend. I couldn't see it; I couldn't hear it. It throbbed like a sudden pressure change, shook my vision as if my eyes were seizing, and forced me to my knees with a searing, burning cold that made me want to scream.

I dared not make a sound. Distracting him in the middle of this... no, I dared not make a sound.

When the air ripped open, it wasn't the usual portal. It didn't just look like a tear in space, a gap in the fabric between worlds. It wasn't just a hole in nothing. Something glimmered in that dark, distant and colorful and carnivalesque, but I had no way of knowing what it was.

Bran turned. He was sweating, breathing hard, but smiling like a cheerful kid. "Take my hand."

Wind howled through that hole. It sounded like a voice, alone, grieving.

"Sure!" I said with as much cheer as I could fake, and I took his outstretched hand.

CHAPTER 13

The Wall of Time

THE PRESSURE ON MY EARS didn't let up as we stepped through the portal to the Guardian world. Correction: as we stepped through to this place that I still didn't believe *was* the Guardian world, but I'll be damned if I knew where it was.

Look, it's supposed to be simple. There are five total worlds, Earth and its four parallels: Zenith, Umbra, Dream, and the Silver Dawning. Yes, the stars and sun and other astronomical things are different in those worlds, but the official explanation is that they're from a vastly different time—so far in the past or future that the galaxy has changed around us.

I should mention there are other theories about parallel worlds, too. Really unpopular theories. Largely about them being somewhere else in space, not just time.

It's not that those theories don't make sense—it's that they're terrifying.

Those parallel worlds and pocket dimensions are supposed to be *spatially* in the same place. Bran's little kingdom, for example, is on a hill that mimics the hill in Wales exactly. The Silver Dawning's major cities are all where human cities are. The mountains are in similar places (or were before some mad magician moved them), the oceans are in the same places (or were before some mad magician—you get the idea).

The parallel worlds are each supposed to be the same planet, just modified. That makes it controllable. That makes it safe. Sure, the stars and suns and moons are different, but we sort of gloss over that, you know?

This place was definitely not in any of those known five. At that moment, stepping through that perilously powerful portal with Bran, I could no longer gloss over anything.

The sky was dark purple-red, like a bruise, and in it were planets and stars. Not like you're thinking. There were no pretty white dots. These were globes, monstrosities, gargantuan spheres so close in the sky that it felt like I could freaking fly to them, wild colors licking across the atmosphere like some unholy hybrid of lightning and the aurora. Below them, the ground seemed nearly dead, warm and reddish soil crumbling under our feet, stretching all the way to distant, bare mountains silhouetted against that strangely red-purple sky with no evidence of trees or water or any habitation.

There was no "sun." There were those planets, or whatever they were (look, this broke all my understanding of how physics and magic work) and clouds of... something bright sparkling purple-blue between them.

Bran shook like a leaf.

That's not something I ever thought I'd feel. "You okay?"

"No." He shook his head. "This feels... I don't know. Something's missing. Whatever it is, I need it. I don't think we can stay long."

I turned in place, every step sending up little puffs of dust. "So where's the wall of time?"

"Hell if I know. We're going to have to look for it. Ahh—" And that little sound was the only warning I had.

His human illusion fell away from him in shreds and tatters, burning up like flash paper before it even hits the ground. His form grew, changed, shifted; and suddenly there he was, Shadow's Breath, a foot taller, brick red, covered with those wide, dark cracks that seemed so much deeper than just the inside of his body. Black horns curled above his head, catching the light in a polished gleam. His eyes—still blue—bulged, enormous, weirdly pretty.

He froze and looked at me, and expressions flickered across his face too fast for me to catch them—maybe fear, or worse. Nothing good.

I remembered: my uncle told me he was ashamed of his natural form.

"Hey," I said. "It's okay."

He stared at me, and the flickering light in the depths of those cracks seemed to flicker faster. "What?"

"If that illusion is a strain to keep on here, leave it. We're good. Come on, man. It's not like I didn't know what you looked like."

There was that expression again: that *was* shame.

I gave him my best dubious look, hands on hips and eyebrow arched. "Do not tell me you've got some sort of body-image issue with your own species."

He looked caught now. "It's not... in fashion," he finished lamely.

"Uh-huh. Come on. Let's find that wall and get out of here."

I can't say he looked relieved, but he did look thoughtful. "You're not normal, you know that?"

"Says the guy whose grandfather is trying to eat him. Come *on*, Bran." Told you I could ignore the kingliness most of the time. It's good for my sanity and his humility.

He made a sort of huffing sound. "I'll carry you."

"You'll what?"

"I can go a lot faster than you can." He stomped one foot—pardon me, *hoof*. "Trust me."

Eh. If it sped this up.... "All right. But no funny business."

"As if life since I met you has been anything but funny business." He picked me up and swung me around onto his back like I weighed nothing.

That was a little dizzying, but after that, it was easy. Note that I did not say *dignified*.

He loped with frightening speed, an uneven jog that covered ground so fast the wind nearly glued my eyes shut—and I could tell just from the way he moved that this wasn't nearly as fast as he could go. He just held my legs (the politeness was appreciated) and I tried not to throttle him, and we both looked for the wall of time.

Whatever that was. No idea what it looked like, but if it was anything like the single stone Crazy Kanon McCrazyface had pulled out, we'd sure know it when we saw it.

How big was this world? I don't know, but if it was the same size as the others, this wasn't gonna work. "See anything?" I called.

In response, he skidded to a sudden, dusty, and violent halt.

Someone was there.

Okay, I hadn't expected that. Look, there was *nothing* in this place; no buildings, no remains of buildings, no foot prints, no trash, nothing that indicated anyone had been here in thousands of years. But up ahead of us, right now, stood a guy.

A guy with a weird shape. Took me a moment because his wings were black, and they almost seemed like strange shadows.

A man with four wings. Dark skin, jet-black hair, black wings. Four of them, in case that wasn't clear.

I knew what I was seeing, but I couldn't believe it. It was like turning the corner and seeing a dinosaur, or a dodo.

Four wings? Impossible. They were supposed to be extinct. Nobody's seen the Broken in at least a hundred years.

My mother and teachers and everybody else said that was a good thing because those wings have a particularly frightening power: they stop magic. They stop it. Cancel it. Turn it off. And not just magic. Electricity. Gravity. Heat, cold, inertia, anything you can think of that exerts force or requires energy or creates it, they can just... *stop* with those wings.

And one was alive. Look at that. Standing right there, be-winged and alive. Bran and I would have quite a story to share once we totally survived this and lived to tell about it.

Bran spoke first. "Greetings. Among the Mythos, I am Bran of the Shadow's Breath, Lord of Crows, Echelon of Darkness, and Heir to the Darkseed. And you?"

The figure stirred. He'd been so still that the sudden stretch of his wings—not unfurling, just sort of widening—startled me. "Among the Mythos, I am Adam, of the Saqalu, Guardian. Why are you here?"

Okay, that was a new one. Of the shaka-wha?

"We come to return that which was stolen." Bran knew how to play this game. He held up the stone, or whatever it was, and oh, how it shone! Colors kaleidoscoped across it with frantic speed, as if it wanted to be home. "This was taken. We have come to give it back."

"Taken by whom?" said Adam the shakalaka, or whatever he was.

"The Raven King. We have brought it back."

"Kanon is still the Raven King?" asked Adam, who apparently was at least somewhat up on current events.

"Yes."

"Your service is appreciated. Can you fly?"

"No," said Bran. "Normally, yes, but if I do, I can't carry her."

You may have noticed I was being ignored in this conversation. I was fine with that. We Kin aren't big players. Of course, now I couldn't hide anymore. I waved. "Hi."

"Hi." Adam's lips barely curved for a moment, then straightened again. "I will have to help you, then." He paused. "Dive to your left."

To Bran's credit, he did. He didn't hesitate—he just leaped, smoothly, effortlessly, coming down gently enough that I was barely jostled. And before I could say anything about *that*, the ground burst open right beneath where we'd just stood.

A thing—a worm-thing, a sort of centipede-eyeless-monstrosity thing—flailed out of the soil and whipped around, all clacking pincers and horrible bafflement that we were no longer there.

Bran let go of my leg, stretched his arm to the side, produced a long, curved blade the color of ebony out of nowhere, took one long step forward, and sliced the thing in half.

The top of the centipede-worm-thing hit the ground with a *thud*, sending up more puffs of dust.

It all had taken about two seconds. Bran held his arm out again; the sword disappeared. "Thanks for the warning," he said casually, like we did this every day.

Adam's face didn't change. Knowing, sad, too wise, too calm—
"Farewell, Exqator," he said to the still-twitching body.

Oh, hell, that thing was a *person*? "Friend of yours?" I blurted, ignoring Bran's warning leg-squeeze.

"Relic. The last. Mad as the rest of us." Adam's smile would have
been sweet without his eyes. They did something then—something I
can't easily describe, the irises expanding, changing shape, until the
black circles of his pupils sat in glowing blue that was no longer round,
but snaked away from them like the rays of a stylized sun, tapering
curves twisting to the edges of his eyes. "You are no threat, but he...
could no longer tell the difference." His wings widened again.

Bran kept trembling. He shook as though I were heavy, as though
his power was nearly gone.

"Put me down," I whispered, making it my idea, and he did with a
grateful glance. "So you protected us," I said in the weird silence.
"Thank you."

"I warned you. I did not protect you."

I didn't know how to react to this statement. Guardians protect
stuff. Seriously. It's their thing. "Well, thanks anyway. I'd call it protecting."

"You wouldn't want me protecting you." Adam looked at me with
those terrifying eyes, and the world shrunk briefly to me and him and
air that somehow was no longer enough. I gasped, small, awful breaths
while he looked at me. "You wouldn't want me to do that," he repeated, then turned away, his wings unfurling, huge, huge, so much
bigger than anything had any right to be, and I had trouble focusing
on them—something about them made the air blur, made light waver,
made my magically-imbued eyeballs strain just trying to see.

White tips slid silently from the edges of his black wings like
blades, and he bent those wings then—like hands, or rope, too flexible
to make sense—and slashed the air.

A portal opened. Perfect, thin, a single line barely wider than an
inch.

"Go ahead," said Adam.

We both stared at it. "Thank you," said Bran, and as he walked past me, I saw that the deep flickering in his personal canyons had all but disappeared.

"Leave when you are done." Adam furled his wings tightly; the white blade-things vanished from their edges. "Not all who remain are as capable of rational thought as I."

That wasn't creepy at all.

"Thank you," Bran said again—no, he wheezed it this time—and picked me up, though it had to cost him.

He stepped into that weird line in the air, and though it didn't expand, though it never changed shape, somehow, we slipped right through.

And onto ground just like the one we'd left, except the horizon was no longer empty. In front of us was a Wall.

This deserved capital letters.

Our little stone gleamed and swirled with colors on its own, but a wall of them...

I can't describe it, okay? I can't! I've been thinking how to all this time, and *I can't describe the indescribable.* You can try to picture it, if you like. Twice Bran's height, gently curving away from us, built from a million billion kaleidoscopic pieces, all of them flashing and shifting through every color that's ever been known, shifting with colors and power that I've never known, and every single twinkle or change of color went *right through me* like gentle rays from some kind of radiation gun, taking a little more magic with them every time, every moment, every second.

I don't have a lot of magic, and I don't use much of what I do have, but to suddenly find myself without it left me weaker than I could possibly dream.

I fell to my knees. Breathing suddenly seemed hard. "I'm not old enough for this," I muttered inanely, because I had to say something, had to make a joke, had to try to be funny in the face of the most terrifying thing I've ever experienced.

Bran's red skin looked... kind of gray. Like bricks long after the fire went out. "We need to hurry."

Yeah. Yeah, we did. This world... I could see why it was abandoned. Who could come here? Watches wouldn't even work. Neither spells nor cell phone towers had a chance.

Bran walked up to the wall, closer than I wanted to be, close enough to shove the loose stone back in if we could figure out where it came from. "Katie," he said in a shocked, choked tone.

I joined him as quickly as I could.

Oh.

These weren't stones.

That was a ribcage. That was a skull. That one looked like hand-bones, crunched together in a sort of freaky fist. Other bones. Many, many other bones. Long ones, short ones, ones that had been weathered and beaten until they looked like rocks (and we both stared at the one in Bran's hand for a good long minute). Bones fitted together, with something I couldn't identify holding them in place—it wasn't mortar, I can tell you that.

The Wall of Time (yes, it was capitalized forever now, you'd better believe it) really was made of Guardian bones.

"Where's the hole," I said, freaked, shaking and weak and feeling like maybe I should vomit a little pretty soon.

Bran looked left and right, studying, then pointed: "There."

Something weird was leaking out of the wall a couple hundred feet to our right. It was like smoke, but didn't act like smoke—hovering, undulating, refusing to disperse and spread like smoke, snaking out and down and nearly touching the ground.

Bran ran for it.

I followed. I don't know why we ran, why we behaved this way, except that the sight of whatever that was (Time? Time looked like creepy sentient smoke?) drove us both frantic.

Bran roared as we came closer. We could see the hole clearly, leaking weird smoke with nothing behind it, no flashing or flickering or anything else. He pulled his hand back and just slammed that stone-bone into the hole.

It shouldn't have fit. We should have had to turn it around, figure it out, kajigger it in there and maybe try to find a way to make it stick.

But it fit. It fit, and it jammed in and stuck, and the smoke got cut off like a rope and fell to the ground and shattered like glass.

A wave of something *womped* out from the breaking Time like sound made solid and knocked us both backwards onto the gravel, winded, scraped, gasping.

Silence again.

The shattered piece of time dissolved as we caught our breath, and the spots where those pieces lay blackened, sickened, died.

"We should go home," I whispered.

Bran stood, somehow, helped me to my feet.

We headed back to Adam's portal. The slit in the air was there, vaguely creepy, and let us through without a problem—though it closed behind us. Adam was nowhere to be seen. From here, I could see the portal Bran made—fluttering weirdly in the air like torn sails flapping in a breeze. That was good. I think we both knew Bran had no strength to make another one of his own.

He didn't offer to carry me, and I didn't ask.

We set off at a jog, aiming for it, trying to keep our pace steady. My breath came at a premium; it was like suddenly jumping to eight thousand feet above sea-level and discovering the air was a whole lot thinner there. My very bones shook (normal bones, no glowing there!), but I kept going, kept my eyes on that prize, raised one foot after the other.

Bran fell flat on his face.

Dust rose around him and slowly fell, settling on his brick-red skin. Those cracks were dark now, completely dark.

"Bran?" About-turn. "Bran!" Shake him. Nothing. "*Bran!*"

I tried to drag him; it wasn't working at all—he was too heavy and I was too weak. I tried pushing him, too, wheel-barrow style. I know that makes no sense, but my brain wasn't working right. "Bran, you jackass, if you die here I swear I am *burning your tower down*!" I tried to pull him again.

"Ca-," he said.

I went to my knees, close to his horns. "What? What did you say?"

"Carry," he said, and suddenly wasn't there anymore.

Instead, there was a crow.

Big old corvid, glossy-black-blue feathers, and it lay on its side, breathing too fast. I don't want to know what that transformational magic cost him, but now, we had a chance. I scooped him up (those feathers were too soft to be normal feathers, just for the record) and ran.

I gasped. He gasped. I clutched him like a beaky teddy bear and pushed on.

That portal—was it shaking? It was, trembling in the air, like maybe it was going to close.

Nope. *Nope.* We were not going to die here.

I screamed like a banshee, like a warrior, like a woman who knows how to fight, and I plunged through it as fast as I could possibly run.

And smacked into the wall on the other side.

We fell to the floor and lay there, gasping up at the ceiling in Bran's tower as magic refilled my veins, my bones, my cells, tickling and ir-ritating and warming me up all over.

From above the high fireplace mantle, a beak and glassy eyes peered at me unseeingly. Whaddaya know. I hadn't blown up *all* his birds.

The portal closed with a sort of *shoop*, and the silence here was so much nicer and fuller and warmer that I sighed for joy.

"Good job," Bran croaked. "Now I owe you my life."

"Eh," I said, but you better believe I smiled. This damsel just kicked some butt.

CHAPTER 14

A Very Bad Idea

W E LAY THERE, JUST BREATHING. The blue stones he used in lieu of fire flickered, making no sound, but keeping the room warm.

"I do not ever want to go back to that place again ever in my whole life," I croaked to Bran the bird, still cradled against my chest.

Bran chortled, a corvine laugh, and shifted—growing as he moved, changing, until he was once again human-looking and male and very naked. And also crouching over me. "That was indeed messed up," he sort of purred.

Oh, *boy.* "Back up, buddy."

He gave me a slow, caramel smile I could feel in my toes, then re-materialized his usual outfit of casual jeans and a simple white t-shirt. "Hungry," he announced, and finally moved away from me and toward the fireplace.

I opted to lie where I was.

The single surviving stuffed bird stared down at me, sort of like it was saying, *Hey, I've seen everything, but a lady lying fully clothed on the floor for no apparent reason is a new one on me.*

"Hi, little bird," I said to it.

"That's Crenshaw," said Bran; the sizzle of meat on heat followed. "Only one in this room that survived. Lucky, I say."

"You *named* them?" Now I felt even worse.

"Of course I did. I name everything I collect." And of course, that came with a smirk over his shoulder.

Gods, he was beautiful, and I wasn't talking about his stupid little human costume.

That was a bad thought to have.

"Is there any way to replace the stuffed birds?" I said.

"My *collection* is being pieced back together again."

"I'm sorry." I didn't have it in me to be clever right now.

"You don't need to worry about it."

That was nice of him. Also good, because I had no money. "Bran. Seriously. What was that place?"

"Screwed Central," he quipped, and added a splash of something to the sizzle.

I glared.

He must have felt it. "I guess that was the Guardian world." He rapidly chopped something up—heaven only knew where the food in his living room was coming from. "It fits the Guardians: Broken. Sterile. Deadly. I don't know what my grandfather was thinking."

I sat up slowly, wincing; my muscles burned. "Why did you have that piece of the Wall, anyway?"

"Because he promised me an extra week of life if I could put it back for him. He didn't want to return it himself. What a shock, eh?"

"Wait just a damn minute. We only have a week to keep you alive? Bran!"

"It's going to be all right." He flipped the steaks, the muscles in his back and shoulders emphasized by the tightness of his tee.

"This is not all right!"

"The thing we need to do now is figure out how you're introducing me to Notte so I can get my grandfather off my back for good."

I groaned. "That again? I don't know any vampires. I can't help you. And didn't we already have this conversation?"

"We did." He was already plating. "Now, we're having it again. Red wine?"

"Bran." I put my face in my hands. "No, Bran. We're not doing this."

"I owe you my life now." He approached carrying two plates and two glasses of red wine, all of which he placed on the floor as he sat beside me.

"Bran."

"I can't walk around with a life-debt, Katie. So until we figure out what Cassandra meant, I'll work to piece your life back together."

There weren't enough sighs in the world. "No, you're not doing that."

"Eat. Then we can argue."

He had a point.

We ate in silence for a few. It was so good, so, *so* good, tender fillet and sautéed mushrooms and roasted Brussels sprouts and red wine, and I did *not* moan, but it was close.

Of course, he had no trouble moaning. "Mmmm," Bran rumbled, a tone I swear I could feel in places it was wiser not to think about right now.

"Quit it," I said, and pointed my fork at him.

Bran's innocent look managed to be absolutely lecherous. "Quit what?"

"Bran."

"I'm not seducing you." He pointed with his fork this time. "Just because you're reacting to my natural allure has nothing to do with me."

"'Natural allure?' Really?"

He grinned.

It warmed me right through my center and down to my toes, which clenched—unbidden—in my shoes.

What did we think we were doing? Two people, exhausted, in a dangerous situation, fighting off attraction? This was a bad, bad idea.

I cleared my throat. "I need to go home."

"Something will just capture you if you do. Those prophetic wanted posters are all still active."

He was right. This was downright depressing. "I don't understand what everybody wants from me."

"I don't suppose Death's little sister gave you any clues." He met my gaze and held it, unblinking.

"None."

"That's useless."

I laughed. "Yep."

"Maybe that upcoming decision is what got all the seers losing their minds," he murmured, tapping his chin.

"So you agree they're full of nonsense," I pressed.

"Aye."

"But you still think *Cassandra* is right?"

"She's an echostone. She's not your average seer who can be misled or confused. She's right."

"I'm not so sure she is."

So of course, he pulled her out of his pocket. Where she'd been when he was naked, I'll never know.

"The answer is the Lost Lin," she squeaked again.

"Oh, for crying out loud," I said, and because I am an adult, did not slam my plate down.

"Find her, and she can take you to one of his children. From there, your path will be easy enough," said Cassandra.

"I don't know any vampires!"

"Hey. Be calm." He took my plate and my glass (empty—that hadn't been a good idea on my part). "She isn't wrong. This is going to work out. And I promise I'll get you your life back when this is over. Somehow."

"You're not touching my life. I earned it. I fought for it!" Was I shouting?

He just looked at me, gaze steady.

Damn him. "Look, I... It's not a 'we.' We aren't a 'we.'"

He said nothing.

"I'm not asking for help," I added.

"I know."

My glare and his frustrating patience got us nowhere. I sighed. "So what do *we* do now, prince of stubbornness?"

"Step number two will be Notte. Step number one is actually getting the seers of the world off your back." He stood and offered his hand.

It felt like we kept doing this—offering a hand, waiting for the other to take it. "I'm not going to get rid of you, am I?" I said at random.

"Nope."

I took his hand.

I made the mistake of looking at his dark skin against my pale yellow. Our skin together would be beautiful, pressing close, maybe slippery with sweat—

Whoa, there, Katie Lin. Rein it in.

He was seven, eight hundred years old. I'm twenty-three. This was not a young adult novel, and 'we' would not work.

It would be fun. I know it would. But it wouldn't be worth what came after—including impregnation, which he'd long ago made clear was his goal. Whether he meant it or not, I couldn't let that go.

I released his hand and stepped back. "How do we get the seers to stop?"

"We send out a broadcast. I have a cousin with connections; we can make sure they know they've been manipulated. The downside is I can't take you with me to see her."

"What?"

"She lives deep in Umbra. The only way I could bring you there is if we dressed you up like I owned you, and while I would enjoy that, I'm pretty sure you'd never forgive me."

And then there was the reminder that he was not human, nor did he abide by any sane rules. "Uh. Yeah. Let's not do that." I gave him a suitably horrified look. "So what am I supposed to do, chill in this place?"

"No. I've got an apartment in Manhattan; nice place, secure, well-built to stand up against both searching spells and attacks—got dragon's blood and silver from the Fey worked all through it, along with charms and all kinds of security. Maybe it's not as good as Guardian bones, but you'll be safe there."

I was too tired to fight with this. I took a slow breath. "It's got a bed? And a shower?"

"Several of both."

"Sold." I really had no interest in wandering around Umbra, especially not in costume. "It'll work. Sure, why not."

"It will work." His eyes softened. "For what it's worth, I'm sorry for damaging what you worked so hard to build."

I stared. "Was that an apology? Who are you and what did you do with Bran?"

"I am the king who owes you his life."

Wow.

I expected him to smirk, wink, be generally annoying. He didn't do those things, and the kingliness, the *muchness* of him swept over me like a warm tide.

I lost whatever I'd been going to say. The moment sizzled, pulled tight between us, scared me, tempted me.

And what came to my mind was not the touch of human skin beneath my fingers, but the craggy, tough flesh of the Shadow's Breath, the exploration of all those valleys, the warmth and solidity of his true form, not this silly illusion.

Oh, no. Oh, *no.*

He broke eye-contact first. "Let me grab a few things. We'll be in New York in no time."

I didn't trust myself to answer him.

I was in trouble. So much trouble.

But I'd be damned if I let him know it.

It was a pretty simple delivery. Bran walked me to the doorman— a sweet-looking middle-aged man who was actually a deadly Naga—

and made it clear I'd be staying in his apartment until he said otherwise.

"That's just in case," he added to me. "I'll be back this evening." Then he left.

The apartment was really nice, one of those co-ops in a building older than the Great Depression. And I could feel exactly what Bran had been talking about: the walls hummed, the floor gave off gentle heat, and even the windows felt deliciously shielded against any searching from the outside.

Also, this place had to be worth twenty million dollars.

Marble floors. Seventeen-foot-high ceilings. A *terrace* (it was the penthouse, so why not?) showing me both Central Park and the Hudson River, delicate chandeliers sparkling above solid dark wood furniture made more solid-looking by the eggshell-white walls and minimal artwork.

It was the exact opposite of his gloomy, crowded tower: filled with light, and simple furnishings, and utter elegance in that understated way that screams class.

I loved it at once. Who wouldn't?

The shower I chose had eight heads, by the way. *Eight.* Oh, yeah, baby.

He had clothes of all sizes in the closets, fit for any gender, and I tried not to think about why he'd bother stocking the place like this. Bran is a collector, always; whatever he collected here, I could only hope I hadn't been added to the list.

The kitchen—with huge, white cabinets soaring out of my reach and a fridge big enough to hold my car—housed every food I could want, magically preserved against decay, so I made myself some dim sum and went to bed.

I really thought he'd be back by morning.

He wasn't.

So, I waited. I watched television, goofed around on the grand piano, hung out on the terrace pretending I owned the place and knew how to choose champagne.

Still no Bran.

He had a library, but it was sort of basic literary classics from the Ever-Dying, the Fey, and People of the Sun; really standard you-should-have-read-this-before-college stuff. Eh. I wasn't that bored.

I considered calling Danner and Danner to see if I'd lost my job yet, but the mild possibility that some unpleasant person could be monitoring phone lines kept me from it. I considered going out to find a public phone (they *did* still exist) and calling the number on the card Joshua gave me, but then I remembered I didn't have my wallet—it was still lost from when Bran swapped out my clothes in the Silver Dawning.

Dammit.

At least I had plenty of cash. Bran had thought to give me a whole satchel-full before taking off, but to use it, I'd need to leave the apartment. The last time I was out there, a vampire tried to eat my face. I wasn't sure I was up to more random meetings.

I enjoyed the shower again. Went to bed. Woke.

No Bran.

Day four was spent fretting. I'm not proud of it; it's just the truth. I barely ate. I didn't sleep well that night, either, and all my dreams were lousy.

One dream in particular took the cake. And also changed everything.

Ready for this? Take a deep breath. It's about to get weirder.

I'm not the type of person who has really interesting dreams, you know? Many among the Kin do; it's one of the things we just have to deal with as part of our mixed and maddening heritage. I have one sister who regularly dreams the weather for the following week, twin cousins who either start or finish one another's visions, and several old schoolmates who make a good living peddling themselves out as fortunetellers.

But not me. That bug never manifested in my genes. I have never dreamed the future, and in my family, if you haven't done that by the age of twelve, you're not going to, ever.

That's why I knew this wasn't a prophetic dream. This crap was happening *right now*.

In a glittering purple cave, painfully sharp like the inside of the biggest geode ever, six dragons loomed: three red, three black, none bothering with their smaller forms. In full draconian splendor, they stood around my uncle Merlin and a tiny, white dragon no bigger than a kitten.

My uncle was in full-on old-man mode today, rocking the white beard and hair, wearing some bizarrely cheap-looking robe of shiny purple material covered in yellow stars. Also a pointed hat, because he thinks it's funny.

He looked so small between the dragons, so cheerfully harmless, but he wasn't. He could kill them without even snapping his fingers. He's Merlin. He's more powerful, possibly, than anyone on Earth—so he gets to dress how he likes. He also gets to host weird meetings involving prophesied lords.

On his shoulder stood a tiny star-white dragon, the one who'd brought Bran and me together in the first place: the fabled Starling Child, the dragon born to bring the Red and Black clans out of their centuries-long war and into peace. Also known as Vesuvius—Suvi, for short—because he'd once puked fire all over my shoes.

Suvi huffed and strutted along my uncle's shoulders, clearly unconcerned that he was smaller than the adult dragons' littlest claws, and I don't know what he squeaked at them, but they reacted as if he'd pronounced himself king.

They bowed. All six dragons bowed with front legs bent. Two dragons leaked angry smoke from their nostrils while doing this, but all bowed their heads to Suvi. When they did, this purple-crystal cave flashed, blinding. Suvi jumped on top of my uncle's head, his tail straight out with startlement.

Then the scene changed.

Suddenly, I was looking at Adam—Adam, talking with a dark form I thought maybe was a member of the Dream. Adam looking grim, Adam looking angry, Adam spreading all four wings (had I ever seen such a glorious sight?) and launching off into the air.

And then, just as suddenly as changing a channel, Adam disappeared, and instead, there was Kanon.

The Raven King sprawled naked in full Shadow's Breath form on some huge throne made of veined red stone, staring at a cauldron of rippling liquid—water? Oil? I had no clue—and *in that cauldron was me,* sleeping in bed, my image warping slightly with the ripples.

Beside him stood the vampire who'd attacked us on the street in New York. I don't like terms like "haughty beauty," but she embodied it, and she spoke angrily to him—without fear—and gestured violently at the cauldron. Kanon said nothing, leaning on his fist, ignoring her as he watched me sleep.

Watched me sleep right now. As I dreamed.

I stirred, and my rippled image stirred in the cauldron.

But I couldn't wake up. Instead, the vision changed once more.

There was Bran. He stood outside a run-down building in an alley flecked with bright but filthy paint, an alley almost made cheerful by the abandoned lanterns strung overhead, an alley made hopeless by the piles of garbage and homeless, starving people all around his booted feet.

He looked grim, really grim, and his black, buckled coat was gray with dust. He knocked on the wooden door—which shook and shed flecks of itself as he pounded—and when it swung open, he stepped inside.

I caught the briefest glimpse of a struggle. Of him, bursting out of human illusion and into his full and deadly form, roaring silently as he struggled with something in that dark place.

The door slammed shut, cutting off my vision.

I sat up shouting Bran's name, reaching for him. Reaching and shouting, half-awake, half-asleep, reaching as though desperate to pull him out of that horrible building, out of that danger.

And everything—

Everything around me, everything in the room—

Traffic outside, the clock on the wall—

The position of the planets, the push of the wind—

It all. Went. Backwards.

The scream crammed itself back into my throat, into my lungs, pushed me back down into the bed and under the covers, and tried to pull sleep back over my eyes. Sound twisted, a reverse Doppler effect as traffic swarmed astern. Stars cranked backwards in agony. My heart hiccoughed blood the wrong way through my veins.

It was all going to tear apart.

I fought it, pulled, like trying to stop a runaway truck with my heels dug into the dirt. No, no, no, what was happening, no—

It stopped. Somehow, it stopped.

My blood, boiling as if it had been radiated, burned through my veins in the right direction. My heart pumped normally, traffic resumed its usual route, and the second-hand on the clock clicked forward at a proper and appropriate pace.

And I lay there, sick, overheated, absolutely scared out of my mind. I wanted to deny what happened, but I couldn't because I'd *felt it.*

I'd done that. I'd pulled back time like pulling open curtains. Reached out with some part of myself and *changed time.*

Maybe if I didn't move, it wouldn't happen again and everything would be okay.

Maybe I was kidding myself and I'd just broken the universe. I made a sound that wasn't quite laugh or cry and covered my mouth.

I needed help. I needed help *now.*

"Bran," I whispered to the empty room. "Get your ass back here or I swear I'll hunt you down myself."

I didn't think he'd appear, and he didn't.

Bran was in trouble, and he had three days left before his grandfather tracked him down. I may have been terrified, but Bran was the damsel in distress tonight. I couldn't wait. Bran couldn't, either.

It didn't matter how scared I was, or how out of my league. It was time for *Katie Saves Her Own Damn Self,* part two. If I survived at all, at least I'd have a helluva good tale to tell.

If I didn't, well...

At least I'd go out with a bang.

CHAPTER 15

The Clamshell Was Right?

I WASN'T THINKING AS I PACKED.

Rifling through Bran's closets produced a hold-all duffle-bag—the kind that takes whatever you put in it and never weighs more.

That was cool, but I wasn't exactly staying in an armory, and the moment I stepped out that door, I could be dealing with Kanon, his vampire girlfriend, or worse. Not to mention whatever was powerful enough to take down Bran.

What was powerful enough to do that besides his grandfather? Seriously. That wasn't a small question.

But the answer didn't matter. I was going after him because I was out of my mind. I'd apparently been out of my mind most of my life anyway, so at least I was consistent.

Scissors, coffee mugs, towels, shoes.

Every damn knife he had.

There were no poisons or charmed items I could find. Someone more enterprising might have dug into the wall to get at that blessed copper and silver wiring, or to make some kind of a paste out of that protective plaster from the walls themselves. Not me. Instead, I packed a wheel of cheese and two candied apples, a cheese grater, about sixty *har gow* dumplings, two loaves of rye bread and a pound of pastrami, and a metric ass-ton of dried noodles. Why not?

If I found Bran, he'd need calories. This would help, I told myself calmly and rationally and not at all while crying.

Water, water, water—enough bottles to hydrate us both for a few days, though it took a while to pack them. Every time I opened the bag to put something inside, the appropriate pocket made an appearance— so I had to fit each bottle into little wine-pouches sewn to the sides.

Speaking of wine, that was a good idea. Red, because reasons.

I packed salt, because there were magical uses for that, and you never know.

I packed the few tools I found around the place—a hammer, needle-nose pliers, and a Phillips-head screwdriver.

I packed clothes for various climates, several pillows, and some bedding.

Then I had no more reason to wait. The duffel hung comfortably from my shoulder, just heavy enough to keep from sliding off. I even had enough money to let me travel through a local Conflux.

As for *where* to travel, well, that was a problem.

You can't just seek for people, not even with magic. Okay, so I had some of his underwear from a drawer to aid in tracking purposes, but I doubted it would help; the people who'd grabbed him probably had pretty spiffy anti-spying spells. If I could even figure out which world he was in, it would be a miracle.

It was about time I had a miracle. In fact, I was overdue. And so, determined, bolstered, brave, I opened the door to the hall.

A vampire stood in the foyer.

"I'm sorry," he said, and covered his ears, and I yelled and slammed the door and the bang echoed down into the elevator shaft like my beating heart pounded up into my throat.

Not my most dignified moment.

My pulse battered my nerves like unknown footsteps in the dark. Okay, Katie—think. Blood-boy out there couldn't have gotten into the building if he'd meant harm, or so Bran said, and I had no reason to disbelieve it.

Also, this vampire hadn't looked... well-fed. It's not that vampires can't be that skinny—they tend to retain their body-types from when they were turned—but he just didn't radiate power. He was too pale, too tired-looking. I don't think he fed as regularly as he needed.

And he'd covered his ears *before* I screamed.

Oh, for crying out loud. Had he known? Was he another fortune-teller, hot on the trail of the Lost Lin? But that made no sense. Vampires couldn't be seers. Vampires can only be made from humans, and humans can't do magic; once they're vampires, they have access to some spells, but never prophecy. Seers are born, not made.

He'd still covered his ears before I screamed.

No problem. We'd figure this out. I'd let him in, we'd shoot the breeze, make friends, become pen-pals, go on adventures, mail each other cookies for Christmas.

I couldn't even escape through the back stairs, could I? He'd tracked me this far. I doubted I could shake him. I pressed my fists against my forehead, suddenly more tired than I'd ever been, so weary I could just hide in a hole and never come out.

Courage is costly. I wiped the tears from the corners of my eyes and took a deep breath. "Ready or not," I mumbled, and reached for the door.

The door opened with a slow creak that would make haunted houses proud.

He stood there, still too skinny, still too pretty in that way Eurasian boys can be, and his body language was so hunched and diminished it was easy to miss how tall he was. "Hello, Miss Lin," he said, barely meeting my eyes; his own green ones—vampire green—didn't dilate or do anything hungry or scary. "Among the Mythos, I am Night Child, called Jonathan."

"Hi." Nice and polite, reasonable, nothing scary here. He knew who I was already.

He smiled and glanced at me, then away. "I bet you're wondering why I'm here."

"You could say that." I shifted the bag. "I don't suppose you're going to let me leave."

"Oh! Sure, of course!" he said, and backed against the wall as though I needed five feet of clear space to reach the elevator.

What was with this guy? "You're not going to stop me?"

"That's not why I'm here, Miss Lin." His hands clutched each other nervously over his groin. "I'm sorry. I know you don't believe me, and that you're about to leave—since I'm, um, 'letting' you, and then you're going to run into trouble in the street." He mumbled something, I think in Japanese, then briefly met my gaze. "It's going to be messy, but you'll be all right. I promise."

No seers among vampires. Impossible. "Okay, pal." I pressed the button for the elevator, urging it to hurry-hurry-hurry.

He smiled, then looked away again, but made no move toward me.

The door slid open. I stepped in. The door slid shut. And unless I was crazy, his shoulders relaxed just as the doors closed, as though he found this conversation every bit as scary as I did.

This guy was officially weird.

Downstairs, I hurried through the marble hall, past the blind wooden cherubim, through the patches of colored light shed by the stained glass in the walls. I couldn't slow my breathing. I was leaving the safe space—the only safe space I had for right now—and I had no clue where I was going. And had Jonathan's words been a threat? I had no idea.

They weren't a prophecy, though. Nope. They were not. I'd already seen too many rules broken on this adventure. Just imagine waking up one day to find the laws of physics no longer apply; it would suck, wouldn't it? Let me tell you from experience that it would. Big time.

The cheerful green awning of 211 Central Park West shaded me from winter's bright sun, but I still had to take a moment to adjust;

snow cast the light back at me like some kind of spell, and my eyes watered in self-defense.

Someone moved next to me, right up against me as though he had a right to my personal space. Someone breathing like a bull.

"You are Lost Lin," he said in heavily accented English, and I looked up to find a minotaur there—bull-head, golden nose-ring, slobbering lips and all—in a bright blue North Face jacket.

"Nope," I said, and tried to pull away.

His grip cut off circulation in my arm. "There is bounty out on you," he said. "Five golden crowns and barrel of heirloom wheat. What you do to make such wealthy men mad, eh? Eh?" And he howled a laugh.

Where was the doorman? Gone, that's where, and I really hoped he'd just gone to take a smoke break or something. "Buddy, you are making a huge mistake," I said.

"No, no, I think you bring great bounty, eh?" He thought this was hilarious. Magic swirled around him, keeping his true appearance hidden from humans; and how often do people interfere when they see a woman getting bullied by a man, anyway? Not often enough.

So I reared back and kicked him between the legs as hard as I possibly could.

Did I mention I'd stolen a pair of steel-toed boots before leaving Bran's love nest?

He bellowed and went down, and his illusion spell popped along with his concentration. An answering bellow from across the street warned me just as his partner came galloping into traffic, utterly incongruous in jeans and outsized Italian boots, and either he didn't see the speeding taxi or he didn't care. It smashed into him going at least fifty-five and stopped as if it had run into a concrete barrier, lifting from the back-end not quite enough to flip over but definitely enough to hurt whoever was inside.

The second minotaur roared, grabbed the taxi, and tossed it onto its side as if it weighed about as much as a dining room chair.

Normal people were getting hurt now. This wasn't acceptable. If I went back into the building, they'd just try to get in after me, and probably attack anyone who got in their way—including human police officers.

Courage has a cost.

"Hey, ugly! Hey, over here, you big heifer!" I jumped up and down, waving, then turned and ran.

Their hooves pounded behind me like a stampede.

Screams. Something crashing. Bellows, curses, shouts. I ran faster, keeping them moving. If they just didn't kill anyone, if at least I could keep them from doing that—

That's when Jonathan appeared. He did that *thing* vampires do, suddenly swirling to physical form from dust motes, and the fact that he did it in bright noonday sun told me he was no baby bat.

"Stop," he said to them, softly, sweetly, completely uselessly.

I ran past him, but the sounds made me look.

A horrible *snap*, a break like bones of the earth cracking. As I slid to a stop, snow flying, a horn landed by my feet, sticking up in the snow like a demented signpost.

Oh, dear. This *had* gotten messy.

The minotaurs ran away limping, leaving red in their wake, and one of them was definitely missing a horn. Jonathan stood there—I kid you not, *shivering* in the snow like he'd just found himself there by accident—and when he turned to look at me, I saw none of the wrath, none of the rictus, none of the violence I'd expected.

He looked exactly like he had in the foyer: apologetic, pretty, desperately shy. "I'm sorry," he said, "but we really should get going if you don't want to be roped into their arrest."

I had no doubt those two would be arrested by magical law enforcement. "Are you in trouble?"

"Me?" his eyes widened. "Oh, no! Not at all. Nobody really saw me."

For real? "How did you know they were waiting for me?"

He closed the distance between us, slipping a little in the snow. "I didn't. I mean... I saw them, but they weren't waiting. They just got lucky."

"There are no seer vampires." I didn't yell it. Are you proud of me?

"I know," he said, but now wouldn't meet my eyes again.

Damn.

He chewed his lower lip, then pointed. "That way is safe. If we go anywhere else, we'll be caught."

What was up with this guy? "Fine. Fine! Lead on! What the hell! I've got nothing to lose anymore!"

He looked up slowly as though I'd said something profound. "But you do." And he began walking.

Two of him could fit in my jeans, and I am not a big person.

Who the hell was this guy? I may not have vampires in my social circles, but I'd met quite a few, and they were never like this. That combination of desirability (the reason they were chosen) plus years to perfect self-presentation tended to lead to suave, confident people. This guy was pretty enough (in a really... wispy sort of way) to qualify, *I guess*, but he was so weird. Not confident.

And, I was pretty sure, hungry.

Not a seer, though. Definitely not that.

He led the way to Amsterdam Avenue, never saying so much as a word to me. He didn't even pause to check behind him, but I'm sure he knew I was there.

I was following a vampire through the city. This was insane.

He seemed to know where he was going, though, and I kept a comfortable distance behind him as he stopped for "don't walk" signs (clearly, not a New York native), let people pass in front of him, and said, "Excuse me" to anyone who came too close.

Wow.

The place he finally stopped at was a little bakery and restaurant on Amsterdam. The warmth made my nose run, and I fished a tissue out of my handy-dandy bag as he got us a table.

We were lucky. I knew this place—very kitsch and normally full. I told myself he absolutely had not known there'd be a table available.

We sat across from each other, silent until they brought us a basket of teas and hot water.

"Oh, finally," he said with the first cheer I'd seen, and made himself a cuppa.

His hands were beautiful. Distracting. I shook my head to clear it.

"So," I said.

"I know this is a lot to take in," he said softly, sliding the honey jar toward me. "And I'm sorry. There wasn't another way to do this, and you're so paranoid at this point that ordinary measures simply won't work." His eyes widened. "I'm so sorry. I mean... that came out terribly wrong. I don't think you're paranoid."

I pointed my spoon at him. "You can be paranoid if they're all out to get you."

"True. And they are. And it isn't your fault." Jonathan peeked at me and back down again. "My family name is Sumeragi. I'm..."

The waitress came.

We got scones.

Bran was languishing in a dungeon, wounded minotaurs were probably screaming my name to magical law enforcement, and I was ordering scones.

"It's okay to cry," he said, and offered me a handkerchief in my favorite color—robin egg blue.

Speaking of color, I could feel mine drain from my face.

"Please," he said. "I picked it up for you this morning. I promise it's clean."

"You're freaking me out, Jonathan." I took it. Used it.

The waitress gave us both suspicious looks when she came back, but we smiled and assured her all was well. "Family drama," I told her with the fakest laugh I have ever made, but she bought it. She still kept an eye on our table as she left. Remember my earlier statement about a woman in distress? Too often, only other women care. But that's a rant for another day.

Jonathan's head hung, and he played with a little spill of sugar on the table, making runes. "I'm sorry about all this. I wouldn't get involved at all, but now that my father is in danger, I can't wait. Please forgive me. I hope you'll hear me out."

Cold. It was warm in here, but I felt cold. "You don't mean your human father, do you?"

He smiled—and there, *right there*, was a hint of the monster inside him. "No."

I shivered. My nipples peaked; I can't tell if that was fear or something else, but Night Children affect everybody that way. It's one of the reasons they're so freaky.

I focused on my scone for a little while. This scone was worth it. Yowza. No wonder this place was always packed.

"Better?" he finally said, though he'd barely eaten a bite.

"Yeah." I realized I hadn't eaten since last night. No wonder I'd felt shaky. "You wanna explain anything?"

"I have to, or you'll never listen." He didn't seem offended or offensive as he made this statement. "I don't blame you, either. So here is the whole story: I was a seer in life."

"Nope." I shook my head, chewing delicious scone, finally asking myself if everything I'd ever learned was a lie or if this week in particular was just screwed.

"Only three Kin have been turned in all of history. It's never happened any other time, so you don't need to be afraid of it."

"I don't need to be afraid of it because it's impossible." I couldn't budge on this for a very important reason. Vampires? *Night Children*? Do you have *any* idea how terrifying they are?

They can take humans and turn them into magical beings.

Nobody else does that. You don't become something you're not. You're born what you're born, and that's that—unless you're a human, because then you can become a vampire.

Humans can't use magic, period. It's not in their genetic code; electric eels can use electricity and that's not a common trait, either. The other Peoples can use magic and humans can't. It's not difficult. But something fundamental changes when they turn into Night Children.

Vampires stop aging. Their eyes all go the same green. They need human blood—*need* it—and now have a second nature called the Beast, which makes them completely bonzo-loco insane for the first year or six of their new lives. If they can't get control of that Beast and find themselves again, from what I know, they're put to sleep. Permanently.

I've even heard that Notte—the first, the most powerful, the "father" of all of them—buries some of them underground, letting them sleep for years until they can be a little more sane.

Who knows, though, really? It's all a mystery. They change humans from one thing into another, and if they could do this to any People other than the Ever-Dying (whom, the biased assert, really needed a hand up of some kind), there wouldn't be any kind of truce or peace or calm.

If we thought they could turn any of us into them, there'd be war.

"Only three?" I whispered, suddenly wishing I hadn't eaten anything at all.

"Yeah. Only three. Me, and two siblings, brother and sister. It's never happened any other time, I promise." He rushed to assure me, to calm me, to give me any kind of comfort in this.

"I won't tell," I found myself saying out of the blue, all of a sudden, not at all what I planned to say. But it was true, wasn't it? It is. I wouldn't tell anyone who mattered about this. It's not this guy's fault his genetic makeup accepted that of the Night Children.

"Oh, I know," he said, meeting my eyes again with his own wide ones. "Now, here's why I'm here: you have some lost time inside you."

Hearing it stated that bluntly was less than kind.

It hurt. Hurt my skull. Twisted something in my spine. Settled in my stomach like mercury, slippery and poisonous. "Okay."

"I think your uncle can get it out, but we have to be careful. If it escapes—say, if you die—then it'll go wild, and no one knows what it'll do. Not even us seers."

"Okay." What else could I say?

"Right now, unless things change, you're going to chase after Bran, and Kanon will let you do it because he's going to use Bran to catch you. He knows that time got into you."

"He WHAT?"

Tables quieted as their occupants paused, glanced my way, then decided I wasn't worth their time.

I leaned over, getting my scarf in the butter. "He *knew*?"

"Yes." Jonathan only seemed to show surprise when concerned he'd said something rude. "It's complicated. He needs your particular genetic makeup—Kin—to be able to take in time. And while there are plenty of other Kin, the others aren't... um. Isolated. And Bran likes you, so hurting you is a benefit."

My sigh was long, slow, and far from patient. "So that son of a bitch is behind all of this."

Jonathan hunched. "There's more. He's a pawn, I know that much, but that's all I can clearly see. I'm sorry."

Kanon was a pawn? Of whom? Of what? I didn't want to meet that guy, whoever he was. "Don't apologize. Unless it's your fault. Not your fault? Then don't say you're sorry." Anger coated the room with red, flickering as if the edges of my vision were on fire. "What's your problem, anyway? You could kill anything that bothered you. Why are you acting like someone's beating you with a stick?" Was I really yelling at the guy behaving like an abused child? Geez, Katie....

"It's okay," he said. "I know you'll feel bad about it for a while, but it's okay. I... when father..." He took a deep breath. "Father didn't make me. Ravena did."

Holy hell.

And now I saw the difference between learned deference and true fear, between sweet and shy hesitation and barely scabbed-over terror. I met his green-eyed gaze, and I knew why he feared. I had met her, and she was crazier than crazy. "Damn," I whispered.

He nodded. "She made me, but he took me away from her. He... I wasn't being treated well." And he went silent for a long moment, swallowing repeatedly, as though her name brought bile to his mouth.

Yeech. And I thought my family was FUBAR.

I shuddered as I exhaled. What the hell had I avoided in New York? Bran saved me in more ways than one when she... *Dammit*. She was there because Kanon sent her. She grabbed Joshua because she and Kanon were spying on me.

Joshua.

Now I was breathing too fast. I sent him home to keep him safe, but in doing so, had I sent him in to her jaws?

Jonathan took a slow breath and continued. "All I know is Kanon needed Bran to take you there, to Meginnah—the Guardian world. He knew time would infect you there."

It was all coming together now, or at least, part of it. "And all the seers prophesying things, getting everybody after me?"

"They're doing it because they're terrified. Look, Katie. Listen. Please. If you hear nothing else, please hear this: what we see is the same thing—that somehow, *somehow*, in two days' time, you die. The time is released, and it goes wild—and I don't know what it does to father." His voice caught. "I don't know, but he goes mad. He... he loses everything that makes him... *him*. And after that, we can't see anything."

Someone dropped something in the kitchen, but we didn't jump. A woman laughed to my left; to my right, four pampered upperclass children whined about their *pain aux raisins* and insulted their caretakers. Outside, a passing car's horn arced in a perfect Doppler effect, followed by a pedestrian's curses in Arabic.

I couldn't move.

He gave me time, waiting, even blinking slowly, as if to tell me I could figure it out at my own pace, but I couldn't, I *couldn't*, we were running out of time for maybe everything in the world, and I *could not*.

"What do you mean, you can't see anything?" I finally whispered.

"I mean there's nothing. I see..." He sighed. "You might as well know everything. Here." He pulled a cell phone from his pocket, fidgeted briefly with the screen, then handed it over.

There was a portrait on this screen, a picture taken of someone's painted work. I know what Notte looks like; it's like being in England

and knowing what the Queen looks like, or in America and knowing what the President looks like. You know the face of important leaders.

But I've never seen Notte like this.

He always looks young, too young to be the ancient and unaging father of all vampires, with big brown curls and soft, beautiful eyes, with a poet's face—to quote my uncle—who looks like he'd cry over the fly instead of hurting it. Well, I recognized the beauty; I recognized the curls.

I did not recognize the being painted in this portrait.

If someone took the essence of rage, took the devil, took all the bias and hate and racial injustice and starving fury and vengeful wrath and scorned women and jealous men and greedy children and every single horrible angry furious thing that ever existed and *compressed it to this moment*, it would be that face.

That face, which is Notte's contorted and somehow wildly freed, lunging at the viewer with eyes locked so it's impossible to look away and his hands hooked like claws, with those slender fangs—normally so subtle—out and long and primordial somehow like a sabertooth's, and you know—looking at this, *you know*—that when he reaches you, he will not drink you like a latte on a fine French evening, but he will rip you, rend you, tear you limb from limb until he can lick your still-warm blood from your shreds.

I made a small sound and handed it back. "*That's* him?"

"Never. But it might be. If we don't keep you alive." He calmly put the phone away—didn't even glance at it, like he's seen it so many times it's just not an issue anymore.

"Then what is that? Who did that? Where did it come from, if he's not that now?"

"I painted it." Jonathan blushed, but met my eyes. "That's my gift. I paint what's to come; that's how I see it."

"What, like... automatic writing?"

"Something like that." He shrugged, visibly pleased and shy at the same time.

I'm not sure I'd like that gift.

I couldn't shake the image he'd painted. It was too vivid, too real. "Okay. So. What do we do?"

"To be honest, I'm not sure. From here, I can only see a little ahead at a time; we've changed your course so strongly that I don't know exactly what to do." He wriggled a little, a kid before a great unknown. "Everything still goes dark in two days, but *we still have those two days.* That's important."

"Let's save Bran." First things first. Hey, I had less than forty-eight hours left to live? Fine. But I was going out doing what I wanted to do, dammit.

Jonathan shook his head. "I'm pretty sure Kanon is counting on you doing that," he warned.

"Of course he is. I don't give a damn. I am not leaving Bran to die, do you understand?"

"Katie. If you go and Kanon kills you, we *all* die. Do *you* understand?"

Ooh. The kicked puppy could bite back. I held his challenging gaze, insanely pleased that I'd summoned a little spine from him. "Then we're at an impasse. Because you know what? I'm pretty sure you're not about to force me into anything."

He paused. "Please."

"Don't ask nicely. It will get you nowhere."

"Then at least let me go with you. Nobody's expecting me. Nobody knows I exist."

My eyebrows crawled toward my hairline. "I guess they must keep you under wraps."

"They do." He smiled, a sneaky little expression that shows his true heart in glimpses.

"What did you do, climb out a window? Wait. Do *not* tell me your creator knows you're here." I could not deal with Ravena today. Or ever.

"No! Father took me from her years ago, like I said. I asked to come to the new dragon coronation, and Father was so happy that I wanted to 'join the world,' as he said, that he told me to come. He's at the coronation right now, waiting for me."

This was the point I started laughing and crying at the same damn time. So Suvi—

My baby dragon, the little guy I'd rescued because my crazy uncle sent him to me to keep him safe—

The baby dragon who'd sort of introduced me to Bran, because Bran kidnapped my uncle (and that was somehow okay because of *reasons*)—

That little dragon whom I'd seen in my dream really was being crowned. And that meant everybody who was anybody might have to be there.

The connections through all this, all my life, suddenly shone before me like a glowing, fiery knot of life and death and knowledge, and I couldn't see where those strands led or where they came from, but it was all connected, all of it, and overwhelmed, I reached for it, fingers already tingling in anticipation of such power, such life, such intricacy.

"You see the Tapestry?" he whispered.

Reality slammed me awake, and I froze with hand in the air, reaching toward nothing. My mouth was dry—it had been hanging open. "What just happened?" I croaked.

"You saw time. It's in you, remember? It just showed you part of itself."

"That wasn't time, that was..." I had no idea. "Did you say 'Tapestry?'"

"That's what we call it." He smiled, eager now, eyes bright, and in that moment looked so beautiful I could see why crazy Ravena took him. "I don't know how it works; even when we change what's to come, we find those threads there, too, like those changes were always woven in all along."

I'd just seen the tangles of *time?* "I can't get into this." I shook my head. "Fate, choices. If I think about that right now, I'll freeze, and I can't afford to."

"I know."

"I mean it, Jonathan."

"I know. Hey—I'll get this." He pulled out a wallet. "We should probably go."

And here it came. "Go where?"

"India. Bran was in New Delhi."

That... was strange. "He was going to Umbra. Are you sure?"

Jonathan nodded.

Bran's weird cousin must have told him to go there. But why?

Jonathan said nothing as he hailed the taxi, taking us to deeper into the city where he swore an unwatched Conflux could swoop us to New Delhi. He knew precisely how much time we had, now that we'd made a decision. Apparently, fortune-telling was easier when someone's path was set.

I just felt sick. I figured, given all I now knew, feeling sick wasn't an unreasonable use of my time.

It didn't help that I wanted to see that glowing knot again. I needed to—but I was afraid. I was afraid that I'd touch it, and then...

Something bad.

We're coming, Bran, I thought, hoping this wasn't wrong, hoping for a way to get this time-stuff out of me, wondering if the Guardians knew what had happened to their wall. Wondering if Adam cared.

I suddenly had a feeling Adam wouldn't be okay with this—and as I blinked, with every blink, a glowing thread seemed to stretch out from me to him, pulling us together, tying our futures.

Nope. Denial time. That wasn't real.

Because if I believed it was, I would sit down on the curb and cry.

"Here," whispered Jonathan, and gave me a chocolate bar—my favorite brand, from Switzerland.

That really didn't help.

CHAPTER 16

Operation *Katie Saves the Whole Damn World*

EVERYONE WAS ALREADY TALKING about the minotaurs by the time we got to Columbus Circle.

"Can you *believe* they did that in front of the Ever-Dying?" was the primary gist, and while most of the magical citizenry seemed inclined to laugh it off, not everyone was so easily amused.

The Mythos *does* have magical police. They look different from world to world, from country to country, kingdom to kingdom, and People to People. But across worlds, across dimensions, over all government and jurisdiction, law enforcement takes only took one form: the Hush.

The word originally came from some ancient word meaning *sweeping* or *keeping clean*, but over time, it morphed as words do—and at least in English, included the finger-to-the-lips gesture of silence.

The Hush scared the crap out of me.

Yes, there are other self-policing groups out there; mess with the Sinaa of South America or the Zimwi of Kenya and you'll find out really fast just what kind of justice they serve. But the Hush are interworld; they're multi-government, legally empowered across the board, committed to the single purpose of making sure the humans don't know we exist. Why? To keep us safe, of course.

You probably think that's laughable. We have *magic*. And we're afraid of bullets?

Some of us are afraid of bullets, yes. And all of us are afraid of nuclear bombs, biological warfare, poison gasses, land mines, knives in the dark—not to mention the loss of all our stuff should some human organization decide we're aliens and they have the right to simply take all of it.

It's a numbers issue, see? There are, what, seven billion human beings living on this planet? Well, the magic-users of the Mythos are a little... less numerous than that. Last count, between the worlds, including the Kin, we had about one billion total. Altogether.

We just don't reproduce as fast. Some of us never reproduce at all. And we never really recovered from the First War, which I think I've mentioned before. But that's beside the point.

Jonathan and I hurried downtown with our heads down, just two magical nobodies trying to make our way, and I strained to hear if the gossip tree had figured out just why those minotaurs went on that rampage in front of the gods and everyone.

Ah, there it was: "They were chasing some chick?" blurted the leftmost head of a cyclops.

"I thought they didn't do that anymore," opined the right, his single brow forming a *w*-shape of worry.

Ha! They do, but not for the reasons you guys think!

"This way," Jonathan whispered, and dove abruptly into Gray's Papaya on Broadway.

Well, it'd be silly to argue at this stage of the game, wouldn't it?

He bought me a medium papaya shake but nothing for himself. I confess a little envy at his easy-access bank account—but that's what happens when you're part of a family like the Night Children. Then he stood there, staring awkwardly at help-wanted posters while I sipped.

Outside, footsteps. Someone ran by, boots heavy, but otherwise silent.

I didn't turn. No reason to act guilty. Or maybe I was supposed to turn, and pretending I didn't care was a bad sign? I was terrible at this.

"Come on," said Jonathan.

"Hey, vampire—I got something you might like to drink, if you change your mind," whispered a waiter.

"No, thank you," Jonathan said sweetly, and off we went.

"What, blood and papaya?" I muttered as we turned down the street, ducking under the tarp and scaffolding that seemed ubiquitous here.

"Actually, yes. It's surprising."

I didn't doubt that.

We turned a few more corners, working our way south, out of the heavy commerce areas and back into places where people simply lived. A nasty, stinky phone booth stood on one corner, its handset torn completely off and leaving a quill of wires behind. It smelled so much of urine that no one in their right mind would even want to touch it; every pane was scratched with graffiti in angry, sweeping strokes as if a wildcat had been trapped inside.

There was also a dead, rotting rat in the exact center of its floor. A subway rat. This thing probably outweighed a Chihuahua. Or it had before the roaches got to it.

"Ew!" said Jonathan, covering his nose.

Yep: this was the entrance to our Conflux. Good job, whoever was in charge of making it unappealing.

Confluxes are magical train stations, and they're the best way to travel distances in the magical worlds. Sure, portals were less fussy, but also require great power, and traveling that way left one without paperwork or any kind of legal proof one was *allowed* to do said traveling. Neither I nor Jonathan were important like Bran. We ordinary people needed to take Confluxes.

You've passed several in your lifetime, I promise. The entrances were disgusting places no one without a desire for cholera would ever go near. But if you have any magic in your blood, if you're anything other than pure Ever-Dying, you will still feel inexplicably *drawn*.

We always know where a Conflux is, always. It pulls us in its direction for no obvious reason, and often leaves Kin who don't know they're Kin very confused. Why do they want to wander *that way* toward those woods, or into that abandoned building, or down that hole, or in that cave? It makes no sense. Sometimes, they even follow that urge, and while it's cool to see all the abandoned and terrible things, they can't really explain why they were so drawn to that one spot.

Because it's a Conflux, that's why. Unfortunately, you need specific magic to access one, or wandering into one won't do a damn thing.

What can I say? Among the Mythos, we are paranoid.

"Nasty one, isn't it?" Jonathan said, gingerly tip-toeing over the rat.

"Well, it's effective." I could only hope this thing wouldn't rub old pee-smell on my clothes. It was real pee. Believe me, it was real. "I don't have a wand."

"We don't need one." He closed his eyes for a moment. When he opened them, the green irises gleamed like Christmas lights in a dark night, and something else—something I couldn't place—in his pretty, slim face transformed to feral.

He did not look at me in that moment, Jonathan. If he had, I might have squeaked; prey-response is strong in those of us who are small and easily squished.

The Jonathan who raised his slender painter's fingers wasn't the same Jonathan who bowed and apologized and shied his way through life. The Jonathan who smiled now—revealing white needle-sharp teeth that ever so slightly changed the shape of his lips—was not one who ever bowed down, or hunched his shoulders, or excused himself for being alive.

This was the Jonathan who ate life.

"Wind," he whispered.

And the wind replied.

I couldn't hear the words. Didn't matter; I felt them, felt the response, the caress, the weirdness of sentient air that fit every rumor I'd heard about the Night Children and their relationship with the wind.

The phone booth began spinning.

It whirled around us at dizzying speed while breeze played with my hair and slipped through small openings in my clothes. I settled my bag on my shoulder; I wasn't spinning, and I wasn't going to get dizzy while this nonsense was going on.

It whirled faster and faster, blurring the New York streets and brightening them until the miserable walls of the phone booth pulled away, widening, expanding, melting into the dust-flecked sunbeams and dark marble of a magical travel-station.

People walked all around us, hurrying to wherever they had to go. Fairies chimed in their little glass globes, casting light in a bored and minimum-wage kind of way. Fresh coffee, tea, and various ciders piped their scents in competition with falafel and pretzels and other snacks for sale. Gold scrolling on the walls drew the eye to the ticket booths built along the walls.

No Ever-Dying anywhere in sight. Plenty of walking trees and custom winter coats designed to accommodate things like faces in people's chests, tall green wisps who still needed tickets in spite of corporeal challenges, talking dogs and cats with wings, and many, many people with trunks or tentacles or multiple hands selling tickets or gewgaws or I ♥ *New York* t-shirts.

In other words, normal.

I couldn't decide if I missed the presence of humans or not as I followed him.

Jonathan—back to himself now, to my relief—possessed an eerie sense of precisely where to be at the right time. Serpentine, he scuttled around lines and through ephemeral gaps in holiday crowds, somehow avoiding eye-contact with every single salesperson so that no one hawked anything in his direction.

I stuck to him like glue.

He paused, avoiding an accident with a runaway luggage cart, swerved to avoid a stroller with at least six baby salamanders crawling all over it, and finally stopped in front of a ticket booth that miraculously, suddenly, shockingly found itself without a line.

How... no, I knew how. I just didn't want to believe it.

"Two tickets for New Delhi, please," he said, taking out his wallet again.

The goblin behind the counter studied him for a moment, the sort of hungry look some people get around Jonathan's particular brand of helpless prettiness. "Sure about that? It's the Vedic games. Nobody sane goes there right now on account of maybe getting eaten by a giant snake or something."

Vedic games?

"I'm aware," said Jonathan, holding eye contact. "Two tickets, please."

The goblin looked Jonathan up and down and shifted his weight, chewing the inside of his cheek.

"Two tickets, please." Steel under fluff; brick under velvet. The unmovable hidden by softness and sweetness and sorrow.

The goblin laughed. "Your funeral. What's she, your lunch? Never mind; I don't wanna know." The goblin handed the tickets over—thick parchment, oblong with cut-out corners and scripted in gold. "Next!"

Jonathan darted away. I hurried after him, but something in my gut wouldn't shut up. *Vedic games.* I had no idea what those were, but they sounded... important. And we were flying right into them? Oh, this was getting complicated.

The queue for the portal wasn't too bad, given the time of day. We took our spots, moving forward a few steps at a time, and I finally summoned the courage to ask. "What the hell are Vedic games?"

"They're sort of like Olympic games for various aspects of the Hindu pantheon," said Jonathan. "They fight to the death—sort of. Everyone comes back, so it's not really death, but the winners get to lead for the next five hundred years, so it's a big deal."

Ah, the games immortals play. "And Bran is there?"

"Bran is near there. So is the dragon coronation, and Father. I still can't see beyond two days from now, but I know it all happens there, in New Delhi."

That image of glowing threads in an impossible, perfect tangle shivered through me, like it was sliding fingertips along my every nerve.

Two days. Somehow, I knew that was as long as I could last before something truly epic happened, and it would probably be bad. My chest still hurt from my time-adventure this morning. I hadn't intended to pull time back in the first place; if it happened again, I didn't know for sure if I could stop it.

Was I even on mission *Katie Saves Her Own Damn Self* anymore? Nope, it had morphed. Apparently, it was now *Katie Saves the Whole Damn World*, because if I did this wrong, everybody would die.

I could do this. I had to do this. Kanon targeted me because he assumed being on my own made me weak. Well, bad news for him; being on my own made me my own woman, and *that* was never weak.

Especially when it came to things that really mattered.

CHAPTER 17

New Delhi

I LIKE NEW DELHI. I don't know it well, but my school took a trip here when I was fourteen. Fun fact: the reason for that trip scared the dickens out of my classmates, but I think it's one of the reasons I eventually decided to run away.

New Delhi is what they call a "smart city," which means the whole place is wired for optimal efficiency and communication. It has some of the best free city-wide wireless connectivity in the world. Their entire public transportation system runs on natural gas. Their metro is one of the most efficient on the planet, second only next to New York's. Every public agency is synched up to the same smoothly-operating database.

It's also one of the greenest cities on Earth, with more than twenty percent of its land still covered by forest—which means People of the Dream live there in large numbers, which *also* means the artistic and creative output of New Delhi's citizens is second to none.

All this efficiency and brilliance took the Ever-Dying a while to build. They had to tear down and revamp and re-invent, but when they were through, they had a city that retained its ancient culture while reaching tall into the future sky.

I *loved* it.

Of course, the point of my school trip was not to love it. The point was that the Ever-Dying were catching up, and their technology and raw willpower (and the push to succeed, driven by their ridiculously short lives) would soon put them on par with magic-users, and when that happened, there'd probably be war.

I can't argue with that. It might happen. I know how my people would feel if entire worlds we knew nothing about suddenly appeared and were like, *Yo, we're the creatures from all your scary stories and more powerful than you ever knew and sometimes we eat you, but hey, it's all good, right?*

Still, I saw New Delhi as hope for the future—that the Ever-Dying could fly with the rest of us. That we could all be as equal as we're supposed to be, and finally share our worlds.

My teachers saw it as oncoming doom, terrifying and probably filled with weapons of mass destruction.

We're both right. But that has nothing to do with the rest of my story, so on we go.

The actual trip through the Conflux was easy. We queued up, handed over our tickets, and stepped into the swirling, dizzying purple light of the goblin portal.

I really like Fey portals better. When Fey make them, you jump in and slide, like you're skiing, and it's all beams of light and prettiness. Goblin portals drop you on your ass.

There's a sensation of falling—a rush, an upheaval of up-down sensation—and when you land, if you're not careful, you tumble right off your game and onto your face—sort of like stepping off one of those automatic walk-ways in an airport.

Jonathan caught me so I didn't perform a pratfall. Let it never be said I hold too tightly to my dignity.

We arrived late, after eight at night. Street vendors were still open with plenty of fruits and toys and tools and delicious fried foods, but

I couldn't even think of eating. We'd wasted enough time. "Where's Bran?"

"We have to go this way," said Jonathan, which seemed like a very carefully worded statement. I ground my teeth and followed.

The marketplace was busy, time of night be damned. Crowds of people—some native, some not, some human, some not—laughed and talked and shoved their way through, purchasing everything from fried potato cakes to furniture, and in such colorful company, Jonathan and I earned not so much as a glance.

No one seemed to be recognizing my face. I suspected Jonathan was carefully directing us. "You're spooky, you know that?" I said.

"I know." Resigned, that's what he was, which didn't really make me feel any better.

He dodged and ducked, avoiding piles of rolled-up carpets and noisy vehicles, pausing to pet a friendly elephant before slipping between booths into a dark alley I was pretty sure was supposed to be off-limits to customers.

"Here's your next choice," he whispered to me as I huddled close. "We can go to the dragon coronation, or we can go straight to where Bran is and try to get him out ourselves."

I stared at him. "What, this is my choice all of a sudden?"

"It has to be." He hunched his shoulders, and I swear no puppy I've ever seen could do those eyes better. "I'm sorry, Katie. Every time you make a choice, things... shift. If I try to influence your decision, it'll all change again, and then I won't be able to see anymore. That's how this works."

"That's how *what* works?"

"Seers. Prophecy. It's not... people think it's like looking in a bowl or something and just watching what plays out, but that isn't it at all." He wrung his hands, hunching closer. "True seers like Cassandra actually know what's going to happen—I don't know how. The rest of us just see the possibilities."

The possibilities at the end of each glowing, tangled thread.

"My uncle always called it 'very good guessing.'" I sighed. "I guess that makes sense."

"Doesn't matter if it does or not. I can't tell you what'll happen. But you have to choose."

He wouldn't tell me more even if I bullied him. Dammit. "Fine. Fine. Let's go and check out where Bran is. Then we can decide if we need help."

And as it turned out, Jonathan had a tell: he chewed his lower lip.

Ah-ha! Maybe I could get info out of him after all. "Won't work, huh?"

"It, uh. We won't be able to get help? Maybe?"

He looked so caught that I couldn't help laughing. "You're terrible at this, Jonathan. Worse than I am."

He shifted from foot to foot, looking both amused and caught.

"Fine. Take us to the coronation then."

"That's your decision?"

Why the hell not? "Yes."

Relief relaxed his posture. "This way." And we were back on the street, weaving between sellers and buyers, squeezing between people who had no idea that I was here to rescue a king, squeezing past beings who had no clue that inside me was something that might unweave time—and that I was following a dude who couldn't possibly exist.

Hell of a night, am I right?

Jonathan filled me in as we walked. The dragon coronation was happening in the human world, which is very weird. Seriously; this kind of thing usually takes place where we're safe—a magical place, filled with our own protections and our own people. Well, this occasion wasn't following the rules. We were staying in New Delhi, and we were going to somebody's house.

Okay, *penthouse*. Same difference.

I had plenty of human money from Bran—specifically American dollars—but nothing I could use for the Mythos without trying to go through an exchange service. I didn't exactly know where the banks were here.

Fortunately, I didn't have to. Jonathan's never-ending supply of credit provided me with a colorful and formal *saree*, and we used a small charm to make my duffel bag look like a prim little lady's clutch complete with fake diamonds.

I didn't know how to put the *saree* on. Jonathan did.

"What exactly did you do in your former life, anyway?" I said, arms out, as he wrapped and tucked and flipped silk around me like he'd done it all his life.

"I cried in a dungeon," he said.

I paused. "What? Are you serious?"

"Yes." He shrugged.

My heart ached. Where could I even go from that? Had Ravena done that to him? "I'm sorry. Wow. For a long time?"

He said nothing.

When in doubt, snark. "Way to kill the conversation, Jonathan."

Still kneeling, he flashed me his sneaky little smile. "*Sorry.* Ha, get it? Saree?"

He was okay. I don't know how, but he was okay. I guess Notte made a good therapist.

I groaned. "Not funny."

"Sure it was. Ready?"

"To march uninvited into a dragon coronation? Sure, no problem."

And he grinned like a naughty cat. "But we are invited. I told you Father extended an invitation to me, and your uncle already left one for you at the door because you're his."

I wasn't *anybody's*, but if it got us closer to helping Bran... "Why?"

"I might have told them to." He looked defiant.

"And you can't tell me what's going to happen when we go in."

"No." And he was back to guilty.

I looked up at the night sky, at the spotlights sliding along the undersides of clouds, at the distant blinking lights of airplanes. "Fine." Deep breath. "Let's go."

CHAPTER 18

Party Hearty

WELCOME TO LIFE AMONG THE MYTHOS: it's either quiet, hard-working, keep-your-head-down-and-your-loyalties-clear kind of stuff, or it's lavish and ridiculous and way too expensive.

Jonathan and I were the only ones to arrive at these apartments on our own two feet. People arrived on flying carpets, or via their own wings, or riding gryphons (who do *not*, despite rumors, take mice in lieu of tips), or in chariots made out of gold and charmed to be as light as if they were made of wicker. I couldn't imagine the layers of magical charms in place tonight to keep this shindig hidden, but so far, it was working.

Jonathan and I walked; both our invitations were there under our names, like he said. And every step we took, my gorge rose higher in my throat. Mentally, I ticked off my problems:

- Kanon chose me with the creepy-ass goal of infecting me with time. Why? Hell if I knew.
- Someone we couldn't see and didn't know was pulling Kanon's strings for reasons unknown. Even creepier.
- I was likely to die in a day and a half, releasing time like a bomb.

- Notte was apparently going to go crazy.
- All the seers were involved. Maybe their strings were being pulled, too?
- The vampire lady was with working Kanon. Was she the mastermind?
- Joshua was probably in trouble with said vampire lady. Because of me. I'd have to deal with that later.
- Death's sister was involved. For some reason.

At least the part about seers finally made sense. My bet was they'd been trying to prevent me from getting near that loose spill of time and destroying the fabric of reality. Well, *that* had all worked out well, hadn't it?

And where was Kanon now? Well, as we walked through the door and into the most elegant reception I'd ever seen in my life, I already knew the answer: *here.*

Of course he was here. It was only the most important dragon coronation ever. Where the hell else would he be?

This felt like walking into the lion's den. I could barely breathe as we exited the elevator, but the penthouse took my breath away regardless: it had been magically expanded to the size of a palace, up and out, and the reason was clear: dragons. And a few oversize trolls. And two small giants, faces sweaty from the strain of keeping themselves small as possible (which isn't very). All this required a lot of head room.

Every single person here was decked out like the night sky over Norway. I looked good, don't get me wrong—I have a body-type that works well with an outfit like a *saree*, midriff exposed and all, and the light blue and bright orange we'd chosen made my skin glow. But damn. *Damn.* I was outclassed.

Try to feel your way through this. Imagine stepping into a party and coming face to face with the President of Russia. Or the Paramount Leader of China. Or the Supreme Leader of Iran. Or the Prime Minister of England.

Kanon was here, all right, across the room—he was in his old-but-hot Jeff Bridges guise and rocking a simple black suit that probably cost more than my car. Twenty feet away from him was Xu Kai, *defacto* head of the People of the Sun and an ancient green dragon whose whiskers constantly moved in a breeze only he could feel. And over there was empress Mer'Qel, who'd single-handedly stopped the mer-people infighting in the Pacific and brought all those clans together under her iron fin. The softly glowing collar around her throat and luminescent white fur on her shoulders kept her both two-legged and breathing, and her ability to be here—so far from the ocean—was a clear show of power and dominance.

Over there was Sovereign Aloeric. And there was Shah Achaemenid. And there was that lion-guy who somehow took care of both Koreas and all the pocket-universes connected to them. And there was that leopard-skinned shape-shifter who watched over so many people-groups on the African continent. And there was The Serpentine, the pale and scale-skinned queen who protected the gates to Naraka.

Half the Vedic pantheon was represented here, too—lots of blue skin and golden breastplates, multiple arms and bows slung over shoulders—hopefully, just for show. They were the secondary stars of this party, gathered for their weird twice-a-millennia games but dropping by to honor the new dragon king.

This coronation was *that* big a deal. I was not joining some simple hoity-toity party. I was in a gathering for the rulers of the known worlds.

And where was Bran? Not here! *And he should have been.* This was his kind of party. I suddenly hated his grandfather for doing this, for taking this away from him, for putting us all in this position.

At the same time, I kind of wanted to hide in a closet. I was not worthy to work in the kitchen of this place.

"Deep breaths," said Jonathan, whose weird, slim beauty worked in this atmosphere, and I followed him as he maneuvered through the crowds.

Kanon saw me. Raised his wine glass. Kept talking to whoever. I didn't scream. Are you proud of me?

Bumped into someone. Jaden. *Jaden,* looking saner than he had (though his eyes still shone with cracks of bright orange), who smiled and nodded at me—which caught the attention of all the Fey around him, who naturally wanted whatever he wanted, and suddenly looked at me like I was a desirable thing.

"Keep moving," Jonathan said suddenly, gripping my arm painfully tight as he yanked me sideways.

We stumbled across the floor almost too quickly for a formal gathering like this, but I saw why a moment later: *she* was here, too. Ravena, The vampire lady. The crazy chick who'd tried to eat my face in New York, who'd possibly harmed Joshua, who'd created Jonathan, and who now glared daggers at me from the far wall of this enormous room. She stood in the company of a tall, broad-shouldered Japanese man—another vampire, *of course*—who stared hate at Jonathan, too.

It was like we were the only four in here. This was a mistake. A big mistake.

"You could have warned me!" I hissed without moving my lips.

"No, I couldn't," Jonathan insisted, looking desperately around. He was tall enough to peer over a lot of heads, and I did not have that privilege.

Crazy lady and her big boyfriend started toward us, slowly, the implacable killer-walk done so well in horror movies.

And the temptation struck for the first time: *just pull it all back and never go into the damn party in the first place.*

I could do it. It would only be a couple of minutes. We could go the other way, rescue Bran, storm after him in force and... and...

I was out of my mind, and whose voice had that been? *I* hadn't thought that. I had not. Pull time back? Really? Really? Why would I even want to do such a thing? What the hell was going on? "Maybe we could go out a window," I joked.

"We're safer in public," said Jonathan, still scanning the room and studiously avoiding the hard, green-eyed stare of the approaching duo.

"I know, I'm kidding," I muttered, and then I came face to face with a tiny white dragon riding on an old man's shoulder.

"Katie!" exclaimed my uncle.

"Maaaa!" squealed the dragon.

"Uncle!" I cried, and flung myself at him.

He held me tightly, laughing for show, but his hands on my back shook.

Suvi crawled right off him and into my hair. "Maaa, maaa," he kept squeaking, and bit my ear.

"Ow! Quit it. Uncle Merlin... we're in so much trouble."

A new voice behind me answered: "So we have heard." It was a young voice, smooth, calm and calming. I couldn't place the accent. And from Jonathan's loving gaze past my shoulder, I already knew who it was.

I plucked Suvi off my shoulders (his kitten-like claws caught my *pallu* and nearly pulled it off) and cradled him before turning around, slowly, trying to breathe, half-sure the room was already spinning.

There he was. Notte.

Without a question the oldest being in this room.

Without a question one of the most powerful, if not *the*.

Without a question an eternal mystery. He started the vampire race, the Night Children; where he came from or how, nobody knows. Friend of the wind. "Father" to thousands. And he looked younger than I am and ready to either pose for sculpture class or break into tearful poetry at any moment.

"Father," breathed Jonathan, and fell into his arms.

Notte held him, rock-solid, and in my wild state I found myself amazed by the way light played in the deep auburn curls of his hair, and the way his skin actually looked a little more green-olive in undertone than I'd ever seen anywhere—*not* a sickness color, but a natural one, unfamiliar though it was.

He also wore a blue velvet suit, which was a little weird, but hey. He'd long earned the right to wear what he wanted.

My uncle stepped between us, smiling. Behind him, the crazy woman stopped, her face twisting away from beauty and into something not too different from a crocodile's.

"My friend, may I introduce my niece, Katie Lin?" said uncle Merlin, gesturing to us in turn. "Among the Mythos, this is Nox Eterna, the Blood King, father of the Night Children, called Notte."

I *might* have made a crazy high-pitched laughing sound before recovering myself. "An honor, oh Nox Eterna," I squawked, bowing slightly, suddenly crazily aware that Cassandra had been right all along, except Bran wasn't here, and this guy was supposed to help Bran, but I couldn't just blurt that out, there was *protocol* to be performed here, and we were in the middle of a party for—

Was Suvi *purring* in my hands?

He was. Kneading slightly, rubbing his teeny-tiny diamond-shaped head against my collarbone. Purring. "They purr?" I blurted.

Merlin chuckled at me. "So they do! It turns out most dragons are trained out of such behaviors when young, but I've been... letting him explore his natural instincts."

Suvi nipped the air in front of my face as if in agreement.

He looked pretty much the same as he had when he'd hatched on my kitchen counter: round bellied, soft-skinned like a frog, though he'd acquired a rainbow sheen of scales over his pearl-like color. His teeny wings seemed impractical, but he could fly with them, and his diamond-shaped head still sat on a proportionately over-long neck, barely balanced by his over-long tail.

Kanon watched us all sidelong from one side of the room. Ravena and her dude watched from the other.

Screw protocol. We were going to die.

I stroked Suvi's back and geared up, ready to ask for help, to beg for aid.

"Father, we're in so much trouble," said Jonathan, and I exhaled in relief. *He* was family. *He* could say whatever he wanted.

"So Merlin has said. And it appears to me that we are being... watched?" Notte suggested.

"Um," I said.

"Shh. We see it." Merlin whispered this against my ear, his familiar hand on my shoulder. "We see it, and probably half the people in this room do, as well. Don't. Do. Anything rash."

Rash? What, like releasing the time-infection I carried like a bomb? Never. "What if *they* do something rash?"

"The balcony," Notte said, and somehow in silent agreement, we all headed that way.

I glanced back. Ravena and Kanon *both* came after us slowly. In no rush.

"Quickly, Katie," Merlin said, and now his smile was gone. "Everything has gone wrong—it's clear someone has a hidden hand in the works. What have you done and where have you been?"

You have to know my uncle to hear those words the way he said them: no blame. No accusation. Just concern.

"Bran came to my door." I swallowed. My stomach felt... not-great.

"The Crow King?" said Notte, his perfect green eyes widening (I would kill for lashes like that).

"Yes, sir. He had Cassandra with him—"

"The echostone?" my uncle said.

Kanon and Ravena were closer. I quit being polite. "Please stop interrupting. We're out of time. Kanon wants to eat Bran. Cassandra told Bran to come to me, that somehow I could introduce Bran to you, sir"—I nodded at Notte—"who could then protect him from his grandfather."

Neither of them interrupted me, which seemed like a miracle.

Then, "Father," whispered Jonathan.

"Hush," said Notte.

"So Bran came," I said. "Kanon attacked. Bran... Bran got me out of there, and we ran. But then that woman—Ravena—attacked us in New York."

"If she had attacked, you would be dead," said Notte in a quiet, damning tone.

"I know. She was keeping us on the run. Look, long story short, Kanon rigged all of this to get me into the world of the Guardians."

Notte gasped.

Surprise from an ancient immortal being? There's something you don't see every day.

"What?" breathed my uncle.

"He wanted to get me near the Wall of Time." Saying it made it real. "He wanted to get me close to a hole he'd... burrowed into it, somehow. And I got infected. Or something. I don't know, but I did something to time this morning. I didn't mean to."

Ravena and her bodyguard stopped outside the patio, not coming in, just eyeing us. Kanon stopped some forty feet away, talking to Jaden. I was suddenly glad Aiden was nowhere to be seen; I didn't want him hurt, and I had a terrible feeling people were about to get hurt.

"That explains events from a few hours ago," Merlin said.

"Indeed." Notte blinked slowly, reassuringly. "Continue."

As if I could do anything else. "It's all Kanon's fault, except someone is behind him and we don't know who," I rambled. "And Bran is trapped, and this isn't the whole story, but Kanon is *right here* and someone is pulling his strings and he's going to do something terrible." I clutched Suvi. "I know what I saw. He's crazy. And he's been watching all of us."

Notte sighed deeply. "I feared as much. Merlin?"

"Yes. Quite. We'd best get this over with. Oh, oh, oh, come now, let go, that's a baby, let go..."

Suvi didn't want to let go of my *saree*, but with gentle manipulation, we got his claws loose. He watched me longingly as Merlin carried him back out into the crowd.

"What's happening?" I said.

"The coronation. After that, everyone can leave; it is the last socially responsible step," said Notte as though all this made sense to him.

Jonathan trembled beside me, shaking like a two-by-four while a train passed. His gaze wasn't on Ravena. It was on the guy with her.

"What is your deal?" I muttered to him.

"He's m... he's...." He shook his head.

Great! Some more confusion to cap this day.

"If I could have your attention, ladies and gentlemen!" my uncle spoke from the center of this enormous penthouse. His magically-enhanced voice carried, not loud at all, but as clear as though he stood right beside me. "It is time to fulfill the purpose for which we have all come: the crowning of the prophesied Starling Child!" He held Suvi up in both hands.

Suvi chirped like a little puppy or something.

Applause came, politely if not enthusiastically. The dragons around the periphery rumbled—a grown-up version of that purr, I suddenly realized—giving their own measure of applause.

"When Sharada, the great queen mother of Red and Black dragons, told me this was coming, naturally, I thought she was kidding," said Merlin with a smile. "Who knew this particular prophecy was literal? Ah, the vagaries of truth and prophecy; one never quite knows which string to pull, am I right?" And he winked at me.

Memories of a glowing, tangled mess of time and decisions flashed through my mind, and I finally really understood that *he saw those strings*. He knew what I was feeling—though *feeling* right now pretty much applied to stomach-upset. Ugh; maybe I'd needed to eat a little more than some papaya juice, a scone, and chocolate today. Heartburn, anyone?

"I certainly never dreamed it would be my honor to be involved so closely with this." Merlin shifted Suvi to one hand, and with the other, pulled something small and silver out of thin air. "Starling Child, called Vesuvius by she who hatched you, do you accept the life-long responsibility set before you?"

That seemed so... sudden. But obviously, he'd been prepared, as had all this crowd. Suvi stood as tall as he could (short, stubby legs being what they are) and held his teeny head high.

The blast came from somewhere to my left, violently purple, distorting everything through its putrid light, and in the brief shock of its brightness, my uncle and the baby dragon both disappeared.

The room went crazy.

Fountains of fire from dragons on both sides geysered through and over the crowd, aiming for one another but hitting plenty of bystanders in the process. Those who could blip out did, magically fleeing before further harm was done. Those who couldn't threw wards up or started fighting back, blasting dragons, blasting each other, starting more fights by the simple accident of trying to stay alive.

Bodies all over the floor, bodies in once-fine clothing now burned and crispy, bodies bleeding yellow and green and blue and black, bodies tripping survivors who tried to flee on foot—

"Uncle!" I screamed, and tried to dive into all of that because I'm a fool.

"Pardon," said Notte, and did... something, I don't know what he did, *something*, but a wind like I've never known picked me up and just neatly deposited me on the street below.

It took me a moment to realize where I was, it had been that fast.

My uncle was up there, and maybe he was dying.

I ran for the door, unhindered since the guards were gone, screaming Merlin's name and Suvi's name and Jonathan's name and looking for any sign of them in the people fleeing the lobby.

I nearly got trampled by the half-dozen troll diplomats in torn suits (trolls change shape all the time, especially when stressed, and their tailoring bills are astronomical), dove out of the way of two smart red dragons who were making for the hills, and decided the elevator would just take too damn long.

The penthouse was only fifteen floors up. I could do that.

Running in a *saree* is never a good move, and furious at its restrictions, I hiked the pleats over my knees and ran.

I didn't know what I was doing. I had no plans what to do. I just couldn't leave my beloved uncle to die up there on the floor, surrounded by horror, and Suvi... he was just a baby! Who the frick would try to kill a *baby*?

The same ones who'd tried to smash him as an egg. The same ones who'd been determined since that prophecy came about that he would *not* unite the Red and Black clans, but would just be another footnote in the sad, sad history of the magical worlds.

Prophecy. Very good guessing. I'd never considered that a prophecy like this might not happen, but now, I did. It wasn't a certainty— it was a guess. A guess based on threads seen, on knots *theoretically* untangled, but it was no guarantee.

Suvi. Merlin.

I ran.

CHAPTER 19

On My Own Again

THAT'S THE THING ABOUT MAGIC: when fights happen, they're usually pretty quick.

Wars aren't quick, of course. They're more like two giant guys in a contest of strength, pushing against each other until one finally weakens. Fights are something else. They're a few blasts. A few explosions. A few well-timed fires, and it's over and done.

The room was full of dead when I arrived.

I tried to hear if anyone was moaning, breathing, crying out, something, but my own breath was momentarily too loud as I tried to catch it. I was Kin. I could do fifteen flights of stairs. That doesn't mean it was recommended.

The attacking dragons had taken their battle outside. Thunder (ha, "thunder," sure it was) echoed outside in an unseasonable storm, and the sky flashed white, blue, purple. The Ever-Dying would no doubt have their phones out already, taking video.

Not my problem.

I hopped and scuttled my way to the center of the room, where they'd been. Where I prayed they weren't anymore. My hands shook uncontrollably and my stomach burned, but I dared not speak—who knew what attention I'd get if I did?

They weren't there.

There wasn't even a stain where my uncle had stood, and absolutely no indication of little Suvi—not so much as a shed scale.

I cried then in silent, ugly sobs, my body shaking, hand over my mouth. Merlin was maybe the most precious person in my life, and I'd nearly lost him. Hadn't I? For all I knew, he'd known this was going to happen.

No one else I recognized lay up here. I checked a few bodies for pulses, for breath, for anything, but there was nothing but blank eyes and empty veins. This was a lot of dead potentates. This was going to be a war. I couldn't see that it would be anything else.

Who had sent that purple bolt? Damned if I knew.

Take it back. Pull back time. Just a few minutes. You can save everybody if you just—

"Okay, who the hell is talking to me? I'm not going to listen, so you can just cut it out!" I yelled, because I know my thoughts, and dammit, that was not me.

No answer. Didn't think there would be one, but now I'd announced my presence, so I needed to scoot. I made my way back down and outside.

More dead littered the stairs, none of them remotely human.

More dead in the lobby, including the innocent doormen who'd done nothing but be employed here.

Several humans dead in this other spot—menial laborers, caught in crossfire or trampled.

Out in the street, there wasn't a sign of anyone magical. I guess on one hand, I should have waited for Notte, but seriously? Anyone with loved ones in the battle would do what I did. And Notte's big on family, so I know he wouldn't be surprised I wasn't there.

But now I was back to square one. My help was gone with the wind (see what I did there?) and Bran was still missing and time was still inside me. Oh, and some freak was talking in my head, but I couldn't care less about that.

I had to find Bran. And do... oh hell, I don't know. Something. Wave a stick. Shout a lot. I didn't even have my wand; this was the stupidest situation I'd ever gotten myself into. And *then* I had to find someone who could get the time out of me. Maybe Adam. Maybe going back to the Guardian world... hey, why hadn't I thought of that before? Even if they couldn't take it out, they could contain it, protect the world from it.

From me.

Was I really talking about banishing myself to a freaky non-magical world to live the rest of my days out gasping and miserable and doing no one else any harm?

Yeah. I was. I'm not really sure if that counts as heroic.

First things first: Bran.

No, Bran was second things second. First things first was figuring out my resources and what I had to work with.

I moved away from the building (alarms and distant emergency vehicles were already on the way, and I had no time to play twenty questions).

It was easy enough to find a dark spot to change my clothes, carefully and regretfully untucking the *saree* and folding it. I doubted I'd ever have a reason to wear it again.

When I opened my bag to put the *saree* away, I found a surprise: Jonathan had left me his wallet, a ziplock baggy of black diamonds, and a wand.

A wand. *A wand!* This changed everything.

Wands are crucial for Kin. They focus our magic—and they're made of cold iron, which I know seems completely backwards from what everyone thinks they know, but it's true. I'd left mine back in New Hampshire; truth be told, I almost never used the thing, and it had gotten more than a little rusty.

But this one was pristine. Beautiful shape. Slender enough not to be overly heavy. Pointed at the end for jabbing various spell materials together like a magical shish kebab.

Jonathan, when did you have time to do this? Damn, boy.

I know Notte got him out of there. I mean, of course he did; everybody knew family came first for that guy, even at the expense of the world. Still. I hadn't liked the way Ravena's companion looked at him.

I mean, yes, Jonathan was beautiful; pretty much all vampires were beautiful—it was a combination of current vampires choosing future vampires that interested them, plus whatever the vampiric process did to them. They just came out alluring, like so many magical beings are. You learn to get used to it. Still. I hadn't liked that look, with its angry and possessive heat. And I also hadn't liked that Jonathan—unlike the rest of his oddly self-effacing sweetness—was genuinely afraid of him.

My own story had crossed a whole lot of others tonight, and far too many of those had come to an end.

I tucked the wallet and black diamonds into my clothes so I wouldn't lose them. Then I used the wand to create a sling for it inside the winter coat. It was twelve or thirteen degrees Celsius (in the fifties Fahrenheit for less civilized folk), and my coat was perfectly acceptable winter-wear. No need to resize my bag into the knapsack; I tucked it into my pocket and walked down the street.

Behind me, the building burned; I don't know how it caught on fire, but it did, and sirens wailed all around. Dragons clashed in the skies like thunder or exploding gas lines.

It would all have to be covered up, but that wasn't my job. And at least while that was going on, it might draw potential attention away from me. Winning!

Who was I kidding? I hadn't won a damn thing.

CHAPTER 20

The Hush

I SHOULD HAVE EXPECTED THEY'D FIND ME. That didn't mean I was in any way prepared.

I avoided the ambulances and police, hid from the media and helicopters, but I couldn't avoid the Hush. The Hush don't work with pyrotechnics or pizzazz. They're quiet and quick, which is necessary when tracking down violent criminals who could, potentially, turn you into chocolate.

All I know is they tackled me from behind, hard, and I went down on the sidewalk as if an elephant had dropped on top of me.

I hit my head. Shouting covered me as the world spun, and the burning in my gut *rose*.

Ever wrestled a hog? It's like that: too big to wrap my arms around, too big to fully control, but dammit, I had to.

Tight, Golem-strong arms pulled me off the sidewalk and into a waiting pocket dimension, one designed for interrogation and incarceration, and I wrestled with the time inside me trying to burn its way out with every ounce of my focus.

Who else would have the job of quieting the mess back there, somehow stopping the dragons from whatever the *hell* they were doing in the sky and convincing every human being it had just been a freak lightning storm? It had to be the Hush. They'd tracked my aura because I was alive in a room filled with the dead. Bloodhounds, all of them.

Burning, burning, I wanted to vomit time all over, but I would not.

Hands pulled at me, grasping, stealing, searching me from head to toe, and dark, gravelly voices demanded answers.

Then, sudden silence.

I ignored it all. Soothing the time in me was like soothing some wild bear, half-mad from the loss of her cubs; it seemed impossible, but I had to, I had to, I had to do it.

And suddenly, they dumped me back on the sidewalk.

I curled up there for a while, wrestling my inner time.

Hours passed. I don't know how many. I know people stepped over and around me, which seems heartless, but it's also true.

I know time passed. Time I did not have—so that when I came back to myself on that cold, hard sidewalk, I realized we were probably mere hours away from the moment of trouble Jonathan predicted.

The thing about sleeping on the ground nobody tells you is how much it hurts. That hardness isn't conducive to the human(oid) body. Moving like a thousand-year-old woman, I creaked my way upright and staggered to lean against a wall.

They'd taken the black diamonds; why? I have no idea. They'd left me Jonathan's wallet, and they'd also left a note. Oh, but you have to read it. You won't believe this otherwise.

DEPARTMENTS OF INTERWORLD LAW ENFORCEMENT
DIVISION 58B
CODE BLUE SAPPHIRE
EAST

PRIVATE: For Nox Eterna, the Blood King, father
of the Night Children:

Sir,
We regret to inform you we apprehended one of
your Children's blood-providers less than a
mile from Incident No. 58426 28B-DRAGON. While
we have determined she was not involved with
the Darkness-based magic that began Incident
No. 58426 28B-DRAGON, we feel it advisable to
caution you that your children must take more
care with their toys. Had she not been Kin, we
would have had every reason to suspect her.

We wish for no animosity with you. Expected
visitation from Lord-General Ramses Al-Benumm
tá Oman will occur at your place of residence
within the next week. No reparations are
expected at this time.

Your great health,

Salis Kamialtárd of the Hush
Junior Deputy Commissioner
Division 58B, Code Blue Sapphire

I stared at it like an idiot. They thought I was Jonathan's lunch and had somehow wandered off on my own. What. The hell.

I noticed there was no mention of the black diamonds. Bribe money, maybe? I had no idea.

What I knew was this: I'd just encountered the Hush and survived because my impossible vampire-seer-friend had left me his wallet. I didn't buy for one moment that my People made that much of a difference here, no matter what spell had been cast. That would be implying that innocence mattered to these folks.

Wait. They'd said someone of the Darkness cast that purple spell. Kanon? Had Kanon tried to take out Suvi and my uncle? What the hell for? What was going on?

Was I really vain enough to think he'd spark off an international incident just to get me to vomit time all over the place?

Panic threatened, but I fought it down. The Hush had left me my bag and my wand and my clothes. Sore, miserable, unsure what day it was, I staggered down the street, and I probably looked like perfect prey for criminals apart from the mad-dog gleam in my eyes.

I realized she was following me about a block later.

It wasn't like she had any reason to let me know she was following me. Death's little sister was weird, no doubt, but I think she wanted my attention—letting her essence slip past, wafting death and terror past me like some weird odor. Fine. I stopped walking and waited for her.

Nephthys—or whatever her name was when she had teeth between her legs—walked casually from shadow to shadow, somehow avoiding the powerful street lights and never taking her eyes from me. She still had galaxy-hair; stars swirled in her tresses, unnerving and beautiful and wrong. She wore the tattoos down her chin this time, and the Polynesian facial structure, so I guessed she was Chompy McChomp-Pants right now, too.

She stopped right in front of me, eye to eye, nebulas slowly spinning by her ear. "I am Hine-nui-te-pō," she said.

"I heard your real name is Dis," I said. Somewhere along the way, I apparently lost my ability to be polite to powerful people. That's not a good thing, for the record, but she took it well.

Her skin darkened, her features changed, shifting smoothly into a broader, older, haunting form. "Perhaps you should call me Beletseri." Her skin changed again, taking on the hues of sunlight reflecting on dark water, and her hair twisted around her neck to form a rope. "Or Ixtab." And one more time—once more—she changed, skin turning blue, face turning young and fierce and so utterly sexual that I wanted to pee with fear and fall at her feet at the same time. "But I personally like this one best," she finished.

"Kali?" My voice cracked.

"For now." She smiled. "Have you made your decision?"

Was she here for the Vedic games? Did she qualify for them? I neither peed nor knelt, but I trembled. She stepped close enough that her breasts pressed against my coat, and don't ask me how, but her nipples poked through like stones.

"Well?" she said.

I swallowed. "Uh. No, I don't think so."

"Pity." She moved, and the belt of skulls around her waist rattled like some kind of morbid invitation. "I'd love to know what you decide."

"I don't know what choice it is yet. Makes it a little hard to answer that question." I think I was slurring at this point, but she didn't care, and I was too busy focusing to apologize.

"Oh, you don't know?" She looked away from me, her arms moving and somehow multiplying or reflecting themselves in the air so they went from four to eight to sixteen. "Oh, my timing is off," she said. "It won't be for another hour."

I had an hour to live. Or decide something. Or find Bran. Whatever it was, an hour wasn't much. "Could you maybe give me a clue?"

"No." She smiled, and suddenly, she shrank down, lost her color, became a small, blond girl—the epitome of every creepy child every Hollywood movie has ever produced. "That's not how bets work. My winning depends on your choice. Bye!" And she wriggled her hands and disappeared.

But as she vanished, she left something behind.

That's the thing about making bets: you want to win, and if you can do anything to stack the odds in your favor, you'll do it. Sometimes that's taking "lucky" items into battle, like a rabbit's foot or the scale of a living gorgon. Sometimes, it's cheating. Like Kali (or whatever her name was), who had just left me a map on the sidewalk in rapidly disappearing shadows.

I stared as the darkness shrank, eaten away by the bright street lights, trying to memorize what it showed me. The location wasn't far. What else could that map go but to Bran?

Okay, lots of things, I know, *shut up.* I had to believe this. I had to try. It was that or wander the streets, hoping for hints from the sky.

The battle still raged overhead, by the way, greater than any thunderstorm and far more colorful. Were the Vedic games still even happening? Who knew?

The shadow-map disappeared, and I turned on my heels and jogged.

I'm coming, Bran, I thought, *if that's where you are.* I was coming, and I wasn't going to give in to the weird voices or temporal urges, and I wasn't going to quit looking, and I *was* going to ignore the burning that had now moved from my chest to my stomach to my spine, and after Bran was safe and my uncle was safe (*he was not dead, damn the world*) and Suvi was safe and Jonathan was okay, I would go back to the Guardian world (yeah, I didn't know how, that bridge could wait) and nag Adam until he fixed me or locked me away.

And then I'd sleep for a thousand years, because I was really sure I'd need it.

CHAPTER 21

Very Good Guessing

REMEMBER THAT DREAM I had with Bran? The vision where he'd been pulled into some creepy room? Well, Death's sister's directions led me right to the door from my dream.

There it was. Same dirty lanterns. Same poor people trying to stay warm in garbage, slowly starving in a world that had enough to feed them but not enough care to try. You have no idea how weird it was to see a thing from my dream in real life. I mean, I *knew* it was real. Of course I did. But it was still weird to *see* it.

It wasn't the only door in this alley. Identical to all the others, it was somehow crowded, somehow dirty, though the paper lanterns overhead spoke of a different time, of some kind of hope that had at least passed briefly through here.

Don't get distracted, Katie.

So, I wondered. Should I walk up and knock? Try to find another entrance? Attempt to sneak in?

I had my wand, but Bran's magic hadn't been enough to protect him. Neither had his physical strength.

I backed out of the alley and circled the block.

This whole place was nasty, an abandoned place for abandoned people. There were so many doors; I had no way of knowing if they all led to one huge room or what. Pulling out my wand, I tested lightly, trying to see through the walls around that specific door, but of course, they were warded. At least I could see through the walls on either side of that protection; normal humans lived here, surviving, barely hanging on, conducting their blessedly ordinary lives.

They didn't have to know about the dragons in the sky. I mean, maybe they believed in dragons in the sky of some kind or another, but they didn't have to actually know about them. Lucky bastards.

Okay. The whole place was warded, so there was only one way in. Here's where I had a weird choice to make, and I had to wonder if it was the one Death's sister meant: did I blast the door down and go in, bluffing? Or did I take it for granted that this, like so much else, had something to do with me, and that I could offer myself as trade and get Bran out that way?

Ah, but both were deadly. If I bluffed my way in and got killed, time would get loose and do who knows what to the world. If I traded myself and was summarily sacrificed... same difference.

The clock was ticking. The Hush had eaten what spare time I had. And no, I wouldn't call them for help. Seriously? No. They were just as likely to lock me up instead of whoever had taken Bran. Besides, I was pretty sure they were busy dealing with the mess of the coronation. I was on my own.

Screw this. If I went in blasting, they'd be likely to blast back, and that was no good. While it might not be glamorous, I had only one reasonable step in front of me, and I was going to take it.

Even though it made me shake.

Even though my stomach and back and heart were all still burning (was that time, eating from the inside out? Maybe! Today was full of fun surprises).

Even though I could never hold my own against powerful things that held someone like Bran prisoner.

Damn this. Damn them.

Katie Saves Her Own Damn Self had expanded to three-point-oh: *Katie Does What Needs Doing.*

Because nobody else could.

"Hope you're proud of me now, mom," I said for reasons best left unexplored, and knocked on the damn door.

Knock, knock.

Who's there?

Katie.

Katie who?

Katie who doesn't know what the hell she's doing. Punchline!

The door swung open, absolutely silent even though an eerie creak would have been better, and it swung into absolute darkness.

But Katie had her wand! That provided options. "Hello in there," I murmured as I raised my helpful magic-stick, its tip glowing bright red as though just taken out of the fire. It cast light on a claustrophobic room that hadn't seen occupation in at least ten years. I assumed that with confidence because it takes a while for bodies to turn into bones.

Skeletons lay along the walls, neatly lined up skull to toe, their pale white radiuses and ulnas crossed over their rib cages as if folded gently at rest.

Sure. Why not. If you're going to be creepy, you might as well be fastidious about it.

I waved my wand in a wide circle, over my head and before my feet, checking for traps (as if I could detect anything powerful enough to grab Bran), checking for dangers (as if I could defend myself against anything powerful enough to grab Bran), but I found nothing except a risk of fungal infection from breathing in here.

I was Kin. I could handle this air for a while, even if the proverbial canary died.

The boards creaked ominously under my feet, but what really freaked me out was there were no signs of a struggle. The dust rose in puffs, no matter how slowly I walked. Where was the mess Bran must have made? He went down fighting; I *saw* him do it, and I knew—

Oh, dear.

The bones were clean, and I'd assumed old, but those streaks on the walls were definitely not. Some kind of dark green color—blood comes in all shades among the Mythos—and it seemed more fresh than not. None of it glistened or anything, but the few bugs that had made the mistake of coming in here to taste it (and die, because *of course* whatever had bled in here bled poison) lay in leg-tangled repose beside the skeletons. They were also lined up, by the way, wing-tip to multi-faceted eye.

Okay. Definitely creepy. They should have gone with the door-creak.

"I'm coming in now," I said, gripping my wand so tightly that my hand hurt. "I'm not here to cause a fuss. I just want my friend back."

The back wall opened.

I mean... *opened.* Not like a door. It parted in the middle, *rolling* away from its center like weird rugs, and behind it was bubbling, silent darkness.

Umbra? No, Umbra never leaked like this, with edges of quiet shadow nipping along the rolled-up walls as if hungry or greedy or both.

Complete silence. No *Step into my parlor* statements. Nothing. Not even the "use the time" voice in my head was speaking.

I was holding my breath, I realized. That had to stop.

"I'm just here for my friend," I said again, stepping closer.

Nada. Just bubbling, hungry darkness.

"I don't want any trouble," I said, as though I could cause any.

I checked the rolled up wall with my wand. According to my little investigation spells, it was a portal. A portal to a black hole, maybe.

So I put my left hand in it.

I had to test it on living flesh, okay? And I'm right-handed, and I needed my feet to run. What other option did I have?

I put my left hand in, and that darkness licked along it like gentle caresses, like something terribly cold and terribly dry that should have been soft and warm. Something that seemed to be *pulling* the life out of it, out of my hand, leaving it aching and old and stiff.

I yanked my hand back and shook it, briefly freaking out—only to see it was fine. It tingled, but it was fine.

Gut instinct said it shouldn't have been fine. I think if I hadn't been infected with Time, it might have become a neatly cleaned skeleton-hand.

"I should let you know, mystery-host, that if Bran is not in there, I am personally going to cave your head in with my wand," I said.

Empty threat, but for some reason, the darkness listened. It roiled apart, boiling and bubbling, to reveal Bran on his knees on a flagstone floor, arms chained behind his back, horns jagged as if broken, though at least the flickering in his cracked form seemed strong and vibrant.

Just as quickly, the darkness closed in, hiding him from view.

Okay. That was really clearly a tease.

You know, I'd thought it was silly to consider this could possibly be about me. Now I *knew* it was. No, I was not comfortable with it, but my comfort didn't matter.

I sighed, slowly. Deeply. Nobody thinks they're going to die at twenty-three.

Survive where canaries die, I ordered myself, and stepped into the boiling dark.

It was like being swallowed by a thousand dead tongues.

Everything was touched. Everything. Gag-worthy, putrid, strangely dead, like stumbling on a desiccated corpse in the woods that you tell yourself is just a deer, when you know it's not.

I screamed, gagged, spasmed in disgust as if I could just shed my flesh and run away. But I couldn't, and instead, I landed on cold, hard stone next to Bran.

He had no power left in him for illusions. His true self stared back at me, horrified, fractured, trembling, stunned at his lack of ability in the face of...

Three women?

I can't say they sat on thrones, because that isn't quite true. But I can't say they sat on chairs, either, because that exsanguinates the grandeur. Whatever they sat on, it was older than chairs and older than thrones. Maybe older than the rocks people first called chairs, older than the logs they claimed from old forests to rest their bottoms above the earth.

The seats were old. *They* were old. And a single, solid pulse banged through this hollow, compressing my eyes, slowing my own pulse, forcing everything to follow its old, sick will.

"We are the Norns," spoke the middle of the three.

The Norns? The puppet-masters? The ones pulling Kanon's strings?

Yes. They weren't gods, no, they were not, but what they'd become was worse. Old, ancient, powerful and crafty, and with every pulse, their alternate vision tried to force itself upon me, a weird reality where a thousand thousand threads all converged on this one snarled spot, knotted and frayed and fragile.

Not gods. Spiders, seated in the tangled heart of the Tapestry.

"Weavers," disagreed the left-most woman—no, *female*. She might have held a nearly human form, but she wasn't even close to what *human* means.

That moved me. Faced with something *in*human, with creatures intricately enmeshed in the mess of eternity and forever-holding, I saw the beauty and preciousness of short-lived frail human life even more sharply.

"You lie!"

"Enough!"

"Fool!" they cried all at once to my appreciation of mortality.

A very large part of me wanted to believe their words. No, not believe. *Become.* Become what they said: a liar, too much, a fool. Their fingers danced over the weft and weave of who I was and barely slid off before changing things. They nearly made me what they said, just by the power of their words.

No one should have that power. Certainly not them.

"We have brought you here," said the first.

"Brought you," said the second.

"Here," said the third, and I knew their words were true—at least, in that.

The *wrongness* of this impossible room and its string-bending boundaries tore at me, stretching, threatening to rip me in two. "Why?" I said, because *who I am* would not be silent, not accept fate, would not let them run rough-shod over everything I'd fought so hard to be.

"Why?" they answered back, distressed at my pushing, at my fighting, at my insistence on being *me*.

And that's right about when I had enough with all the dramatic and poetic and epical baloney. "For frick's sake, just give me my friend, and let us leave!"

It was like the world stopped turning.

No one ever spoke to them like this, not since they'd figured out how to read the signs and choose the right threads, the right paths, directing and controlling and commanding at the center of their nasty web. Well, they weren't controlling me, bucko. Never me. "So. We can go?" I said.

They shrieked.

The heat in my belly rose again, searing through my whole system. My eyes boiled, my womb sizzled, the hidden places between my toes and at the roots of my hair burned. Burned, but did not burn up; I was being... consumed? Becoming something new? I didn't know, but it was terrible.

And wonderful.

And terrible.

"Katie!" Bran couldn't look at me anymore, and he seemed stark, cast in the light of my *selfness*, and I was so bright that the flickers in his flesh were hidden.

"Give it to us!"

I looked toward them, toward these three whose fingerprints I could now feel on *everything*, in everyone I knew, yet I knew they weren't truly gods any more than I was. "Why should I?" I demanded.

And they showed me.

They showed me the world since the First War, split in two and hidden on either side of a curtain.

Showed me how hard they'd fought and how strong they'd struggled to keep the magical out of view of the Ever-Dying humans, to keep us safe, to keep all the Mythos safe.

Showed me what they'd surrendered, the paths taken and eschewed, the choices made.

And they showed me something coming *soon*.

Tonight, the dragons would fight with no more care who saw them, with fear of losing their agency, with hate for one baby white dragon.

Tonight, the Vedic pantheon, bereft of elders who'd been insulted and harmed at a party, would choose sides at random because they did not know whom to blame.

Tonight, the Night Children, long under quiet siege for the freakish uniqueness that made them *them*, would face Kanon, who came against them with the might of all Umbra beside him.

Tonight, humans would stare up with their cell phones at things so fantastic that disbelief kept them from scurrying to safety, while television crews and internet podcasters and grandmas with dusty eight millimeter film recorded things the world had never seen in their living memory.

Tonight, governments would rise in panic to debate whether this was World War III and to question whether anyone would or should drop a bomb on a hugely populated country out of raw paranoid fear.

Tonight, the curtain would be torn.

And none of this had happened yet.

"We knew this would come!" the first fate shrieked, her young hands like claws.

"All will end!" The second.

"Comes to a mistake, a single mistake." Third.

"We can repair it." First.

"We can rewind it." Second.

"We can make it like it never was." Third.

Hands, claws, talons reached toward me, reaching for me, beseeching and commanding and threatening and warning.

"Give to us that which was stolen."

"Give to us that which was lost."

"We will give to *you* what you desire." The third tried so hard to wheedle with her tone, to whine, to simper, to smile.

But they were out of the loop now, and I knew all.

I'd never be able to hold onto time, and that was okay. I didn't want to hold onto it. But I could see now—see how delicate threads lead to thicker twines and stronger braids and, at last, an end to what was. I could see how this was the moment when everything changed between the people of the Mythos and humankind (the curtain torn), and yet the genesis of this was not now.

It all went back to one single *choice*.

To a moment thousands of years ago—

Notte—young Notte, standing and grieving and wailing over a battlefield of ash and blood, of bodies he'd loved, of those he'd created as family, and those he simply knew.

*His enemy, Kanon, on the battlefield's other side, wearing armor made of magic rocks and glowing runes and all manner of evil souls and sacrifices, coming for him with glee, glee, **glee** that Notte should grieve because Kanon had killed the ones he loved.*

A choice.

What. The hell. Was this.

"That is the time!" shrieked the first.

"The moment of decision!" shrieked the second.

"The moment to be changed!" shrieked the third.

Why was this the moment *why was this the moment* **why was this the moment**

I couldn't... I couldn't *keep* it. I could almost grasp the pattern in my thoughts, almost follow the threads and the many ways they wove, but no. I couldn't retain it in my silly mortal mind.

That was all right. I didn't need to. I got the picture.

"Give it to us!" they cried.

They had used me. As a vessel. They were no gods, and even these Norns could only control a few paltry strings at a time—not enough to counteract something this big. But there *was* a bank of time available, wasn't there, in the Guardian World? Time they could use to reverse the damage, time they couldn't reach on their own.

They used Kanon and his hatred of Notte to do this. Somehow, reversing that moment in Notte's life would erase tonight—and erasing tonight meant that there would be no moment of revelation for humankind.

They wanted to keep the curtain whole. I got it. I understood. I knew what they wanted.

"We will give you what you want!" And they dared show me images of my father (*that's* what Dis was talking about) as if they could give him back to me, returning my childhood happiness the way it used to be before I realized he was scum.

I was not that little girl anymore. "You picked the wrong vessel." I raised my arms, glorying in this moment, struggling to seal it in my mind, because pretty soon, I wouldn't remember anymore. "My father? You're going to hold my father in front of my face as trade-off for something I want anyway?"

And I could see how they'd gotten lost in the whole, lost in the knots, lost in the ideas of nations and Peoples and eras, and missed the teeny, tiny thread of independent thought.

They had no idea who I was, just what I was. And that was their expensive and foolish end. *I wanted the curtain torn.*

This power was nice (and terrible). I'd never feel like this again— so eternal, so immortal, so all-knowing.

I didn't want to. I liked being simply Katie.

I pointed at the left Norn. "Screw you."

At the middle. "Screw you."

At Bran. "You're okay."

And the right Norn. "And screw you." And then I took Bran and *went away.*

I just knew how to do it, how to access all the natural power I refused to acknowledge because of the problems it would bring. But right now, using it only made sense.

The burning extended even to my tears now, which felt like searing red paths down my cheeks.

"Katie!" Bran called me, but I could barely hear him. We were outside. We were in a public square. There were people. Fountains. Statues. Why had I chosen to be here? I couldn't remember anymore. I'd chosen to come here, to this place, but why?

We were not alone.

A crowd stood around us, shouting and pointing as the sky tore overhead and as dragons warred, as magical beings cried out and wove protection spells around themselves and clusters of humans, as everyone feared and stared and bled and trembled. Dis waved at me from the edge of the crowd, in her little-girl form, bouncing on her toes.

"Get down!" shouted Jonathan from somewhere, and so help me, I ducked.

Purple power flew over my head, distorting the world like strange glass made and melted right in front of my eyes. It hit the ground, somehow missing everyone, and exploded. Stone and dirt sprayed; everyone ducked, screaming.

"Why won't you *die?*" bellowed Kanon.

They were all here. My uncle. Baby Suvi, trying to flap out of his hands and get to me. Notte. Jonathan. That guy who freaked Jonathan out. Ravena. Jaden. Aiden. Quinn.

People. So many people. So many threads, thousands, millions, billions of tangles and weavings and frayed ends and I—

I couldn't—

I couldn't hold it together for much longer.

"I can't much more!" I screamed, grammar be damned.

"He's coming!" someone cried, I don't know who.

Kanon marched toward me with a big curved thing like a dinosaur's claw, aiming for my middle to tear me open and release the time, and I saw the threads: Notte would be caught up in it, but it wouldn't be like the three Norns thought, oh no, it would reverse him, it would rewind him, it would turn him into something he'd been back before anyone could even remember and that would be the end because he would eat the world.

I screamed and fell to my knees, gripping my abdomen, and my arms glowed like heated bronze as I held the world's death in.

And it all happened so fast—

Suvi pulled lose from my uncle and clawed Kanon's face.

Kanon batted him aside with a roar and swung the claw down.

Jonathan got in the way—must have moved before Kanon even started—and then it was Jonathan gutted, Jonathan split in the middle with that big wooden hook, and me screaming and that guy-friend of Ravena screaming and Kanon screaming—

I blacked out for a moment. It was burning in my brain now, and getting hard to concentrate.

Hold it in, Katie.

All my will, my stubbornness, my essential bull-headed *self* leaned against the door to time and kept the damn thing closed.

Wind swirled, dust whipping aside to reveal Jonathan in the arms of that other guy, who poured his own blood from a self-inflicted wound into Jonathan's mouth murmuring *nomu, nomu, nomu*—

Kanon panted like a bull, hook raised and bloody, but he did not bring it down again.

Notte stood between us.

"You have broken the truce, my old friend," Notte said, and his soft voice *carried* and *hurt* and *pounded*.

"He's alive! He's fine!" Kanon snarled. "You know you were my target!"

"Yes," said Notte calmly. "But you did not harm me, did you?" And the next words sent ice-nails up my spine one sharp, frozen syllable at a time: "You. Hurt. My. Child."

And Notte *gusted* at him, Notte *surged* at him, Notte became dust and wind and hunger, and enveloped Kanon with so much raw power that pieces of flesh went flying off into the screaming crowd in chunks and goblets and plates.

I couldn't hold it anymore.

The door inside me burst open, shattered, nothing left for my will to push against—

And the wings came down. Black wings, and time splashed against those wings and stopped like a breeze against a brick wall.

Cool darkness rushed through my veins, replacing. Repairing. Relieving.

Time for a nap.

Boy, was it nice to find thoughts parading across my mind in an orderly and ordinary fashion when I woke.

The walls were a sort of faded yellow paint. Cracked plaster made up my low ceiling. Traffic sounds—engines, horns, voices—rose in the distance.

It felt so ordinary, so human, so normal. Everything hurt, which wasn't normal. But I could think clearly, and nothing burned, so that was okay.

It sure sounded to me like the world was still alive.

Bran's warm, strong hand touched my forehead, stroking my hair. "There's the hero," he said softly.

My muscles had apparently turned to leather while I was out, and I found myself surprised my neck didn't creak as I looked at him. "You're alive, too, huh?"

"Yeah. Thanks to you." He stroked my hair again, gently, but did not smile. Then he held out his hand, and Suvi leaped off it to land on my chest.

"Baby!" I said, and kissed his little head. We spent a few minutes like that, reuniting, baby dragon and the lady who hatched him, but even during this, I couldn't avoid the truth: something was different.

I couldn't place it. Something just felt strange; not bad, necessarily, but abnormal. "What happened?"

"You did the impossible. You held time itself back until Adam could come to contain it."

"Who called Adam?"

"I did." Bran shuddered. "Went there first. Thought we'd need a backup."

"You went to Meginnah *alone*? Are you crazy?"

"Not anywhere near as crazy as you. And I think it's my turn to ask what happened now."

"So the Norns are probably out to get me," I said.

His jaw fell open. It turns out he hadn't been able to see the three beings who held him. Which probably meant that without time inside me, I couldn't, either.

It was time for explaining.

I talked, and Suvi curled up under my chin like a kitten, purring in his sleep. I couldn't remember everything—those future glimpses were gone—but I remembered enough. "I don't know what happened to them," I said. "It's probably too much to hope they just blew up or something."

Bran leaned back and rubbed his eyes. "I'll find out."

"It's not on you to find out. So what happened with the dragons?"

He eyed me. "The Red and Black clans were brought to heel by the Hush and the Sun. Half the Vedic pantheon broke the law. Numerous members of the Darkness followed Kanon and panicked when he died. A lot of people are waiting trial now."

"Geez," I whispered. "And Suvi?"

"Officially crowned. He's the king of both clans; but that's beside the point. It's out. Magic is revealed. There's no way it couldn't be after that. No amount of magic could cover up a mess like this."

Time could have. But I'd stepped all over that chance.

Traffic continued its noisy current, people going about their lives, probably a lot more scared than they'd been before. But I heard no mobs. No unseasonable storms. And we were clearly still in the human world, so that seemed good.

I know I made the right decision. "Where's Merlin?"

"Your uncle? He's on TV."

If I'd had a drink, I would have sprayed it. "Television?"

"And computer screens, and phones, or whatever." Bran smiled slightly. "Someone had to be a negotiator, and... well, he's pretty likeable. He also has a good handle on Ever-Dying cultures, which is something very few of us have."

"Finally admitting there's something you don't know?" Apparently, my internal filter was still bluescreened.

His eyes widened. "Maybe," he allowed.

He was getting used to my bluntness. Score one for Katie Lin.

"The Ever-Dying are being told part of the truth." Bran bent over and rummaged for a moment. I recognized the hold-all bag I'd brought from his apartment. Judging by the empty bottles and wrappers, he'd been enjoying the bounty I'd brought.

And then, he handed me my cellphone.

My phone! My very own phone! The one he'd taken from me in New Hampshire! "I could kiss you," I said to the phone.

"Really?" said Bran dryly.

"Hush." I checked the news.

Boy, he was not kidding: this was a mess no one could contain.

Emergency meetings of the UN and NATO and every other organization. Crazy laws being passed, demagogues rousing the rabble. Protests, violent outbreaks, at least a dozen buildings firebombed or burned down out of fear that they were secret magic headquarters.

But so, so many were preaching peace.

I blinked away tears as I scrolled, reading article after article of Ever-Dying humans risking their short, weak little lives to build bridges with the magical strangers. Of humans getting between mobs and fairies, humans hiding Fey who'd been attacked, humans pointlessly trying to protect dragons who could protect themselves just fine, but were so shocked at the gesture that they let it happen.

Yes, there were plenty of crazies with guns or pitchforks or whatever, but far more humans were trying for peace.

Wow.

"We don't know yet if there will be war," Bran said, leaning back so his wooden chair creaked. "Or even if there should be. We're in talks—maybe we should just withdraw from this world completely. It's not like the Ever-Dying could bomb Umbra."

"Maybe." I wouldn't put anything past humans. All they needed was time. "Quick question: are all the seers dead? Did their heads explode? Do they still know anything that's coming, or is it all up for grabs?"

"Ask her yourself," said Bran, and put Cassandra in my hand.

"Beware," squeaked Cassandra. "Beware the teeth that drop!"

I groaned. "Good to see all is normal."

"The teeth that drop?" said Bran.

"Long story. Maybe *you* should ask her *yourself*."

He laughed.

Apparently, I'd survived the pointed tongue and the orange eyes. Kanon and Jaden, maybe? So Ravena was still on the prowl, or... Honestly, I had no idea.

Maybe it didn't matter. Cassandra may be an echostone, but I'd seen how time really looked. Her guesses were good, but they were still just guesses.

And for no reason, I was done with illusion and mystery. Just done. "Bran?" I said.

"Yes, Katie?"

"Gimme your real face."

He froze.

I pointed at him. "Don't try to out-stubborn me, Bran. I'm sick. I demand succor. Give me your real face."

He exhaled slowly, morphing up as he did, changing, growing, until his real form sat where the "human" one had. Cracked, horned, frightening. "Weird woman. Happy now?"

His horns were still broken.

I did something I'd wanted to do forever: I reached up and palmed his cheek, sliding my thumb over his lips. Soft lips; I hadn't expected that, what with the plates and cracks and infernal fires, or whatever they were. Beautiful. "Happy. Are you gonna be okay? Those horns look like they hurt."

He just stared at me like I'd grown six heads.

"Earth to Bran? Fine. Subject change. Is Kanon dead for real?"

And he grinned like a kid in a candy store. "More than dead. My grandfather *lied*." He leaned in. "He never had the strength to open a portal to the Guardian world at all, never mind prying a stone from the freaking Wall of Time."

"What? Then how did he get it?"

"Ha! I don't know. He bought it off someone. I'll find out who. Ha!"

"But you opened the portal."

"I did! Ha!"

"So you really are stronger than he was."

"Ha!"

I laughed with him. What a hell of a revelation. "What was his problem with Notte, anyway?"

Bran snorted. "Hell if I know. He thought that if he released that time, Notte would no longer have the mental wherewithal to fight back. My fool grandfather thought he could win. Fight him down. Kill him. That's why he brought that wooden hook to the final battle. Wood is the only thing that reliably hurts vampires, you know."

I shook my head. "And what happened to all that time that was in me? Please don't joke about this and tell me it's the year eight thousand twelve, because I don't think I could handle it."

"Adam took it back."

"Took it?"

"Just drew it out of you." He made a motion like pulling taffy, gaze distant. "Said 'greetings, old friend,' to Notte, and then just... flew away."

"Great. Well. Okay. Wow."

"It was eating you, Merlin said."

"Ew. Well, I hope I was tasty."

He made a face.

I made one back at him, then sobered. "I'm sorry about your grandfather."

"Are you really?"

"No. He was crazy. And a jackass."

"And weaker than I am." Bran couldn't stop grinning.

Suvi nibbled my fingers, my chin, the ends of my hair, evidently reassuring himself that I was alive and well. Oh, and he'd been "crowned"—a silver collar sat around his neck, elegant, pointed in a downward-v and utterly royal. I loved the way it sat against his teeny-tiny barrel chest. "I'm okay, baby," I told him, petting his little head.

"You'll be back to well soon," Bran said with a slow, wicked grin. "Your uncle's been working on you. You should've seen yourself six hours ago. Wrecked, filthy. You smelled."

I flattened him with my expression before *moving right along.* "Is Jonathan okay? That creepy guy had him, last I saw."

"Yeah, they. Well...." Bran leaned back, chair creaking as he crossed his massive arms. "They're a couple of weirdos."

Something about the way he said that made me laugh. "Excuse me?"

"They've got this love-hate thing going; it's miserable and unsatisfied on both ends. Maybe because now Notte has Jonathan, while Ravena has that guy—whose name is apparently Seishiro." He shrugged again. "Anyway, he was keeping Jonathan alive. They parted ways after. It was messy. Yelling. Crying. Gesturing. You'd have loved it."

Wow. Funny how your life crosses paths with other people, and sometimes you forget that they have a whole other life outside of whatever adventures you had together. "Complicated, huh?"

"Complicated."

He wasn't wrong. I realized something right then, though I didn't say it: Jonathan's painting *had* come true. Notte had become that... that nightmare Beast while killing Kanon. What's more, Jonathan probably knew that would happen when he threw himself in the way of that weird wooden hook thing.

That little sneak. I sincerely hoped he wouldn't use his powers for evil.

Bran sighed slowly and looked out the window. It was such an ordinary room; nothing on the walls, just a bed and a dresser and blinds covering the window. Late daylight filtered through, accompanied by hints of traffic beyond.

"Not all of us are exposed," said Bran suddenly, "but enough. And the revelation definitely did not happen the way any sane person would have chosen to do it. Everything is different now."

"A dragon war probably wasn't ideal, no."

"Yes. A dragon war—all over this." Bran pointed at Suvi.

Suvi bit him.

I laughed.

"Brat," Bran said, shaking his hand. "Anyway, it's a mess."

I didn't doubt that.

Things were going to happen. It would get bad for a while, but the thing is, *they were already bad.* We'd been strangled, living in fear of being found out, paranoid and punishing our own People for existing.

This had to happen. My few glimpses of the knotted, tangled mess of time kept slipping from my mind like buttons off broken threads, but I still knew that with the curtain torn, in time, things would get good again.

It's funny: a while ago, my uncle had told me enormous trouble was on the way. He also told me I wouldn't see it coming.

Well, he'd been wrong, very good guessing or not. I saw it all. I could only wonder where else he'd been wrong and where that would lead. Very good guessing is still only guessing, after all.

"To the future," I said at random, and touched the back of Bran's hand.

And the big scary monster blushed. The light flickering in his cracks turned *purple.*

I could live with that.

EXTRA STORIES

Visit <u>RuthanneReid.com</u> to join the newsletter and get short stories and exclusive chapters in your inbox!

The following short stories give a glimpse of what's to come.

Beware the Teeth That Drop

THERE ARE REPERCUSSIONS for everything we do. I think you know that. But sometimes, the things that hit us aren't our fault at all. I think you know that, too.

So did Joshua.

Bran *finally* remembered to give me my things back, including my wallet, and I *finally* got brave enough to check in on my work situation.

You'll never believe this: I hadn't been fired. Why? Because we'd *all* lost our jobs.

Kanon blew Danner and Danner to smithereens; it was lucky nobody got killed, but the official word was some kind of problem in the heating system—a gas leak. Oh, and the manuscripts were considered part of what got blown up—which meant no one was looking for me thinking I was a thief, which meant I did not need to go on the lam.

However, old Mr. Danner had decided this was the final cherry on top of a miserable winter-cake (and his sister needed full-time care now, the poor old dear), so he'd simply opted to take the insurance money and close down.

I got a reference from him, happily. A good one, too. So I could go anywhere. Guess where I went? No, not Boston—that would be too forward. But I was willing to go to New York.

Leeching off anyone wasn't my style, so instead of crashing at Bran's place, I took my reference and my sweet smile and I hit the pavement for a job. Mind you, the cash he'd given me didn't go to waste. I could *just* afford a room in a tiny place in Queens, which was a win! With Roommates, which wasn't as much of a win, but this wasn't so bad. Besides, I knew I wouldn't be there long.

I called the number on Joshua's card, but he never answered. It never even went to voice mail.

I called the law firm in Boston. Joshua never showed up for work. They didn't know where he'd gone, either.

I asked my uncle to look. A terrible waste of resources, I know, right in the middle of this big thing, but if he was in trouble, it was my fault. I expressed an interest in Joshua. I put the spotlight on him.

No sign of him. Guilt in my gut.

Okay, I told myself. Life goes on. No problem. No panic. No worries, right? People change phone numbers all the time, especially with the world in chaos. And it was in chaos. The personal violence was what bothered me—humans attacking other humans, thinking maybe they were taking out monsters in disguise. Monsters attacking each other, sometimes harming people in the area. But on the whole, it was okay. Tense, but no nuclear bombs yet, which is always good.

There were so many laws and contracts being drawn up (not to mention weapons being stockpiled and/or dismantled) that legal courier jobs sprang up all over. Much money and jewels and wealth exchanging hands/claws/tentacles required trustworthy hands, and I owned a pair of such hands. Employment was stable.

And I was not ready to sit in an office again for a while, so.

Months went by. I made money, saved up, planned to move back to New England.

Countries nearly went to war, then pulled back. Vast magical potentates stepped out of impressive flaming orange clouds, then had to sit down in uncomfortable plastic chairs while they suffered through political briefings.

It was tense. But spring came, and that lifted everybody's mood.

I love New York this time of year. Spring had just edged around the corner, and most of the snow melted. The sun was super-bright; and just for the record, NYC's human population was handling the magical revelation a lot better than many places.

There was a lot of, "Eh, whaddaya gonna do about it?" and "Is your money green? Then screw the color of your blood, man."

Eminently practical, New Yorkers.

I had a good routine. I, the working woman, was now a delivery-person for a law firm near Columbus Circle on the west side. Primarily, they used me to hand-deliver important documents, since having a runner was quicker and more secure than relying on some third-party service.

I got exercise. I got to keep an eye on how how humans were dealing with things. And I got paid. Winning!

I also had a... date?

No, not a date. We'd agreed it was *not a date*. Bran and I just both wanted Portuguese food again, although since humans knew nothing about the Shadow's Breath yet, he had to go in disguise—and under the constant whispering fear that the humans would figure out a way to see past it, making everybody awkward really fast.

All pressures aside, we honestly just thought it would be a good idea to go for Portuguese together. Why not?

So, more than a little nervous, I worked that afternoon until just two hours before our not-a-date. I wasn't fully sure I wanted to do this with him, but the thought of avoiding him felt awful. So I thought and

I walked, missing Joshua, wondering about Bran, letting Columbus Avenue near St. Paul's provide my backdrop.

I glanced at Fordham theater, glanced the other way to gauge traffic.

That's when she hit.

Caught me right around the middle, intentionally hard, beating the air out of me and lifting me off the ground so fast no one saw. Smashed like a battering ram through a wall, bricks and glass flying everywhere. Barreled down, down through the floor, into the basement of the cathedral, where she threw me to the floor like garbage.

Light streamed jaggedly through the ruined building. Water sprayed from broken pipes and electricity sparked from broken cords. I'd broken bones; if I'd been human, I'd be dead, but I managed to cough, gag, breathe. And yes, I knew who it was before she started talking.

"You ruined everything," Ravena hissed.

"St... stereotype," I gasped, fumbling for my wand, hands shaking, hearing sirens in the distance, wondering why she'd opted to not just kill me.

She crouched down, glorious and deadly as an ancient lion, her irises glowing green. "Your uncle loves you. This will be the beginning of his sorrow." She vanished. Reappeared. And in her arms, spasming, spitting blood, was Joshua Run.

Joshua.

I should have known.

He reeked. His clothes were torn. Blood, blood everywhere, on him, dripping from his hands, from his teeth—

His eyes had gone green.

He groaned, seeing me, smelling me, smelling my nearly-human blood spilling from tears she'd caused slamming me through a freaking building.

"Smile," said Ravena. "You're a Lin. Chins up, now."

My heart stopped. How did she know my mother used to say—

Joshua lunged at me.

I whipped my wand around, protection spells active, but oh, they cost me, they cost me, and as he ricocheted back and smashed through furniture, screaming, I screamed, too.

Oh, Joshua, Joshua... His life was done. Even if he recovered from this and found sanity, nothing would be the same. He'd lost it all. Joshua, Joshua—

He leaped up, unharmed, irises glowing and fangs out, and came at me again.

This was his Beast. He wasn't in control at all. "Joshua!" I blasted him back, bones crunching terrifyingly inside my body, barely able to grip my wand.

Howling, he flipped over like a thrown doll and smacked against the wall before bouncing upright again.

"Joshua!" Sirens closer, so much closer, screams outside, curious people coming. If he saw humans, he'd kill them. They smelled better than Kin. I couldn't knock him out. Couldn't hurt him. "Joshua!" Maybe I could keep him occupied until—

Joshua had always struck me as a crazy-quick learner, and he proved it now: he *went to dust*. They're not supposed to be able to do that so easily—to just lose corporeal form like particles floating in a sunbeam—but he did it, he w*ent to dust*, and that innocent-looking dust-cloud came right at me.

Protection spell—but it was barely enough this time, and we both went flying.

I landed hard, bruised and broken, blackness stealing life from me for one terrifying second.

He reformed solid, bounced, crashed, howled like an animal, leaped to his feet again, and stood over me, hands like claws, frozen.

He stood with recognition in his eyes.

Ravena wasn't here to command him. Maybe, just maybe— "Joshua!"

There were voices outside. We had no time.

"Joshua! You know me. You're better than this. Fight it! Joshua, fight it!" Now who was the stereotype? Me, but it didn't matter.

He made a strangled sound with horror in his eyes; he *did* know me. He also knew what he'd done—what she made him do. He knew. And it was a hell I couldn't even begin to comprehend.

"Let me help you," I said, though that didn't mean anything, because what could I do beside bleed and try to keep him from attacking anyone else?

Suddenly, he screamed.

Joshua staggered away from me, hands gripping his head, tripping over the detritus of what we'd broken. "NO!" he howled.

And then he was gone. Just gone.

Nobody screamed outside, which meant he wasn't attacking them. Ravena didn't come back.

He was fighting his Beast. Barely made, maybe a couple months at the most, and already fighting his Beast. Incredible.

I sobbed, hand over my mouth, a litany in my head. *I'm so sorry, Joshua, I'm so sorry...*

I had to get out of here. If the humans found me, I'd lose my anonymity.

I staggered. Cast a few quick spells to remain unseen, or at least unnoticed, and staggered more, out onto the street, trying not to cry, guilt warring with the common sense (it was her fault and not mine but I *could not feel that to be true*).

Ravena didn't seem like the kind of person who'd forget who "owed" her, in her mind. And she'd quoted my mother while leaving me to die.

I staggered again, this time around the corner. Got my miraculously-unbroken phone out with shaking hands and called Bran. "Help," I said.

I'm sorry, Joshua.

I'm sorry, all of us.

I'd really hoped we could just get back to our lives, even while the world went nuts with new things and new people, new relationships and struggles for power. But no. Of course not.

Courage always has a cost.

A Hotel Room, a Knife, and a Bottle of Chardonnay

THE HANDLE FINALLY GREW TOO SLICK TO HOLD and slipped out of his hand with such force that it crashed through the thin-screen TV.

Blood from its passage left Rorschach patterns all along the carpet, the dresser, and what was left of the television, but it hadn't been enough. It would never be enough, because Joshua was still alive.

He looked down at himself, at the hamburger of his own flesh knitting together before his eyes, and started laughing. He couldn't die. Could not. Nothing he did would end it, the torment, the hunger, the fear. The burning. He'd thought at least the sun might kill him, but no—it just resulted in horrible pain, unconsciousness, and waking up right back in the hotel room where he started.

Using an abdomen just-healed and muscles he'd tried to destroy, he curled in on himself and wept.

Four days passed, and two times, he'd woken with a new body in the room. Some person he'd apparently taken and killed, though he had no idea how, when, or why. When he grew hungry, he just lost it—lost his mind, lost his memories, and did... horrible things.

And he couldn't die and end it.

His credit card would max out soon. He could only keep this room for so much longer. At least the cold air meant his open window kept the bodies from going bad too quickly, but even so, the smell—

"Joshua Run."

He flung himself off the filthy bed, scrambling backwards, caught and trapped and certain he'd kill the policemen or whoever had found him.

"Stop."

And he stopped. He couldn't *not* stop. The man who spoke owned him with one word.

And what kind of a man was this? He couldn't be more than twenty, with soft curls haloing an angelic (but decidedly masculine) face, wearing a blue suit made of... velvet? Compassion softened this man's green eyes—the most beautiful eyes Joshua had ever seen, though he wasn't into guys as a rule.

The strange man knelt, and whatever power he produced wafted across him like a gentle kiss of breeze. Joshua shuddered, yearning for the unknown, repulsed at himself, afraid, but unable to move; that single word had turned off his ability to run.

"You are afraid," said the blue-suited man. "I know this. You were changed and left here to do harm to others. You were intended as a terrorist attack, of sorts." He produced a bottle of Chardonnay for no reason Joshua could guess and began to work on the cork with his fingernail.

His fingernail. Ordinary-looking, but apparently strong enough to remove a cork.

Joshua's lungs ached with his fast, shallow breaths, and he tried to take a deep one to scream.

"Hush."

He had to obey that, too, but the blue-suited man had not told him not to cry, so.

Apparently unsurprised by weeping, the blue-suited man held out the Chardonnay. "Drink this. Then we can speak."

"What the hell am I supposed to do with wine?" was what Joshua wanted to say. What came out instead was a moan, summoned by the smell of something definitely not grape-born in that bottle.

Blood. It held blood.

He drained the bottle before he even realized he'd reached for it, and this blood... *this blood* was like nothing he'd known, rich and filling and calming, and as he lowered the empty bottle from his lips, he realized the shakes had left his limbs. Finally.

"I have found you," said the blue-suited man. "I am Notte. You were made in an attempt to hurt me, but I have found you before that could happen. I know you are afraid; the self-control you have shown here is extraordinary."

"I killed people!" Joshua said.

"Yes, but not as many as you were meant to kill. You were intended to be madness, uninhibited and unhinged, so that by the time I found you, the dead would be innumerable. Yet you have only killed two."

What was he talking about? "Only?" The room blurred with tears.

"You were meant as a weapon. I will take you as a son." The blurry blue-suited man held out his hand. "Come to me, Joshua Run. Come. Join my family. I will take care of you, and I will ensure you never kill another innocent again."

Maybe the blue-suited man would kill him. Or maybe it would all be worse than before, trained to be a weapon, or who knew? This was like some horrible movie, straight to DVD.

"Take my hand." It was not a command, and it could have been. The blue-suited man who could control him with words was giving him a choice.

Joshua sobbed and grabbed the other man's wrist as tightly as if that grip was the only thing keeping him from falling off a cliff.

He'd almost fallen off; he'd scrabbled and torn out fingernails trying to keep from falling, but as Notte drew him close, the sucking power of that cliff finally melted. Gentle control wrapped around like a blanket on a cold night, tight and safe and warm.

For the first time in days, Joshua slept, and did not dream of blood.

The Bet

S HE'D WON. She'd won! *He* had got it wrong, but she'd won. No way was she going to pass up collecting. Dis was nothing if not thorough.

She skipped her way to father's throne, through the decrepit ruins. Her shadow danced over jagged remains of statuary, castellations born of destruction and too much time. Her syncopated steps tapped by themselves down halls occupied only by dust and shadows. The breeze was her own, and she took it with her from room to room.

Color meant nothing now, bled of its variety and vibrancy by the blue-gray light she breathed. Dis twirled as she skipped, inventing a song immediately forgotten. Conveniently, her back spun toward the ruined throne that sat in geometric desolation. She ignored its empty angles and strangely dust-free planes, facing instead arched windows that opened to nowhere, doors that gaped in darkness her blue light could not pierce, rubble that once represented glory and that no feet but her own came near. Her forgotten song picked at crevices but left them unchanged, and she did not slow until she came to the final empty chamber.

A curtained bed crouched here in squalid splendor. Alone among the ruins, it stood whole, reduced to neither kindling nor splinters. Only the curtains were torn. The stains were barely visible.

"I won, father, and the world still lives," said Dis, no longer dancing, her spooky-little-girl form waxen in her light, eyes hidden in shadow and teeth the same hue as her lips.

There was no reply from the bed, no ripple of answer from the torn and stained curtains.

"I took your bet, and I won," Dis whispered, and her skin warped, pulsated, threatened to twist and change into an alternate form.

But she did not change. "I won," Dis said a third time, and threw.

A single stone arced from her hand onto the bed, and when it landed, its target snapped with a crack so sharp it cut through the silence like an axe. Brittle, ancient bone did not just snap, but erupted, sending puffs of strange white and black clouds to settle on colorless brocade. The white clouds ate into the fabric, sizzling as the threads died, but the black clouds renewed them—just as colorless, just as faded, just as brittle and old.

Dis saw none of this. Her shadow danced back up the hall, forgotten song exploring cracks and doorways before evaporating forever. She skipped higher, arms raised with pointless victory.

She'd won.

It didn't matter how long it had taken.

She'd won. And she'd broken her father's bones.

Dis left through ways and weirs only a daughter of Cronus would know, and she took her light with her. Her song—forgotten—died, and the empty palace closed its eyes for one final time.

About the Series

Step into a 15,000-year history through the eyes of its least-ex-pected storytellers....

AMONG THE MYTHOS is a science-fantasy series covering 15,000 years through the eyes of history's outliers, all the way to the end of the Earth—and what comes after.

Runaway Fey princes, alien Earths and parallel worlds, ancient warriors and know-it-all brats grace these pages with attitudes and truly epic screw-up adventures. There's also science that grants magic to humans... but for a heavy price.

Visit RuthanneReid.com, where you can <u>sign up for **free books**</u> and sneak-peeks in your email, peruse <u>the wiki</u> for trivia, and <u>bug the author</u> for information (and encourage her to write faster).

Welcome to the world of the Mythos.

P. S. Did you read The Sundered? *Visit <u>RuthanneReid.com</u> for questions and answers from readers!*

ABOUT THE AUTHOR

When Ruthanne Reid was a child, her friends were imaginary. Being an adult meant writing them down and introducing them to other people.

She's led a panel at Geek-Girl Con and taught writing classes on world-building and writer's voice. Her blog posts are shared by real live people, and her Twitter following is a pretty darned fun one.

Ruthanne has lived on both US coasts but currently dwells somewhere in the middle, loathing the hot summers and avoiding cholla cactuses. She's happily married, is owned by two cats, and has little else to say in a third-person format. To learn more (and see pictures of Interesting Things), visit RuthanneReid.com.

Made in the USA
Lexington, KY
04 October 2017